And Venus Is Blue

by Mary Hood

How Far She Went
And Venus Is Blue

And
Venus Is Blue

STORIES

Mary Hood

THE UNIVERSITY OF GEORGIA PRESS

ATHENS & LONDON

Published by the University of Georgia Press
Athens, Georgia 30602
© 1986 by Mary Hood
All rights reserved
The paper in this book meets the guidelines for
permanence and durability of the Committee on
Production Guidelines for Book Longevity of the
Council on Library Resources.

Printed in Canada
05   04   03   02   01   P   5   4   3   2   1

Library of Congress Cataloging-in-Publication Data
Hood, Mary.
And Venus is blue : stories / by Mary Hood
p. cm.
Contents: After Moore—Nobody's fool—Something good for
Ginnie—Moths—The Goodwife Hawkins—Desire call of the
wild hen—Finding the chain—And Venus is blue.
ISBN 0-8203-2308-X (alk. paper)
1. United States—Social life and customs—20th century—Fiction.
I. Title.
PS3558.O543 A82   2001
813'.54--dc21
2001025088

British Library Cataloging-in-Publication Data available

The author is grateful for permission to quote from
"Martyrdom: A Love Poem," from
The Difference Between Night and Day,
by Bin Ramke. Copyright 1978 by Bin Ramke.
Reprinted by permission of the Yale University Press.

The following stories in the collection
have previously appeared elsewhere:
"Something Good for Ginnie," *The Georgia Review* (Fall 1985);
"After Moore," *The Georgia Review* (Summer 1986);
"Moths," *The Kenyon Review* (Fall 1984);
and "Nobody's Fool," *The Kenyon Review* (Winter 1986).

For my family,
where I learned

Certainly I would die for you:
that is the easy part, like falling
from grace or off a log.

—Bin Ramke,
"Martyrdom: A Love Poem"

CONTENTS

After Moore

RHONDA COULD DIVIDE her whole life into *before* and *after* Moore. She was fifteen when they met, and thirty now. She had gone to the Buckhorn Club with a carload of older friends and a fake I.D. in her pocket just in case. Moore, a manufacturer's rep, had been standing alone at the bar, thirtyish, glancing indifferently around, looking familiar. Her friends kept daring her, and after a few beers Rhonda threaded through the crowd to ask him:

"You think you're Ted Turner or something?"

It is true he cultivated the likeness, in style and posture, the neat silver-shot mustache, the careless curve of gold around his lean wrist, the insolence: his calculating, damn-all eyes focused always on the inner, driving dream. Because she had been searching so long for her mysteriously lost father, a trucker, she thought she preferred men rougher, blue collar, not white silk, monogrammed. For his part, he knew he was dancing with danger. Still, or perhaps because of that, Moore drew her to him, so close he could reach around her, slip his hands into the back pockets of her jeans, and ask:

"You ever wear a dress, jailbait?" They were slow-dancing, legs between, not toe-to-toe.

"I take my pants off sometimes," Rhonda said. She was pretty fast for fifteen, but not fast enough. That was when and how it began, with her wanting someone, and him wanting anyone. Love was all they knew to call it.

"My problem is I'm a romantic," Moore said.

"I guess I still love him, but so what?" Rhonda told the counselor. They had sought professional help toward the bitter end. The family counselor listened and listened.

"I got married when I was fifteen," Rhonda explained. "A case of *had to* . . . Three babies in five years, tell me what chance I had?" And Moore with such ingrained tastes and habits — sitting for barbershop shaves, manicures, spit shines on his Italian shoes. "What he paid out in tips would've kept all three babies in Pampers," Rhonda grieved, "except he didn't believe in throwaway diapers, said it was throwing away money." But he couldn't stand to be around when she laundered cloth diapers, either, and when it rained — before she bought her dryer at a yard sale — and she had to hang them indoors on strings all over the house, and the steam rose as she ironed them dry, Moore would leave. "He just doesn't have the stomach for baby business," Rhonda said.

Moore said, "I never hit her. If she says I did, she's lying."

"He had this *list,*" she told the counselor. "A scorecard. All the women he's had." She found it the day Chip and Scott ran away.

The boys had made up their beds to look as though they were still asleep in them, body-shaping the pillows, arranging the sheets. They slipped out the window and dropped to the sour bare ground, not to be missed for hours. When Moore slept in on Saturdays, the duplex had to stay holy dark, Sabbath still, and no cartoons. "Boring," the boys remembered. Rhonda made sure there were always library books around, but Chip and Scott weren't readers then. They saw the window as a good way out. "We had a loose screen," Scott told the counselor.

"You've got a loose screw," Chip told Scott. He didn't see getting friendly with the counselor, who had classified him, already, as a "tough case." Chip lay low in his chair, legs spraddled, heels dug in, arms behind his head as he gazed at the ceiling tiles. He was the one most like Moore.

Corey said, "We had fun."

Scott said, "Not you. You were a baby in the crib. Just Chip and me."

Corey told the counselor, "Chip's the oldest."

"Numero uno," Chip agreed. The boys were talking to the counselor on their own, by themselves. Rhonda and Moore sat in the waiting room.

"It wasn't *running away*," Scott explained. "We were just goofing around."

Corey said, "I bet Mom yelled."

"Mom's okay," Scott said.

Corey agreed. "I like her *extremely*. I guess I love her."

Chip said, "Oh boy."

"Moore came after us," Scott said. It had been years but the shock and awe were still fresh.

"God yes," Chip said. "He gave us sam hell all the way home.'" And it is true that Moore had stripped off his belt and leathered their bare legs right up the stairs and into the apartment.

"It was summer," Scott said. "No Six Flags that year, no nothing."

"They thought you were kidnapped," Corey said, in that

slow way he had, as though truth were a matter of diction. "Mom worries about dumb stuff," he told the counselor. "During tornado season she writes our names on our legs in Magic Marker . . ."

"And we have to wear seat belts," Scott added.

"And keep the car doors locked *at all times.*"

"That was because of Moore trying to snatch us that time and go to California — that's okay now," Chip said. "He was just drunk."

"We call him Moore because that's his name," Corey explained. "He says, 'Is *Son* your name? Well *Daddy*'s not mine . . .'"

"He tells the waitresses we're his brothers," Chip said.

"He belted us because he thought we ripped off his wallet," Scott said. "That was why."

"Which we damn well did not," Chip pointed out.

Rhonda had found the missing wallet in the laundry box, in Moore's jogging pants pocket, where he'd left it. "That's when it hit the fan," Rhonda said. She had looked through the contents, not spying, "just exercising a wifely prerogative," and behind the side window, with his driver's license and Honest Face, there had been the record of his conquests, a little book with names and dates.

"I was number seventy-eight," Rhonda said. Not the last one on the list by any means.

When the family counselor spoke to them one-on-one, they talked freely enough, but when they gathered as a group again, reconvening in the semicircled chairs, a cagey silence fell. The counselor, thus at bay, tested their solidarity, fired shots into it, harking for ricochet or echo. Were they closed against each other, or him? He left the room, to see. In the hall, he listened. There was nothing to overhear but their unbroken, patient, absolute silences, each with its own truth, as though they were dumb books on a shelf. He did not necessarily know how to open them, to read them to each other.

"It can't all be up to *me*," he warned, going back in, as they looked up, hoping it would be easy, or over soon.

Moore had said, "All right, then, let's split," more than once when the bills and grievances piled up on Rhonda's heart and she made suggestions. Moore called it "nagging." Sometimes Moore did leave them, not just on business. Perhaps after a fight, always after a payday. He'd be back, though, sooner or later.

"A man like Moore can be gone a week or so and then whistle on back home like he's been out for a haircut," Rhonda said. "In the meantime, he'll never stop to drop his lucky quarter into a phone and call collect to say he's still alive and itching." On a moment's notice he'd fly to Vegas, the Bahamas, Atlantic City, anywhere he could gamble. He never took his family.

"We'd cramp his style," Rhonda said. "He's the sort of man that needs more than one woman."

Moore had been the one to say, "Let's split, then," but in all those years Rhonda had been the one who had actually walked out with full intentions of never coming back. The first time had been early on, while Chip was still an only child, in that rocky beginning year, long before Rhonda discovered that she was number 78, Rosalind was number 122, and Moore was still counting. Rhonda took Chip and drove away, rode as far as she could till she ran out of gas. She had no money, and the only thing in her pocket besides Chip's pacifier was the fake I.D. she had used to get into the clubs. Her learner's permit had expired while she was on the maternity ward.

When she had burned up all the gas, she nosed the coasting station wagon over the berm into a ditch, and ran the battery down with the dome light and radio. This was a side road heading generally toward Alabama, and not much traffic passed. She told the ones who stopped she was fine, didn't need help. When things got dark and quiet, she and the baby slept. It was good weather that time. They were fairly comfortable. By morning Moore had had the State Patrol track them down. They had to be towed out.

"God, he loved that Volvo," Rhonda said.

The only other time she had left him she had learned better than to take his wheels. She walked, rolling Chip along in the stroller. Scott, baby number two, was due in three months. Rhonda headed for the church.

"You know, just to hide out," Rhonda explained, "till I could figure what to do next. The last place he'd look." She didn't count on its being locked. It was raining so she pushed the baby back on down the road to Starvin' Marvin's and bought a cup of coffee. She gave the baby her nondairy creamer, loaded her cup with sugar, and nursed the steam till the rain let up. Then she headed on home.

"Moore don't know about that time," Rhonda said. "He never even missed us."

She said, "Don't expect me to be fair. The kids love him. Ask them. They think he's Jesus Christ, Santa Claus, and Rambo all rolled into one. But you ask me, I'll give you an earful. I'll try for facts, but I can't help my feelings."

She said, "Between jobs he'd get so low he'd cry." Moore was always jumping to a better job, and when the glamour wore off, he'd jump again, sometimes with no place to land.

"I've only been fired three times for my temper," Moore said. "The real reason is I drink a little sometimes. But I never lost a client or a sale. When I did, I made it up on the next one. They've got no kick! Anywhere I go I can get a top job in one day. You kidding? My résumé's solid gold. People like me. They remember me. They trust me."

"He has a bad habit of talking up to his bosses," Rhonda said. "Says all men are created equal and he isn't in the goddamn Marines any more and don't have to call no s.o.b. *sir.*"

"I've got an 'attitude,' " Moore said.

One layoff, with him home underfoot every day, Rhonda took up gardening. "I got a real kick out of digging in the dirt. Anything, just to stay out of his reach. If he wasn't yelling at me and the kids, he was wanting to talk, as in 'Lay down, I think I love you.' We didn't need any more rug rats!"

She made a beautiful garden that year. There was even time for a pumpkin vine to bear fruit. She trained it around a little cage of rabbit fence filled with zinnias. "Pretty as a quilt," she said. "I'd go out there and rake leaves, pull weeds, plant stuff for spring . . . You have to look ahead, put out a little hope, even if you rent." They were always moving. They rented their furniture and TV.

"Someday I'm going to have my own place, great big yard. Put down roots a mile deep. My house is going to suffer, but that yard'll look like a dream come true. I'm tired of praising other women's glads!"

She and her babies would stay outdoors till moonlight, working, enjoying the air, steering clear of Moore's moods. She was still a teenager herself, more like their babysitter than their mother. They played in the leaves, piling them, jumping in, scattering them around by the armloads.

"The way Moore spends money," Rhonda said. "Fast as he can rake it in." He never did without anything nice he could owe for.

"You've got to go into debt to get ahead," he'd tell Rhonda. But somehow they never could get enough ahead to put a down payment on a house of their own.

"According to *Woman's Day,*" Rhonda said, "what married couples argue about most is m-o-n-e-y." She had showed Moore that article about credit counseling, with the local phone number already looked up. He threw the magazine out the window.

"Not down, but *up,*" Rhonda explained. "I guess it's still on the roof, educating the pigeons."

But he did agree to open a savings account, salt a little away for the boys. "The school says they all test way above average and Scott's maybe a genius," Rhonda told the counselor. "I figure we owe them more than life. I *know* we do. What's life if there's no future in it? What did my parents ever hope for me?"

With the opening of the savings account, and the balance slowly growing, Rhonda had begun to feel that they were on their way. Then that fall the tax bill came.

"See, we rent," Rhonda told the counselor. "No property taxes on that. But here was this bill for taxes on a lot in Breezewater Estates! Waterfront high-dollar location." Rhonda couldn't believe it. Since it was near her birthday, she guessed that Moore had meant it to be a surprise. She didn't want to wait. "I tooled up that day, while the kids were still in school, just to sneak a peek. Wouldn't you?"

She drove along hoping for a shade tree or two. "An oak," she decided. "If there wasn't one, we'd plant an acorn. There was plenty of time for it to grow." But when she got there, there was no oak, just pines and a trailer. "Not a house trailer, but a little bitty camper," Rhonda said. No one was home. "But there was sexy laundry of the female persuasion dripping on the line," Rhonda said. Patio lamps shaped like ice cream cones, a barbecue cooker on wheels, and a name on the mail in the mailbox: *Rosalind.*

"I won't say her last name," Rhonda said. "Why blame her? She'd be as shocked to learn about me as I was to learn about her."

Rhonda laughed. "I knew it wouldn't last either. Maybe not past first frost. That trailer had 'Summer Romance' and 'Temporary Insanity' and 'Repossess' written all over it."

Rosalind was Moore's 122nd true love.

"That's how Moore is," Rhonda said. "He can't help it."

She had driven straight home in her Fury, a rattling old clunker she never washed, believing that the dirt helped hold it together. "I could poke my finger through the rust," she said, "but not the mud." Moore hated the whole idea of that car. She had had to cut a few budgetary corners to achieve it — buying it from Moore's father at his auto salvage yard — and from spare parts made its fenders whole again, though of unmatching colors. She paid cash, like any customer off the street.

"No favors," she told her father-in-law. "Except don't tell Moore."

For six months she kept the car a secret, parking it down the block. But when they moved away from there, she had to explain it to Moore when the car showed up on their new street. It wasn't the sort of car you can overlook. She told him his father had made her a deal on it, for two hundred dollars. Actually, she had paid three fifty, but the extra had gone for transmission seals, retreads, and a new battery. The muffler was shot and the car blew smoke, rumbled and shook in idle, and when she gave it the gas, the U-joint clunked.

"You're a goddamn redneck," Moore had yelled, over the racket. "I don't want to see that car in my driveway!" He stood between her and his leased BMW.

"Like rust was contagious," Rhonda said.

All the way home from discovering Rosalind's little trailer Rhonda thought up ways to pay Moore back for the rotten surprise, for using up their savings to make another woman happy. She considered cutting off the sleeves of his cashmere sweaters, or filling his shoes with dog mess. He was particular about his shoes . . . "He'll pay out more for one pair than he gives me for a week's groceries."

Moore said, "I'd rather go without lunch for a month than walk on bad leather."

"He threw the slippers the boys bought him for Christmas in the fireplace. J. C. Penney, not junk! They burned. I couldn't even take them back for credit on our revolving charge," Rhonda said.

"In my line of life," Moore said, "you have to impress people into respecting you. I don't mean pimp flash. I mean class. What people can *see*: tailoring, jewelry, gloves, car . . . Look at my hands, like a surgeon's. And I've got a great smile. A fair country voice too; I could've been a singer. I could've been a lot of things; that's why I can sell — I have sympathy. I'm a great listener."

Rhonda said, "I don't know why I wasted my breath arguing with him when he came home that night. And the funny thing is, we didn't really argue about Rosalind at all. We argued about money. So I guess *Woman's Day* is pretty much on the ball."

Moore had said, "That bank account was my money. I earned it."

Rhonda said, "I earned it too."

Moore said, "Housekeeping?" with a mean look around the kitchen, greasy dishes piled in the cold suds, laundry heaped on the dining table for sorting, and no supper under way.

Thus the stage was set for the final argument, with shots fired.

Corey, their aim-to-please baby, the one they all called Mister Personality now he was nine, told the counselor, "Mom tried to kill Moore, so he left."

Chip said, "In your ear, Corey," but Corey didn't take the warning, just went right on, adding:

"It was Moore's gun. He had to buy another one. She stole it and kept it. It's on top of the refrigerator in the cake box."

"It's not loaded," Chip said.

"That's what Moore said," Scott pointed out. "Then pow! pow! pow!"

"She only fired twice," Chip said. He had watched, the bedroom door open a pajama button wide, his left eye taking it all in, from the first slug Rhonda fired into the shag rug between Moore's ankles to the way the taillights looked as Moore headed west.

"I probably shouldn't have drunk those three strawberry daiquiris made with Campbell's tomato soup," Rhonda said, with her wild, unrueful laugh, "but we were out of frozen strawberries." She was a good shot, even when hammered with vodka. That was exactly where she had aimed. She raised the gun a little, between Moore's knees and belt buckle. "Dead center," she warned. "Don't dare me."

When she and Moore had gone to the firing range so he could teach her how to handle a gun, her scores had been sharpshooter quality. His were not.

"An off day," he had said. "Too much caffeine." He didn't give up coffee, but he didn't take her there again either. It was the only thing in their life so far she had been better at than him. "Except holding a grudge," Moore said.

Moore never took her anywhere much after they were married. She was no asset, pregnant. Before, they had gone to clubs and races. He liked the horses, but he'd bet on anything running, walking, or flying, any sport, so long as there was action. He'd scratch up the cash to lay down even if he had to pawn something. When he'd win big, he'd spend big. "You've got to live up to your luck," Moore said. He didn't like anything cheap or secondhand.

"Like my car," Rhonda said. "I used up my Fury in the demolition derby, so I've got me a Heavy Chevy now, a Nova with a three fifty-five engine, that's what I race. Moore's dad is helping me keep it tuned." She had only been stock-car racing a year, just since Moore left. She had found a job as a waitress at the VFW, working from two in the afternoon till one at night — "No way to keep my health," she agreed, "but I had bills to pay off." She had got them whittled down to five hundred dollars by hoarding her tips and with what she saved on rent by moving in with Moore's father, in the trailer at the junkyard. "It's easier on the boys, anyway," she said. "They can ride the bus to school, and I know there'll be someone there to meet them when they get home, even if I'm at work."

"What I really wanted to do," Rhonda said, "was drive an over-the-road truck. You know my daddy was a gear-jammer, and I'm still not satisfied with what I know about that story. I'm not even convinced he's dead." She thought he might be out there somewhere, and maybe she could find him, in the truck stops, rest areas, coffee shops. "I'd know him," she said. "Something like that, you know in your heart." In any other city she and Moore had ever traveled to, she had slipped away in cafés, gas stations, or motel lobbies to check the phone directory, furtively flipping through the pages, hoping for news. She wore that questing look on her face, always searching the crowds, every stranger a candidate. Moore didn't understand. He called it flirting. They had more than one fight about it.

"Can you picture it? *Him* jealous of *me?* Maybe I did a little shopping, but I never bought any. I'm no cheat," she said. "All I ever wanted was a man who'd be there for the kids, be a real daddy, not run out on me. And here I am living out my life like history repeating itself.

"So how can I go on the road, full-time, with three kids to raise? I can't leave them, don't I know how that feels? They count plenty in my plans, and they know it."

Her brother was in prison in Texas. "Nine to life at Huntsville," she explained. "He's no letter writer." And her mother had dropped out of sight two marriages ago. With no family, and no diploma, she had chosen the best she could, and made the most of her chances. When she read that poster for the demolition derby out at the dirt track, prize purse of one thousand — "That's a one, followed by three zeroes," Rhonda marveled — she had decided to go for it.

Moore said, "I have a bad habit of not taking her seriously, you know? Like night school. She was all fired up over that, too, but she didn't stick with it. I thought racing would be the same way."

Rhonda had dropped out of night school, never getting even close to an equivalency diploma because she was so off and on about attendance. Moore didn't like watching the boys while she was gone, and there was no nursery at the school. The boys made him feel tied down, nervous, even if they slept through.

"I'd give them beer for supper," Rhonda said. The baby

would take it right from the bottle and hope for seconds. "They were good babies," Rhonda said. "And they were *his,* but so far as I know, he never once changed a soak-ass diaper or cleaned up any puke but his own." Night school hadn't worked out.

"Nowadays, they let girls go back to high school when they get married. Regular classes, every day. I don't know if I would have, even if I could have. Maybe just gone back once to show my rings." It was Moore's first wife's diamond. "I knew I was number two, and that he had a past, but I thought I was woman enough to handle anything that came up. I don't mean that dirty . . . Well, maybe. I was pretty cocky back then, before I knew he was keeping score."

She had painted her number — 78 — on the racer's door. "My first demolition derby was my last. I said to myself, 'Rhonda, why spend your life mostly in reverse, taking cheap shots and being blindsided, that's too much like everyday life.' I decided right then I was going to race."

"It's just like Rhonda to think she can get ahead by going in circles," Moore said. "And my old man — Christ! — this is his second childhood."

Rhonda said, "Did he tell you that he thinks his daddy and I are a number? He came back from California and found that I was living there at the salvage yard and flung a fit."

"Did Rhonda tell you that she's living with my old man now?" Moore had returned home in a van. He drove it over to the auto salvage to ask his father if he could crash there a couple of days, "Just till I got back on my feet," Moore said. "The van's a home away from home, I just needed a water spigot to hook to and somewhere to plug in my extension cord. There they all were, one big happy family, churning out to see me like peasants around the Pope. Chip had grown. He's as tall as I am, and Corey wasn't sure if he knew me any more . . .'"

Rhonda said, "He didn't have a word for me. He told his daddy, 'I was just going to plug in to your outlet, to charge my batteries. God knows you've been doing a little plugging in to mine.' He said it right in front of the boys!" Rhonda said, heating up all over again.

Moore's father, trying to joke them past the awkward moment but only making it worse, said, "She's got her pick of dozens of good-looking guys every night at work. Why should she settle for a one-armed, gut-busted, short-peckered old-timer with a gap in his beard?" The gap came from a welding accident years before. Moore didn't stick around to listen to his father or Rhonda explain. He backed the van out and headed away, fast, taking the three boys with him.

"I saw those California plates vanishing down Dayton Road and all I could think was: *kidnapping.*" She called the State Patrol first, "and then every damn number in the world, and threw the book at him," Rhonda explained.

"She hoodooed me," Moore said. "I don't just mean the writ. She visits palm readers. She's put some sort of hex on my love life. I'm telling you, since that afternoon, nothing. As in, zero, *nada.* It's not just the equipment, it's the want-to. I'm seeing a doc. He says it's in my head, says if I lay off the booze and keep up my jogging program —"

"They got Moore back on the road at the wring-out clinic," Rhonda said. "He's looking one hundred percent better."

"— I'll be good as new in no time. I've just got to take it easy on myself for a while. Avoid challenging and competitive situations. I'm not even working as a rep any more.

17

I'm a plain old nine-to-five jerk clerk for B. Dalton. Just till I get my feet back on the ground. Something's better than nothing. You'd be surprised at what-all you can learn from books. I'm reading more now than I did in all my life before, a book a night. What else do I have to do, you know?"

"He was gone a *year,*" Rhonda said, "and he never sent back one penny of child support, one birthday hello, one Merry Christmas. I'm *lucky* his daddy helped us out, or we'd have been on food stamps from day one." It was Moore's father she had called, the night of their battle when Rhonda fired those two shots, the first one burning into the carpet and the second — because Rhonda's attention wandered an instant before she pulled the trigger — breaking the picture window and their lease. His father came right over, asking no questions, taking no sides, with a stapler and a roll of 3-mil plastic garden mulch to tack over the empty window frame. By then, Rhonda had thrown all of Moore's stuff out onto the lawn and was praying for rain.

"Moore's dad is so special," Rhonda said. "He loves the kids like they were his own, and they get a kick out of him too. But I quit going over there to see him when Moore was along. We'd go on weekdays instead. Mainly, Moore just hated going, but he didn't like it when we left him home, either. When he's ticked off like that, it's a pain."

Moore liked things better than he found them at the salvage yard. The junk dealer made jokes about Moore's exalted tastes, saying things like, "You must've hatched from the wrong egg. If we didn't favor, I'd say the hospital must've pulled a switch on us as to babies, but they won't take you back now, so I guess we're stuck." And he'd offer Moore a can of beer.

Moore always brought his own brand, imported, "Green-bottle beer," is what Rhonda called it. He wouldn't drink Old Milwaukee. "A pretty good brew if you ask me," Rhonda said.

Moore used the Old Milwaukee cans for target practice, out behind the junkyard office. "All they're good for," he said.

"He'd have been a better shot if he'd wear his glasses," Rhonda said, "but heaven forbid anyone seeing him in glasses!"

"Sure I wear a gun," Moore told the therapist he was seeing about sexual dysfunction. "While I'm breathing I'm toting. It's legal. I don't go around ventilating people. I just want a little respect, you know? Who's going to argue with a gun?"

Rhonda had hated it when Moore used to shoot up the beer cans in the junkyard. The way it sounded when he missed and the bullet shattered glass in one of the junked cars. The way Moore laughed. Rhonda wouldn't let the boys play outside when he was like that. She made them stay in, watching TV. Moore's father stationed himself at the door, apparently looking at the clouds, talking about the weather like he was a farmer. He had all sorts of instruments on his roof and kept records — wind speed, humidity, barometric pressure, records for high and low, precipitation — and called the television weathermen to correct them when they made a bad forecast. "It was his hobby," Rhonda said, "till he took up racing. He'd talk about clouds while Moore shot those cans through the heart like they were Commies." And the kids would have the TV going full blast. It was crazy. And his daddy just fretting, saying, 'Looks like a son of mine would have sense enough to come in out of the rain.'" Moore got as wild as the weather, sometimes, and he'd stand out in the open, defying the lightning and the kudzu. Every year the vines and weeds grew nearer, creeping over the acres toward the trailer on the hill, turning the pines into topiary jungles. On the junkyard's cyclone fence the boys had helped their grand-father spell out H U B C A P S in glittering wheel covers, and on the pole by the office a weathered flag lifted and drooped in the breezes. This was the flag honoring Moore's brother, who was still listed as officially missing in action. It had, over the years, faded like their hopes.

"Moore and him were jarheads —"

"— leathernecks —"

"Marines," the boys told the counselor.

"His name's on the wall —"

"— in Washington —"

"— D.C."

Moore's father still wore the Remember bracelet. "It's kind of late to start forgetting," he said.

When the boys would beg him to tell about the war, Moore wouldn't say much. He took them to any movie about Vietnam, though.

"We've seen *Rambo* twice, and we're going again," Corey said.

Scott said, "Moore says it's about time —"

"— about *damn* time —" Chip said.

"— we won that war."

Moore's mother had died, not suddenly, and too soon, shortly after Moore and the Marines parted ways. She had, some said, grieved herself into a state. She insisted to the last that she was really ill. She consulted physicians and surgeons in clinic after clinic about the pain. Finally, she found a sur-geon who would listen. "Tell us where it hurts and that's where we'll cut," he said.

She lay on the bed and wept, to be understood and taken seriously at last. Her continuing hospitalization and petition finally convinced the Marines to release Moore, on a hardship. He was supposed to be needed at the junkyard. In his fury at how she had manipulated events, Moore hadn't even come home. The junkyard to him was no future. Within two years she had died, her last surgery — elective — being the removal of her navel, after which the pain finally stopped, and so did she. Moore had married by then, and he and his first wife, Lana, the stewardess, were on a holiday when the news came of his mother's death. He didn't fly back.

"So far as I know, he's never even been to her grave," Rhonda said. "I ask him, 'You want me to run by there and put some flowers or something?' He never did."

After Moore's mother died, Moore's father sold their house in Paulding and moved into the little trailer on the hilltop at the junkyard. He narrowed his interest in life to the weather and his customers. He paid his bills and filed his taxes. He didn't look for much more out of life. He had pretty well gone to seed when Moore brought Rhonda by for the first time, just married.

Rhonda waded right in. "I'm gonna call you Daddy," she said, "because I never had a real one." She hugged him fiercely, and didn't shy away from his rough beard, cud of tobacco, or the stump of his left arm. He never would tell her how he lost it. "I'm no hero," is all he'd say. He let her wonder, through all those years, making her silly guesses, calling him in the middle of the night when she thought of some new way it might have happened, driving by in her ratty old car with the boys, teasing, joking, giving him something to look forward to. Gradually he got interested in things again, like a candle that gutters and then steadies and burns tall. She had to remind him not to keep buying the boys bicycles for every birthday, spoiling them, quick to make them happy, generous with his time and his money. He had been so sure his usefulness was over, he took his second chance seriously.

"Second childhood, I'm telling you," Moore said. "A classic case. I thought when Mom cooled that was going to be the end of him. It was a real shock, you know, coming so soon after my brother bought it in Nam. We were in New Mexico when we heard she had died. Or maybe it was Brazil. Anyway, I wired roses. My mom loved roses. She's where I get my romantic side. Not from my old man, that's for damn sure. Hardy peasant stock."

"Moore's daddy stood by me through some rough times, I'll say that much," Rhonda told the counselor. "I never had to wonder if he'd show up. Like that night after Moore left us and went to California —"

"I wasn't having as much fun as she thought," Moore said. "It's dog eat dog out there."

"— and Corey had some kind of breathing attack and turned blue. I thought my baby was dead!" When she looked up to see who was coming so fast down the hall, praying it would be Moore — "though that would be a miracle," Rhonda said — that he had somehow got her frantic message and for once come running, it hadn't been Moore. It had been his father instead.

"I was glad to see him, but it wasn't the same, you know? I just bawled."

"Aw, hell, honey," he told her, "he'll be back. If he can't make it to the funeral, he's bound to send an armload of roses."

"Maybe, right then, I could have fallen for him, you know? For being there, and being strong, and laughing at heartache," Rhonda said. "But we didn't screw up a good thing. We're still friends, the way it ought to be. He's always been my friend, the only one I ever had, in my corner every round." And now on her team, as she raced.

"I like winning," she said. "The night I won my first race — not demolition derby, but out on the track, running against the others — maybe that was the best night of my life so far. Except the night Moore and I made Corey. I'll still have to call that one the best. He's the only one where it was love, not lust. I still feel good about him."

"They like Moore better than they do me," Rhonda said. "He can give them stuff — trail bikes, waterbeds, tapes. When they're fourteen, they can get him to go to court and ask for a modification in the custody. They can live with him full-time. Chip's old enough now."

"The other day," Moore told the counselor, "Corey was dressing on the run, as usual, and as he passed I called him back. 'What's that written on your shirt?' He's always into something. He looked. 'Just my name,' he said, and headed on out the door . . ."

"His *name*," Moore said. "C-o-r-e-y." Moore shook his head. "I thought his name was spelled with a K! Can you believe it? He's ten years old, and I didn't even know how to spell his name. That's when it hit me. That's when I started thinking."

"I'm pretty much self-contained," Moore said.

"He doesn't even have a permanent address!" Rhonda said. "He blew in from the West Coast in that van —"

"Listen," Moore said, "we're talking custom conversion here, not telephone company surplus. I've sunk twenty-three K in this buggy already." He had pictures of it, inside and out, to show to anyone who cared to see. "Take my word for it, the ladies looooove powder blue shag."

"— with status plates: SEMPRFI —" Rhonda said.

"There are no ex-Marines," Moore said.

"— and a bumper sticker: *If this rig is rockin', don't bother knockin'.*"

Chip said, "Corey thought that meant if the radio was playing too loud!"

"Why do grown-ups act that way?" Corey said.

"You want to know something funny? Rhonda thinks Lana — my first wife — is still around . . . As in, 'not dead.' She thought — all those years — I was divorced."

Lana had died in a plane crash. Not even Moore's father knew much about Lana. She and Moore had been married only a few months. They had been good months, though. They had known each other for about a year, had been flying on Lana's pass — "The airlines give great incentives" — as husband and wife, and they decided to make it official. They married on one of their trips, and it was on their honeymoon that word came of Moore's mother dying.

"I knew I wasn't a jinx or anything. It's luck, and being home wouldn't have saved my mom. But I really took it hard, when Lana died. She begged me to go with her. She didn't want to fly that day. They called her to fill in for another stewardess. She went, of course. Part of the deal. Duty. She was a class act, head to heel. Natural blonde, a lady. She could blush, you know?

"I flipped my lucky quarter — go with her to Orlando or sleep in? — and I still don't know if I won, or lost.

"Don't tell Rhonda what I said about Lana's being dead. She thinks we're divorced. All those years we were married, I told Rhonda I had to pay seventy-five a week alimony. Great little alibi. Kept me in incidentals. I spread it around. I never saved a thing for myself. It all went. I blew Lana's insurance in one week at Vegas. Let me tell you, they're crooked as hell out there, luck doesn't enter into it."

After Lana died, Moore drifted. He didn't see his father again till he married Rhonda and brought her by the junk-yard.

"I don't know why I did that," Moore said. "Like I was asking his blessing or something. Maybe I just wanted a witness, this time. Lana was like a dream. None of my family had ever met her. That's why when she died, I just said, 'It's over.' I didn't want any sympathy. I've got a strong mind. I can control my emotions. I'm no quiche-eater, no hugger . . . I never told anyone, but I put Lana's ashes right there on my mother's grave. I went out there at night, there's no guard, it's just a walk-over. They'd have got along, if anyone could. Lana knew how to treat people. She was Playmate caliber."

After that, Moore didn't think he'd ever feel good again, or want to. "But a man has to get out, meet people, take an interest." Rhonda happened along at the right moment. "Bing-o," Moore said. "I'm not saying it was a case of something's better than nothing — I had my pick — but I'm not saying I didn't fall for her either. It was more a case of body than soul. She could be pretty cute.

"Whatever it was, it was no meeting of minds. It was a struggle all the way, to teach her anything about style. All we had in common at first was the kids. I took her to the museum once. So what did she ask the guide? 'Where's the clown paintings?' And she laughed over Golden Books like she was a second-grader herself. She never got tired of reading stories to the boys. Said it would make them smarter."

"In my whole life, nobody ever read me a book," Rhonda said. "How much time does it take?"

"She saved Green Stamps for a year to get that damn

serene picture, big as a coffee table — white horse, red barn, kids on a tire swing, ducks on a pond, daisies, the whole deal. I wish you could see it! We were married — what, twelve, thirteen years? —"

"Fourteen years," Rhonda said. "We were together fourteen years."

"— and I couldn't teach her a thing."

"I learned how to fix appliances," Rhonda said.

She said, "I took remedial English my first course in night school. After that I picked small appliance repair and automotive. I didn't tell Moore. I said I was flunking history. History couldn't teach me how to wind a watch, much less fix one. You can save a lot of money if you repair things yourself. The library has what they call trouble-shooter's guides. I'd look it up, order the parts, get whatever it was going again, and charge Moore what Sears would've charged me for a service call, thirty-five dollars for driving up in the yard! Not to mention labor. I fixed Moore's adding machine one time. Those guys make eighty-five dollars an hour . . .

"I learned all sorts of little tricks to help out our budget. Moore never suspected half of it. Including me doing his shirts laundry-style. He wanted them just so. But on hangers, not folded. But if he had wanted them folded on cardboard and in those little bags, I'd have figured a way. He never knew the difference. He paid me what the cleaners charge. What I saved like that — including laundry, couponing, repairs, and cigarettes — went into a special fund. He was always running out of cigarettes. He'd give me money and say, 'Rhonda, run to the store and get me some Kents.' I got to thinking. I started buying a pack ahead of time just to save me running to the store, besides which I didn't like him smoking — we'd made a New Year's resolution when I was pregnant with Corey that we'd both quit, and I did, but he didn't. I made him do his smoking outside, not in the house, and yet here I was hiding them for his convenience. What was in it for me? If I think long enough, I'll find an angle. After I wouldn't let him smoke in the house, he kept his cigarettes in the car. I started going out there and taking a pack from his carton, just one pack — and when he ran out of cigarettes, I'd sell it back to him! It all added up. I'm a patient person, generally.

"Anyhow, that's the way I saved enough for the encyclopedia set. I didn't order it right away. I went to the library and asked them which one was best, no doubt about it. It's a good thing I *am* a patient person; they aren't giving those *Britannicas* away. When they finally arrived, I told the boys, 'Anything you ever need to know, begin looking right here.' I told them, 'You won't hurt my feelings any if you wear these out.' They do pretty good about homework, but in the summers, forget it. Scott's the only bookworm I've got. He was reading me about the Appalachian Mountains while I ironed the other day. Did you know, as mountains go, they're *young*?

"I told Moore I won the encyclopedias at a raffle. 'Pearls before swine,' he said. But I could tell he was pleased. He respects knowledge a lot.

"He wanted me to learn. He bought me *The Joy of Cooking,* and that's serious cooking, you know? A page and a half just for pie crust! And what kind of weather is it, and all that hoodoo before you make a meringue . . . He didn't think much of my cooking but I kept trying."

"If she ever loses the can opener she'll starve to death," Moore said.

* * *

27

"When Moore had clients over, everything had to be perfecto. We had honest-to-God butter and cloth napkins. Wine in little mugs on stalks, what-do-you-call-'ems? Goblets, yeah. I told Moore I wasn't going to wheel the food in under pan lids, like at the hospital, but everything else was just what he wanted. The night we got friendly and made Corey, I had cooked Christmas dinner for his crowd. And they didn't show up. Not one of them. Moore thought it was a reflection on him. I said, 'Invite someone else, look at all this food!'

"He said, 'Nobody else rates.' I said, 'How about your dad?' and he finally said okay and went on down to the Quik-Shop to use the pay phone. Ours was disconnected a lot. I had a system on how to pay the bills: rent, electric, water, car payment, Gulf, Visa. Phone was the last on my list, and some months, like when insurance came due, no way I could stretch income to cover outgo. That's why I got so upset at the fancy dress he bought me to wear for entertaining. There I was in that lah-de-dah deal — he wanted me to look high-dollar for his friends: 'No goddamn jeans,' he said — and I could've cried to think what-all he spent on it, and the food too. He went wild when he did the shopping. Anything he wanted, he'd reach for.

"That party dress was something else. I don't know what you call that kind of merchandise; I'm no lady. Light-colored stuff, nothing you'd choose for a funeral or anything. Maybe I could wear it to get married in again. There's just so much you can do in an outfit like that."

"If she gets married again, I won't have to pay alimony, will I? I'm only pulling down minimum wage now," Moore said, "but still I'm saving some. That's better than I've ever done in my whole life. I figured it the other night at Gamblers Anonymous: in the twenty years I've been on my own, since the Marines, I've pissed away half a million dollars. That's conservative.

"Listen, since California, I've tried it all: I've been dried out, shrunk, reformed, recovered, rolfed, revived, acupunctured, hypnotized, and chiropractically adjusted. I've knocked around some: look at me. And I was no Eagle Scout to begin with. The doctor says it's natural to slow down . . . I just don't want to chase it much any more. I've got something else on my mind, believe it or not. I'm taking an evening course at the vocational school: blueprint reading.

"Chip's already saying he's going in the Marines when he's seventeen if I'll sign for him. That'd kill Rhonda. She's been making plans since day one. She's such a piss-ant about money, but I have to hand it to her, she's never been lost a day in her life. She's got this inner compass, and she knows which way is *ahead*.

"I was the first-born son, just like Chip, and I can see a lot of myself in him. He wants to be the leader, set the pace, push things right to the edge, and over. At that age, you don't think about death, or even getting old. I want to tell him things, but why should he listen? Did I? I left home on the run when I was seventeen, and never looked back. I guess I thought the clock would stand still if I kept moving.

"I'm not worrying about any of it. One day at a time and all that crap, you know?"

"I don't trust him, he's up to something," Rhonda told her Creative Divorce group. She and Moore had been officially divorced — "I've got it in writing," she said — for two months now, and he had completely dropped out of sight, paying child support on time, but not, as he had done before the final decree, driving by the house at all hours, or tailing her as she went to work or shopping, or calling to ask the boys if she was alone or if she was seeing someone else. "He was even hassling my boyfriend," Rhonda said, "the one who drives a dozer." Rhonda liked him a lot.

"Jake don't tell me how to drive or dress," she said. She was back on her feet again, had moved out of the junkyard and into a rented cottage with Chip and Scott and Corey. "So far, Chip hasn't talked Moore into filing for custody," Rhonda said. "Things are going too smooth," Rhonda had worried when she didn't see Moore all summer. She raced well, and when she won the Enduro, she got her picture in the local paper. She clipped the article and sent it to Moore in care of his lawyer.

She had cried her eyeliner off. "I looked more like a loser than a winner, but they spelled my name right," she said. She used a red pen and circled the car's number — 78 — and wrote across the picture: BET ON ME!

"I don't know why I did that," Rhonda said.

Then Moore called her at work.

It was her busiest time of night, and she told them to tell him she couldn't leave her post. He called again, in an hour.

"What if I buy a house?" he said.

She said, "You never talked like that when we were married, don't bother now," and hung up. Hard.

Moore called again, in a couple of weeks. "I sold the van," he told her.

"To pay off gambling debts," Rhonda guessed, even though Moore swore he wasn't gambling any more, or drinking either. "He's definitely up to something."

* * *

Toward Halloween he drove over to the VFW in an old flatbed Ford.

"Used," Rhonda marveled. "Moore bought a used truck!"

"What if I *build* a house?" Moore said. His credit was still so bad, he couldn't find a bank willing to take a chance. By then, he had completed the blueprint course at Vo-Tech, and had ordered plans from Lowe's.

When she wouldn't talk to him about it, he said, "Just come on out to the parking lot and see . . ."

When she didn't even let him finish asking her, he yelled, "Just walk out to the parking lot, goddammit! I'm not asking you to go to North Carolina . . ." Heads turned, and Moore sat back down, his face in his hands.

He wouldn't leave. He took a booth and ordered supper and waited. He didn't eat much, Rhonda noticed. The boys told her he had an ulcer. He didn't look much different, only a little more silver-haired. He had a tan like he'd been working outdoors, and he was thin. "Wiry, not thin," she realized. He looked strong enough. She told her boss, as she left on break to go out with Moore to the parking lot to see the truck, "If I'm not back here in five minutes, call the law."

Moore was so proud of that Ford, Rhonda tried to be nice. Conversationally, she pointed out, "I don't get it. It's just an old truck, tilting over under a load of —"

"— cement bags. That's for the footers," Moore said. "I'm doing all the work myself." He had books and books on carpentry. He read late into the night, and dreamed about permits and codes.

"He's building a house," Rhonda told her boss when she went back to work. "Who's the lucky girl?" he asked. Everybody laughed. Rhonda hadn't kept much about her divorce a secret, including Moore's "list." Everybody knew why her race car was number 78.

"I talk too much," Rhonda said, for the hundredth time.

"She was vaccinated with a phonograph needle," Moore used to say.

All that fall he worked on the house. His father helped too, in the evenings — not on weekends, when Rhonda needed him at the speedway. The boys were over there every afternoon now. They'd come home and report: "Roof's on." Or, "There's going to be a ceiling fan." Or, "You oughta see the fishing dock!"

Moore called her at work. She kept her phone unplugged at home, so she could sleep in the days. She had gotten used to night-shift hours, and didn't even mind sleeping in direct sunlight, but she couldn't stand noise. Moore told her, "Chip's getting pretty good with that drywall stuff, you oughta come see . . ."

"Not now, not ever, not negotiable," Rhonda said.

"It's finished," Moore told her at Christmas.

"You bet," Rhonda said.

There was a party going on at the VFW, and she could hardly hear him on the phone. ". . . you always wanted," Moore was saying, when Rhonda hung up.

She told her boss as she went back to work, "What I always wanted wasn't much."

Rhonda was five days away from marrying Jake — his mother had already taught her to crochet place mats left-handed — when Moore fell through the glass while re-caulking the hall skylight. "If he'd just done it right the first time," Rhonda said.

Instead, she spent what would have been her wedding

day at Tri-County Hospital, watching Moore breathe. He wasn't very good at it, but better than he had been at first, when they flew him in by Medevac, on life support. He lay unconscious in intensive care for three days, and the first thing he said when he woke was, "Don't tell my wife."

Rhonda, hearing that, drew her own conclusions as to what he had been dreaming about while in a coma.

After they moved Moore to a private room, Rhonda went back to work. Moore had a week to go before they could remove the stitches, and he was still in traction. Rhonda told her boss, with some satisfaction, "It'd tear the heart right out of your chest to see him like that."

As she went by the bulletin board after signing in, she ripped the invitation for her and Jake's wedding from under its pushpins, and dropped it in the trash. The jukebox was playing "You're a Hard Dog to Keep under the Porch."

"I hate that tune," Rhonda said. Nobody laughed.

To clean up the glass in Moore's hallway, Rhonda borrowed a pair of heavy leather work gloves from Jake. "Keep 'em," Jake said. It sounded final. Rhonda said, "I'll get back to you," but how could she mean it? She had the boys to see to, and work, and the racing season, just beginning. And there was Moore . . .

Nothing had been done at Moore's house to clean up after the accident. Rhonda and Moore's father managed to staple plastic over the skylight.

"Reminds me of old times," Rhonda said, thinking of the night she had run Moore off at gunpoint, and shot out the picture window in the duplex on Elm Terrace. Her laugh echoed hollow in Moore's empty rooms. Moore hadn't bought furniture yet. When Rhonda turned the key and first looked in — she had not been out to see the house

before — she said, "This place looks like 'early marriage.'"
She was determined not to be impressed.

There was no way, that many days past its drying, to get
all of Moore's blood off the hall floor. She scrubbed at it
till her head ached and her hands trembled. Finally she
stood up and said, "I've got a scatter rug that'll cover it,"
and added that to her list.

Rhonda felt funny just being there. Not because of the
bloodstains on the floor — one handprint perfectly clear
where he had lain broken — but rather on account of the
house being built on that very lot where Moore had installed Rosalind in her little love-nest camper.

Rhonda took Moore's last two Tylenol. His medicine
chest had only shaving supplies, a bottle of ulcer medication, and cold remedies. She drank from his glass. While
she was waiting to feel better, she made his bed and hung
up his clothes, checking out his closet as she did — hardly
enough stuff to fill a suitcase. She examined the titles of his
books — mostly paperbacks, mostly how-to's — and prowled
shamelessly through the cabinets, amazed to see generic
labels. Most of the kitchen drawers were empty, sweet-
smelling new wood. She dampened a rag and wiped sawdust out of one. When she found his revolver, she spun the
cylinder — it wasn't loaded — and put it back. She re-
searched the garbage in the cans outside, marveling: "Even
his Pepsi's decaffeinated."

She found not one drop of Southern Comfort, and no
green bottles . . .

It had been the imported beer that finally told Rhonda
where to look for Moore's paycheck, in the closing moments of their marriage, when he had countered her ar-
guments about Rosalind by saying, "You're such a piss-ant

accountant, you'll find this money in fifteen minutes . . ."
and he endorsed and hid his whole paycheck. It was Rhonda's for the keeping if she could find it. He gave her a week, not fifteen minutes. "Seven days," he said.

Rhonda had torn the house apart. Not while Moore was home, watching, but during the days, while he was at work. Sometimes she felt that he could see her, frantic, down on her hands and knees, reaching under the sofa, standing on a chair to look on top of the hutch, probing with her flashlight under the kitchen sink, searching the shoebag, laundry box, flour and sugar canisters. She'd have the house put back together when he came home at night. He'd walk in and head for the refrigerator, stirring through the utensils drawer till he found the can opener, prying the cap off the beer and sighing after that first quenching. He never asked, "Did you find it?" and she never volunteered, "No, dammit," but it was obvious, by Wednesday, that she still hadn't lucked across it. It about killed her to ask him for money for a loaf of bread and some milk. "For the boys."

"I gave you all I had," he said, with that smile she wanted, always, to slap off his face.

Thursday night he brought three paper hats from the Varsity Drive-In. "For the boys." They loved those Varsity hot dogs, but Moore didn't bring any home, just the hats. "I had lunch there," he explained. "Hot dogs wouldn't have kept." Corey cried and had to be sent to bed. Moore was mean in little ways like that, when he had been drinking. And it occurred to Rhonda, on Friday, as her week was about up, that Moore might not even have hidden the check. He might have spent it all, and how would she ever know? It made her crazy to think that. She was rubbing lotion on the carpet-burns on her knees — the "treasure hunt" had taken its toll on her nerves and flesh — when Moore drove home. She ran to the kitchen, and was washing dishes when Moore strode by to get his beer. The rule was: Nobody messes with Moore till he gets his beer. "I don't want to be greeted by what broke, who died, or where the dog threw up," Moore always said. Driving the Perimeter home left him jumpy. Sometimes he went jogging. This time he didn't. He said, after his first swallow, "The week's up."

Rhonda didn't even turn to look at him. What need? She could see his grinning reflection in the window. Before he tipped back his head to chug the last of the Heineken, he added, so smoothly she knew he had been pleasing himself thinking up the words all the miles home, "Since you haven't spent what I gave you last week, why should I give you any more?"

She said, "How do I know you even hid it?" He had lied before. Hadn't she looked everywhere? Turned the house upside down? With the boys helping, like it was a game? Even behind the pictures on the walls, in the hems of the curtains, in the box of Tide . . .

"You always were a lazy slut," he said, laughing. He drained that bottle and reached for another — sixteen a night; he was just beginning. As he raised it to his lips, Rhonda figured out the hiding place. Just like that.

"That's when I knew," she said later. But she waited till Moore had padded into the living room and shoved his recliner back, staring at the world news through his toes, before she made sure.

She opened the door to the freezer compartment — it always needed defrosting, it was the job she hated most — and reached for his special beer mug. He had had a pair of them, so one could be in use, and one on ice, at all times. But she had broken one washing it, and after that, Moore said, "Hands off." He never drank from the bottle, always from that mug. "So why has he been pulling on the bottles all week?" Rhonda asked herself, just as she retrieved the answer from the frost. There it was: the endorsed check, dry and negotiable in a Baggie. She took it out, quick, and banked it, with a little shiver, in her bra.

She needed time to think, to make plans. But he noticed, somehow, that the power balance had shifted. Maybe it was the way she unzipped her purse and slipped her car key off the larger ring and into her pocket. She pretended she was getting a stick of gum. He couldn't have known better, she was so cool. She even turned and offered him a stick, the pack covering the palmed car key. Maybe it was her lighthearted laugh. He looked sharp. Something gave her away. He scrambled to his feet and headed for the kitchen, returning in a moment, incredulous. "You found it."

"You betcha," she said, patting her chest.

"Let me kiss it goodbye, then," he said, reaching for her with both hands.

That's when Rhonda hooked the gun from his armpit holster. Without yelling — the boys were doing homework in the next room — she warned, "Back off."

Moore grabbed her pocketbook and swung it at her, missing, but spilling the wallet and other stuff all over the rug. He snatched up her billfold and dumped it. Pennies rolled under the sofa. She put out her foot and stopped a quarter. By then he had torn up her checks into confetti and tossed them at her, and was bending her credit cards into modern art. "Try making it without me," he said. He slapped at the gun. "It's not loaded," he said.

"That lie could cost you," she said, and fired right between his feet.

* * *

37

"If Chip hadn't opened the bedroom door there's no telling what might've happened next," Rhonda said, to no one in particular. She was sitting on the fishing dock, her feet dangling in the cool lake. She slipped her sneakers back on and started for the house. Moore's father was still on the ladder, stapling weather stripping around the skylight.

"We'll just make it," she called up to him.

They headed back to town to meet the school bus.

"Do you realize," she said at the outskirts, "he's got nineteen windows needing curtains, plus that weird kitchen door?"

Of course, this thing led to that. That's how home improvements go. The counselor had warned them, even before they filed formally for divorce, that what can't be argued or bettered, in therapy, is indifference. "No use pretending it's over when it isn't," the counselor said.

"Or it ain't when it is," Rhonda pointed out.

Her lawyer, when she asked him about it, had said, "I've seen clients replaying their vows in candlelit churches the night before they head for divorce court in the morning. And I've seen newly divorced couples get back together before the ink dries on the final decree."

"Then they're fools," Rhonda said.

She said, "Not me, not for Moore."

"Something's different," Moore said, on homecoming, looking around, easing through the doorways on his crutches. Six more weeks in a walking cast, then therapy. "Then back to normal."

"God forbid," Rhonda said, when she heard that.

* * *

Those six weeks passed somehow. One Saturday Rhonda looked up on her final lap as she raced by in her Nova: Moore and the boys were in the stands, ketchup and chili on their identical T-shirts, red dust on their identical hats, waving mustardy hands, yelling, "Stand on it!" as she roared by. She didn't take the checkered flag, though. She finished third. Cooling off in the pits, she didn't even open the long florist's box Moore handed to her. She laid it on the fender, saying, uneagerly, "Roses."

"Did it ever occur to you —" Moore began.

By then, Corey had the ribbon off and was saying, "Look, Mom."

"I could hardly believe my eyes," Rhonda told her boss. "I could've puked."

It was Levolor blinds for that weird kitchen door, custom made, custom colored, with an airbrush painting on them of Rhonda's racer, a red Chevy with 78 on the door and a driver looking out, looking very much like Rhonda, giving the thumbs-up sign.

"Happy Mother's Day!" they said. Moore's father had the card. He'd sat on it, and it was pretty well bent, but its wishes were intact.

"At that point, there wasn't a thing I could do to stop it," Rhonda was telling the doctor. "I know it sounds crazy, but he should've started right then building another room on the house. It was just a matter of time." How could she explain it any better than that? Was it her fault? Her resolution had failed in a slow leak, not a dam break, but still, the reservoir was empty. "Full circle," she said to the nurse, a fan of docudramas, who had no more sense than to ask, "Rape?"

Rhonda said, "The fortune-teller swore my next husband's name would start with a J."

"Will it?"

"Yeah," Rhonda said. "Jerk."

When she came fuming back from the doctor's, her worst suspicions — pregnancy — confirmed, she told Moore, "I should've killed you when I had the chance."

Moore laughed. "You don't mean that," he said.

Nobody's Fool

FLOYD HEADED up the hill to feed the dogs. They had been hoping for him, pacing the length of the near fence, for an hour. He was that much later than usual; it was his day to shave. A man with the shakes would be a fool to shave fast. When Floyd opened the door to the shed to get the food, Goldie padded down to the gate and poked her muzzle through the gap by the latch, sniffing, her blind eyes blue as the sky. Cinder, the puppy, tromped over the empty pans, dumping the water basin in his clumsy hunger. The bald patch on his hip was hairing over and he no longer limped. He looked as if he had been rolling in ashes. He always could find trouble.

"Now, listen," Floyd said, pleased as he always was by their boiling-over welcome. He staggered a little under the weight of the chow sack. It was hard to open. He tugged at the string, then took out his knife and cut it. He should have done what Ida said, put some food in a bucket and not carried the whole bag, but how could he, after she said it? The bag only weighed twenty-five pounds. That wasn't too much for a man. She was at work. She'd never know it if he didn't do what she said, and why should he? Just because she said?

"It'll weigh even less going back downhill," he told the dogs. They were busy eating. He stood in the open gate, watching them. They weren't doing anything but eat. They ate loud.

"All you think about's your belly," he said.

It was nice weather. Floyd liked spring. He thought he'd get the rake and sweep up those last oak leaves. Ida said for him not to get up on the ladder and do the gutters, but he could still rake. He'd rake.

Then — before he could say more than "Whoa" — the dogs got out, got past him, escaped, tore away across the yard as if they'd been planning it for weeks. Cinder was leading, Goldie at his heels. For a blind dog, Goldie was keeping up.

"Y'all don't," Floyd said.

But they did. Straight down across Ida's rye grass, under the cedar fence, and free, barking out of sight as if they were closing on a coon. Floyd listened for the squeal of brakes — nothing — so that was all right, they made it across the highway, heading for the woods behind the shopping plaza. He could imagine them pelting on like that for hours, till their dinner gave out and they circled back for supper.

"They'll be back before you get home," Floyd said aloud. He hoped so. He didn't want to hear from Ida about it. She'd say he couldn't even manage that, to leave it to her to do from now on.

"I was just trying to save you from walking up here in the mud and ruining your shoes," Floyd said.

He'd remember to mention that, if the subject came up.

Let her think about *that* for a while. "The world ain't all me-me-me," he said.

He stooped to scrabble up the dog chow that had spilled from the sack while the dogs had his attention. He toed the rest over onto their pans and left the gate open.

"They'll be back," he said.

He started down to the house, the sack of chow in his arms like a baby. Ida had been a difficult child, sure of her ways and disapproving of everybody else's, from day one. Things had to be nice and they had to be all her way. Or she'd kick sand. Or do without. Or starve. She was proud. Nice about things, always wanting better. "Like her mama," he said.

Once Ida had gone without her lunch. Refused to eat it. Opened her brown sack at school and announced, "This isn't mine. Someone stole my lunch," in that flash and fury against all things wrong and second best that carried her through high school, chin high, and on past college too, to tell the world, for her living, how it was doing things wrong too. That day, she said, "My mama don't make black banana sandwiches." The teacher sent home a note. Floyd remembered it like yesterday. He laughed.

He set the chow sack against the shed door and sighed. It had been easier on the downhill. "A sight easier," he said. The pain in his shoulder eased in a minute, but he thought he would rest some more before he started raking. He sat on the patio and chewed. It was pouch tobacco, not his usual plug. Ida had bought it for him. She didn't approve, and didn't see any difference. Besides, Piggly Wiggly didn't carry Bull of the Woods, and Piggly Wiggly was where she got double coupons.

"No use in telling you," Floyd told her.

All day long he'd talk to her like that, till she came

45

home from work. They'd eat in silence, or else she'd talk, talk, talk at him. It wasn't always quarreling, but it wore him out, so he'd go to his room and listen to the radio till bedtime. Ida liked her TV in the evenings. She laughed along. Sometimes she talked on the phone at the same time.

It was ringing now.

Floyd spit into his soup can and had a sip of Coca-Cola before he answered.

"Hay-lo," he said. "This here's Floyd."

"I'm Bob, the computer," the voice said. Floyd listened. He didn't know Bob.

"Did you say computer?" Floyd asked.

The voice talked on without pause. It didn't matter if you were listening or not, Floyd thought. He hung up. "Bad as you," he told Ida. He had better to do.

Ida said, "All you had to do was shut that gate."

"I was just trying to save you from some trouble," he said.

"Then why didn't you shut the gate?"

They were driving slowly along. All the yards they passed were empty. Everyone was at work, or indoors, watching TV. There was only one dog in sight — a Doberman.

Floyd said, "Those'll kill you soon as look at you."

Ida stopped the car and got out. The Doberman danced as he barked, his clipped ears, healing in their splints, white as horns.

"Somebody's bad news," Floyd said.

Ida got in and drove them on. They turned left. Her window was rolled down so she could whistle. She beat on the side of the car with her hand. Cinder and Goldie were nowhere to be seen.

"They'll come home when they get hungry," Floyd told her.

"You're the one who's hungry," Ida said. "That's why you want to give up looking." Whatever Floyd knew, she knew better.

Floyd took some tobacco and packed his cheek.

"And don't you spit from that window," Ida said. "I ran this car through the Bubble Wash this afternoon."

"I'd swaller it first," Floyd said.

They went past the shopping center. At the mud lane into the pines where the dirt bikers roared on weekends, Ida slowed.

"You reckon my babies got this far?" she said.

"I hope I'd have more sense," Floyd said. "Why do they dock them dogs like that? Ears and tail too. Didn't leave him more than a nub."

Ida said, turning onto the mud, "It's dry enough. We won't get stuck." She rocked them slowly along the ruts, trying not to splatter her clean car. Floyd sat up straight, his fist on the door handle. They ran over a piece of chrome from a junked car. There was a mattress sagging against a dinette chair. Ida edged past. Then they came to the scrap roofing and old tires, blocking the way.

"Trash is all they are who'd do a thing like that," Ida said. She had to saw the car, back and forth, back and forth, to get them turned around and headed back to the road. When she got to the highway, she blew out her breath and just sat there.

"Ain't nothing coming," Floyd said. "Either way."

"You-can-give-me-a-minute," Ida said, like she was counting out change, each coin clicking down to pay a righteous debt.

"Just trying to help," Floyd said, folding his hands.

"Help like yours I need like a hole in the ground," Ida said. "All you had to do was *shut that gate!*"

Floyd opened the door and got out. He had to spit. He worked on that.

She leaned across the seat and yelled, "You going to run off too?"

He swiveled around. "Better for both of us if I did."

"Wipe your chin," she said. She handed him a Kleenex. She was always right there with her Kleenex, her coasters, her spray wax, her dictionary, her Lysol, her vitamin tablets, her salt substitute.

He turned his back on her. "Ain't good for nothing no more," he said, just loud enough if she cared to deny it. He could set off, walking, if he knew which way was north. He could find friends. He checked the sun, held his hand forth, counting the hours between it and the horizon. He still wore his watch on his grandpa's chain, but it was broken.

"Get in this car, Daddy," she said, gunning it. Next thing she'd be blowing the horn.

"Maybe I'll walk," he said. "I've walked further'n that."

"Right now, Mister," Ida said.

"Many a day," Floyd said. But he was already trembling, like he'd gone miles. That lint cough, the one the mill had retired him for, bent him over, blind. He didn't even notice it any more. He stood up, wiped his eyes, and eased back into the car.

"Pore as a snake," he said, catching his breath.

She just stared at him. "Why do you do this? Behave like a child? I've had students no worse than you. They don't waste *my* time, not a minute. I send them out."

She drove toward home, fast. The tire made a flap-flapping sound on the asphalt. Floyd heard it, but didn't mention it. Maybe they'd wreck.

She heard it too.

She slowed, eased over onto the shoulder, past the sign

that said: BOILD P'NUT AHEAD FRESH HOT GOOD. Closed till summer.

"Well, check and *see,*" she said. "Can't you even do that?"

Floyd got out and looked. There was a piece of board stuck to the right rear tire. The tire went on down to flat as soon as he had kicked the board loose. The long nails left holes like snakebite.

Ida got out and looked, too.

"I don't suppose anyone'll stop," she said. "Why should they?"

Floyd said, "I can fix it."

She didn't count on that, he could see. "I'll trouble you for them keys," he said.

When he got the trunk open and was fiddling with the jack — it had to fit in those holes in the bumper and he couldn't get it right — a truck pulled up behind them and a man in a camouflage jumpsuit offered to help.

It didn't take him long.

Floyd unbuttoned his front pocket and unwadded three bills from his snap purse. He handed them to the man. "Many thanks," he said. "If there's ever anything I can do for you some day . . ."

The man pushed the money back. He laughed. "Keep it, old-timer. Buy yourself some Red Man." He swung up into his truck and drove away.

Floyd stood there for a minute. Ida was already back in the car, washing her hands on a little towelette. Floyd flung the dollars into the sedge. He kicked at one of the bills that fluttered by.

Ida started the engine. "Daddy?"

When he shut his door, it hung up.

"*Slam* it!" Ida said. "Can you?"

Floyd said, "Don't worry about *me.*"

They rode along not talking.

Just before they turned onto the street where Ida's house was, Floyd said, "If you was to need a transplant, I'd be who to ask. You can have anything I've got that'd do you any good."

Ida aimed the car up the drive, braked sharp, rammed the lever into park, then jerked out the keys. "I don't need anything presently," she said. She laughed.

Floyd just sat there, thinking. Ida went on into the house. She didn't look back out, or wonder.

The dogs came home on their own. Ida was out at the fence welcoming them, pouring red-eye gravy on their chow, talking to them like children past nine o'clock that night. Floyd watched from the kitchen door. He couldn't have gravy. Ida read where it was bad for his heart.

Floyd went to his room and packed.

He didn't know whether to tell her or just leave a note, but if he told her, she'd have something to say.

"Nothing I ain't heard," he decided.

He stayed in his room till she had left for work the next morning. As she left, she tapped on his door.

"Daddy? Daddy?"

When he didn't answer, she went on to school. He could hear her muttering, "Like a rock . . . whole place could burn down around him . . . thank Jesus he doesn't smoke . . ." She had to be at school by 7:30.

Floyd waited till her taillights were good and gone. Then he tied up the pillowcase with his extra overalls and Sunday shirt. Ida hated his overalls, hated the very sight and color of denim, but Floyd didn't mind it. He'd spent his life making it, so why should he mind? He was drawing seventy-five cents a day — "A *day*," Floyd said — at the sawmill when he got hired on at the cotton mill for three dollars a day. It made a difference in their life right from the first paycheck. Ida didn't know how to be grateful, that was what it was. Floyd had his Bible in the sack, too, and the photograph of all of them, that summer day at the river when he got himself baptized and stopped drinking for all time. A man could change for the better, Floyd knew. He liked to keep the evidence at hand. He put his knife in his pocket and counted what was left of his pension. He had enough.

He reached down his hat from the closet shelf, and put it on, by touch, from long experience. Floyd knew who he was. He could shave in the dark. His hat had that trade-mark billiard-rack block to the crown. Ida hated that hat. Said a sock cap, like babies wear, was warmer. She bought him one, and a muffler to match. Floyd left it in the box, saying, "Where's my mittens, Mama?" and wouldn't even wear it to feed the dogs.

Floyd dug out his pencil and licked it twice.

Now Ida, he wrote, *dont bother. I done it before and I no how to live. A man has to pull his own weight at least. I done fed the dogs. When I am settled I will let you no.*

Yore dad, Floyd.

He added at the bottom: *no usen caling me,*
                            it'll be long distance.
                            No usen hunting me.
                            I don't like it hear.
                            All you do is fuss.

In fairness, he marked that out so she'd read: *All we do is fuss.*

He set out, walking strong. If a man offered him a ride, he'd consider it. But he felt strong enough for miles, if no one did. When he saw just the right sapling he carved it down some and kept it in hand.

"To scare off varmints," Floyd said, nobody's fool. He read the papers.

He was meeting all the traffic on its way to town jobs. He wasn't going that way. Nobody even slowed. Some of them had on their headlights. The wisps of fog off the river blew into pieces as they drove through it. Even without the traffic, there was a wind. He stopped to put on his extra shirt. As he bent to retie the pillowsack — caught between his legs as if he were shoeing a horse — his hat blew off, skipping along, teasing him into chasing it with his stick.

Then the wind played a trick. Lifted the hat over the railing of the bridge and tossed it up, sailing it out on a curve, into the water below. Floyd watched it settle into its reflection, sinking slow. It was considerably oiled after years, randomly waterproofed by Wildroot. A little fishing skiff putted up to the rocks below the bridge and their mere trolling wake sent it under.

"Adios, hat," Floyd said.

He walked on across the bridge, then, bare-headed, clear-headed, undizzy. There was more to think about than a lost hat.

"I played here as a boy," he told the fisherman at the other end of the bridge. "Used to jump right off the mill into the deep over yonder."

The man looked where Floyd pointed.

The lake covered it now. And the fields he'd run. "Prettiest cotton," Floyd said. He saw the fisherman didn't remember.

"It's this new road," Floyd said, irritated. "It don't go where it used to, just to town and back. Look over *yonder,*" he said. "That hill?"

The man looked again.

"Me and this old boy hauled Book Gravely up it with ropes and mules to be buried close by. Drownded himself in the mill. Nowhere else to swim, but you had to be strong against the tow. Dry summer."

The man said, "Drought, huh?" He was busy with his fishing. He took out a little red and white lure from his box and hooked it on his line. Floyd watched it swing out and down, and the ripples spread wide, from such a little thing.

"Grass growed in the riverbeds so cows could graze," Floyd said. "Only green left in the county." He got thirsty remembering. He wiped his face.

"Things was different then," Floyd said. "Book didn't have no kin and it being hot, we couldn't ship him. We did it as decent as we could."

"Back then, folks was different," the fisherman said. "Cared for each other, you know."

"It's so," Floyd said. He studied the man for likeness. "You from around here?"

"My mama was from over at Rose Creek."

"Maybe she knowed her," Floyd said.

"Who?"

"The lady who come on toward nightfall and laid weeds on Book's grave. We rolled a rock on it to mark it but nobody knowed who she was, never did."

"Weeds?" He was pulling in his fish, a little one, not worth keeping.

"Weeds was all he got, and a fieldstone, but that was more than he might've, considering."

"Mama never said nothing about that," the man said.

"We always wondered," Floyd said.

The man went back to his fishing. Floyd looked out at the lake.

"Nah, mama never said nothing about that," the fisherman said again.

Floyd checked his dead watch. It was a habit, marking time. He always had to be doing something useful, or he felt he was slacking. He said, "I could talk all day," and the man said, "Yeah, I know what you mean. I could fish for a living."

"Same thing," Floyd said. "Back to work, then, son." He took up his sack and headed on up the hill. He told the man, as he went on, "Take it easy on them crappie, son, save some for the rest of us."

Floyd struck off up the hill strong, past the Marina, not looking back. He had to rest his breath, though, at the top. He stood poking at the crumbly shale on the bank by Spain's old place, honeysuckled over now, boarded up.

"Dead now," Floyd said. "I knowed him good as a brother. His little sick wife. All them flowers he growed for her to look at."

Floyd blew his nose.

When the chicken truck stopped, Floyd told the man, "I won't say no," and got up in the cab. He had to leave his hickory stick behind. He glanced back, to memorize *where,* in case he got back by there. "I hope not," he said. They were rolling. The radio was on, and the heater. Floyd sank asleep almost at once.

The lady at welfare said Floyd *had* to tell her his name. He didn't see his way clear to do that. He said he'd manage, then, without her help. Could she recommend a rooming house? She wrote the directions on a scrap of paper and he took that — and his pillowcase — and stepped off toward town, steady as he could in case she was watching from the window. "I'm no hobo," Floyd said.

At the rooming house it turned out he had enough money

for one week, if he ate lean. Floyd knew how to manage that, too.

He couldn't change his Social Security till the next week. The agent only came to the courthouse on Tuesdays. Even so, it meant the next check would go on to Ida's, too late to stop it now.

"If I was to die, mid-month, she'd have to pay it all back," Floyd said. He thought that through, how she'd look when she got the letter saying IMPORTANT and she read how she'd have to miss work to get it straightened out.

"Ida, she hates paperwork," Floyd said.

Every day he walked the streets, looking for work. He got a few little jobs — mainly handyman chores — mainly for widows who couldn't even change the light bulb in their ovens. Floyd had a little problem with that, too, till the man at Otasco told him to buy the heat-resistant bulb. That woman told him, when he came back with the right bulb and explained he wouldn't charge her for his mistake, "You're not too handy but you're sure a man."

He did better on raking. Hammermill had a lot of oaks.

"They bad to hold their leaves till spring," Floyd said, door to door. He had all the work like that he needed. He piled the leaves up and burned them if they didn't want them turned into their gardens. He didn't know anything about that ordinance against burning.

"I ain't from around here," he told the police. They didn't hold him. He wasn't a vagrant. He didn't have any money to pay a fine. They could see that. They didn't shame him into crying or telling Ida's name. He didn't even feel bad about it till he got to his room to rest. He lay on his cot, weak. He couldn't even go out the next day, to straighten out about Social Security. He kept a fever, and his cough was worse.

55

He thought Ida had found him. He thought Ida was spying on him. He told Mrs. Sloane, when she came around to get the rent, "Look." He showed her the markings, their code, the way they numbered his room when they came checking up. She laughed.

She said, "Ridiculous!" just like Ida.

"It's where the cash register tape got in some water," she told him. "The ink's left a stain on your table, that's all."

He knew by the way she laughed it off that she was one of them. He couldn't stay any longer. But he paid her what he could, so she'd think he was going to.

That night he took his Bible and extra clothes and left by the back door, while Mrs. Sloane and the others were in the front room, watching TV. He could hear them laughing.

It was twelve steps down to the back yard. Floyd took them in one. He landed hard on his arm. He crawled back up to the house and into bed before he called for help.

"I heared it snap," he told the doctor.

They didn't know to look for his things. They lay out in the rain all night. His Bible was ruined.

Floyd had paid Mrs. Sloane all the extra he had, and the hospital wanted more. If he gave them his real name for Medicare, he was as good as back with Ida again. They'd call her before the plaster dried.

He wasn't going to be handed back. He had legs.

Floyd walked out of the hospital. It was easy.

"They weren't expecting *that*," he said, getting clean away. He headed back by Mrs. Sloane's, and when she was talking to the milkman, he slipped around and got his things. He took the alleys and lanes, walking like he had business. He had his sleeve pulled down over the cast. He fit in. No one noticed. He staggered, bummed up from the fall, but he kept on going. He loosened up as he pressed on. He could feel the heartbeat in his broken bone. He didn't dwell on it.

It wasn't raining now. That was a good thing. He sat on one of the benches in the park by the post office. He needed to think. He needed his tobacco. His head was clearer than it had been. Day was just getting going. The sparrows and starlings were awake, drifting down from the eaves and clock tower. From the courthouse roof the pigeons rose with a sound like worn-out cards being shuffled. Floyd watched them wheel. He always did like first light best. He felt young. Like he was on his way to school. Or to the mill. And none of the things that went wrong had yet come to him.

Then he thought, But they're behind me, at least, if they had to happen. The *pastness* was something. If he was young, it'd all be ahead, even if he didn't know to dread it. What was ahead now? He didn't know that, either. So it was like being young.

"If ignorance is peace," Floyd said, "I oughta be getting more out of it."

He felt for his Bible. It was swollen and damp, its pages sealed to each other around the photograph of his baptizing.

"Never mind," he said. He knew by heart what was in there. He knew what he had to do before sundown that very night. He stood. After he got moving, he was warmer. His feet woke. He picked up speed heading down the sidewalk toward the railroad. He didn't even feel hungry any more. At the depot he turned south.

It was Saturday. Plenty of traffic going both ways. He got a ride in the first mile that carried him as far as the river. After that, he rode, wind-whipped, with the sun in his eyes, in a plumber's truck that got him down to the four-way stop. There were three in the cab already. He didn't mind riding in back. "Take it easy," they told him.

"Or any way I can get it," Floyd said. He felt good. As if it were home he was nearing, not just Ida's. He walked up the drive fast.

Ida was still in her housecoat and slippers. She answered the door with half a biscuit in her hand. She just stood and stared, without swallowing. She looked hollowed out, like she could use that biscuit and some sleep too, Floyd thought. He saw, in that light, she looked way past grown, on the downhill side, like him.

"Daddy?" She reached for his hurt arm.

"I just have this one thing to say," Floyd said. "Let me say it."

She turned him loose.

"I think I made a mistake about that dog gate," he said. "That's what I think."

She kept staring.

"Next time I won't," he told her.

She still didn't say anything.

"What do *you* think?" he wondered. She had about gripped a hole all the way through the biscuit. She took another bite and leaned against the door.

"You still mad?" Why didn't she say something?

"Talk at me," he said.

If he could just get her started, it'd be all right again. He didn't have to listen.

"Ida," he said, priming the pump, "I threwed away my hat."

Something Good for Ginnie

THE SUMMER Ginger Daniels was twelve years old she no longer needed her mother's feet on the gas or brake pedal to help her drive. She could do it all, big enough and willing. Her mother never knew how to stop her except by going along. Ginnie pushed it to the limit and past, on the straight stretches through the pinelands between black-water ditches, cutting a swath through the swarming lovebugs, her mother riding beside her, not thinking, just answering, "Sure, baby," if Ginnie asked was she happy *"now,* this exact very minute I mean *now?"*

Neither of them knew if Harve Powell ever got elected, but they laughed about his sturdy ads rusting away several to a mile: YOU CAN TRUST HARVE POWELL IN CONGRESS. "I don't know about Congress, but he sure was thorough with his *signs,"* her mother said. Several times they started to count them, but lost track — something else always caught their attention. What difference did it make anyway? They didn't come from around there.

"That was before my time," Ginnie said.

"Don't wish your life away," her mother warned.

On their getaway sprees they sang to the radio and laughed and yelled at cattle in the fields — miles before their courage drooped and they had to turn back. Sometimes they picked berries or wildflowers. Ginnie teased the pitcher plants and sundews with the tip of a reed. She knew just how little or how much it took to cause the involuntary carnivorous snap of the fly traps. She ran through the congregations of sulfur butterflies and they settled on her like petals shattered by wind.

Her mother always told her she was going to be beautiful, a heartbreaker. "If you could *see* yourself," she'd say.

Long before she qualified for her learner's permit, Ginnie was driving solo.

"Why do you *let* her?" someone asked Mrs. Daniels, before her fall.

"She's going to anyway," Ginnie's mother said. "I want her to know how."

When Ginnie was thirteen, her mother fell out of a live oak on a camping trip, way out on a limb after a bird's nest for Ginnie. She broke her back on a POSTED sign, but they couldn't operate immediately; she had to be detoxed first. This was down in Jacksonville, and when the hospital released her, she went to a halfway house. She didn't come back to Georgia right away. Ginnie's father, Doc Daniels, told people it was snakebite. He knew better, and so did the ones around Dover Bluff who always kept up with things like that.

Word got back across the state line that Doc's wife had been feeding her habit straight from his shelves. As long as something's possible, rumor doesn't stop to ask, Is it true? His pharmacy — never number one in town before that — endured harder times afterward. He couldn't afford to reopen the snack bar, closed since integration, or to stock more than a few of any of the items that lay dusting and yellowing toward their expiration dates on the sparse shelves. Most of his regular customers kept charge accounts, usually delinquent, with hard cash trickling in a few dollars at a time from old-timers who didn't feel like driving out to the new mall or from tourists who sometimes stopped to ask directions back to the Interstate.

He had a Coke machine out on the sidewalk that brought in a little income, not much, not reliably. More often, vandals picked the coin box and made off with the profits — and small change made a big difference some weeks. That made Doc shrewd, restless. He got a gun and kept it in his cash drawer. There was room.

He had returned to Dover Bluff several years earlier — had packed up his life entire and moved back home to become his father's partner — even though his father and the store were both failing, and they had never been able to work together before. There was still friction, but not like the kind after his mother died that had driven Doc all the way to north Georgia to establish himself there. Doc had come back thinking that he could turn around the losses, and things had looked pretty good — until the new Interstate opened and business moved east. His father died the second year of their partnership, but Doc left the sign up: Daniels & Son, Drugs. Ginnie was Doc's only child.

Now, with both his parents gone, Doc got restless again. Dover Bluff was a dead end for him, and his wife had never given up hoping they'd move back to the mountains. Doc decided she was right; he was finally free to please himself, and a fresh start for him meant a fresh start for all of them. They stuck it out in south Georgia for another year, making their plans, then moved back to Deerfield, north of Atlanta, where Ginnie had been born.

Doc leased a brand-new building at the plaza south of town and built them a house out in the country — no neighbors — on land they had bought years before, thinking of retirement someday. They returned to Deerfield the summer before Ginnie was supposed to start her junior year. The high school was six miles away. Everything was six miles away, "or more," Ginnie's mother fretted.

"A girl needs friends," Mrs. Daniels said, standing at the window, watching the woods. She no longer used her walker, just a cane.

Ginnie said she didn't care, so long as they didn't make her ride the bus. She wouldn't go to school if she had to ride the bus.

Her mother said, "Be happy, baby, be happy," and Doc said he'd see.

Her first car was a fifteen-year-old Falcon. "I won't," she said. "I'd rather be dead in a ditch."

"You're the type," he agreed.

Ginnie's mother had a more practical approach. "What'll it take?"

Ginnie knew, exactly. "Red," she said. "I want it painted red. New seat covers. And shag. And a tape deck."

"Jesus Holy Christ," Doc said. "You want me to rob a bank?"

Ginnie didn't back down: "You want me to, *I* will."

"She doesn't mean that," Ginnie's mother told Doc.

Ginnie said, tightening her barrette, "I didn't want to go to school anyway. Boring."

"They're going to like you, sugar," her mother said. "You make friends easy, and you already know these kids, went to grade school with them. Remember sixth-grade Talent Night at PTA? They liked you best."

"Well, that's what counts," Doc said.

Mrs. Daniels picked up the keys to the Falcon and offered them to Doc. "It won't always be like this," she said. "This is just the beginning. Look ahead, that's where to look."

When Doc didn't take the keys, and Ginnie stood with her arms crossed, head tilted, not looking, her mother said, "Your daddy finished fifth in his class. He's going to make it right for us, he just hasn't found his niche yet."

"Well, here we all are," Ginnie said. "Hillbilly Heaven."

"When you get back into things —" her mother began.

"Just shut up, both of you," Doc said. "Will you?" He grabbed the keys and went out, cutting along fast down the hill and through the woods.

"He's probably going to throw them into Noonday Creek," Ginnie said, just as he turned back. They could see the white of his tunic flashing far off, a flag of surrender.

"You mustn't hurt people's feelings," her mother told Ginnie. "You won't be able to keep friends if you play like that."

Ginnie watched her father walking slowly back. He didn't come in. He got in the Falcon and drove, hard, toward town. She turned from the window and said, "He's going to do it! Every last bit!"

Her mother hugged her, held and held her. "We love you, baby."

Ginnie was sixteen when Gid Massey fell in love with her. Gid was a man already. Around school they called him "Drool Lips," but he didn't drool. It was just their way of singling him out. He was a strong, tough, slow man who guarded the parking lot, served in the lunchroom, and swept the halls. He was out in the parking lot the first morning of Ginnie's junior year. She wheeled in, late, and backed between two school buses, into the one remaining space, skilled and cool, indifferent to him standing there, watching. After that, he waited to see her arrive, even though she was usually late, past the first bell. He never waved or spoke. When her arms were full of books, she kicked the car door shut. When she had gone, he'd go over and wipe off the scuff on the paint her shoe had left. Her name was on the door, in pink: *Ginnie*. The *i*'s were dotted with hearts.

Gid stopped by the office one day to see if anyone had claimed a ballpoint pen he'd turned in; he always turned in whatever he found, even money. They teased him. Was he going to write a book?

"Letter," he told them, earnest. He talked slowly, thickly. It sounded as if he said *"Let ha."*

Behind his back, they smiled. "He's all right," they said, meaning "not dangerous," meaning "good-natured," meaning "too bad the speech therapist hadn't helped him and a hearing aid couldn't."

Gid watched Ginnie a long time before he wrote that first letter. For practice he ruled the page off, the whole brown grocery sack page, using a two-by-four scrap for a straightedge. He practiced on the scratch sheet till he got it right. He kept the note in his pocket, folded no bigger than a coin. Every day at lunch when he saw Ginnie coming by for her milk, he reached deep and touched that folded paper, but he didn't give it to her. He'd hand her a carton of milk instead, just as always, saying, "Here for you," with an intense look that made Ginnie and her friends exchange sly grins. Once Ginnie said, "You'd think it was heart's blood," and everyone laughed. Gid laughed too, the watchful, mirroring, uncertain, count-me-in laugh of the deaf.

After lunch Ginnie always worked for an hour in the school library, shelving books. He knew that. He had seen her. He had found her with his fugitive glance as he pushed his wide broom by the open door, a glimpse only with each pass he made up and down the oiled planks of the dim hall. He looked from dark into light to find her — the afternoon sun silvering the hair on her arms as she stood watering the philodendron, straightening the magazines on the table, giving the globe a spin as she dusted the quiet world. Ginnie worked in the library every day that semester, penance for misbehavior in study hall. They kept their eye on her, kept her busy. They caught her once in the stacks, kissing Jack Taylor's pale wrist — he'd just had the cast removed. After that, they kept her in plain sight, up front.

Gid Massey swept past now, and she turned, about to notice him in his plaid jacket, pants tucked inside his laced-up boots like a Marine, his head with its lamb's curls ducked over his work, over his secrets.

"Hunnay," Ginnie drawled, loud enough for the other worker to hear and laugh. Ginnie patted her heart, mimicking agitation. She fanned herself with a limp *Geographic*. Anything for a laugh.

She wasn't the one who found the note. The other girl did, and brought it to Ginnie the moment Mrs. Grant's back was turned. It was folded and smudged and tied with blue sewing thread — and it was for "ɢɪɴɴɪᴇ," the ɴ's backward. Ginnie wouldn't read it right then. Let them wonder. She knew how to play things for all they were worth.

All it said, and it made her smile in contempt when she at last unfolded and read it, was PLEASE. The s was backward too. The next day, she stood at the door of the library as he swept. He tossed a little note ahead of his broom; she might pick it up or not. If not, he'd sweep it away. She let him wonder. She let it go almost past, then she plucked it up and pocketed it, her eyes drugged and shining with her secrets. It never mattered much what the fun was, to Ginnie, so long as she had a part in it. This note was longer:

LIKE YOU GINNIE YOU GOOD THANK YOU YOUR FREND GIDEON

Ginnie wasn't afraid of him. She'd never been afraid of anything but missing out. She kept each little thread-wrapped message from Gid in her majorette boots, along with her birth control pills and her stash of marijuana. She couldn't wear the boots any more — they were from long ago. She kept them stuffed with newspapers, the perfect hiding place. Before her parents gave up on stopping her, she used to hide her cigarettes in the boots, too. She smoked in public now, anywhere or any time she wanted. Even at school. That's how she got thrown out of study hall. Three days suspension for not using the smoking area, and a semester in the library — in the peace and quiet and order of Mrs. Grant's cedar-oiled rooms, among timeless and treasured-up thoughts — because of how she had sassed Mrs. Pilcher, the study-hall keeper, who wouldn't have her back. The library was a compromise. It had taken a little for Ginnie to get used to Mrs. Grant and the silence. She had to learn how to look busy, to keep the librarian off her back.

"I thought things were going better with me and you," Mrs. Grant said, the day she found the fifth note. Gid had left it in plain sight on the poetry shelf.

"Between you and *I*," Ginnie said. "Isn't that correct?"

"No, it isn't, but how would you know?" Mrs. Grant said, walking her to the principal's office. Ginnie had the note, but Mrs. Grant wanted it back.

"It's a federal offense to tamper with the mails," Ginnie said.

"No way, sister," Mrs. Grant said. "No stamp, no postmark. You lose that round too."

Ginnie opened the note and wound the thread tightly around her finger, round and round.

"Untie it," Mrs. Grant said. "It'll cut off the circulation and your finger will turn black and fall off and you won't be able to wear a wedding ring."

Ginnie laughed. "What do you care?"

"Hush now," said Mrs. Grant, as they entered the office. Ginnie said, "You're not my mama."

The principal brought it all to a head by saying, "Last chance," and reaching for the note.

In the hall, Gid Massey swept by, not looking in, but knowing. He couldn't hear much of what was going on, but he knew Ginnie was in trouble, and he hated them for making her unhappy. He leaned against the wall, trying to hear what the secretary was telling Doc on the phone. He caught Ginnie's voice, too, but no words. The principal said, "If you *don't* —"

There was a struggle and a chair overturned. Gid heard the principal cry, "Stop her!" and "Don't let her swallow!" and then things speeded up. The school nurse came running and, as the door swung shut behind her, he saw Ginnie's foot rising through the air to kick. The nurse came back out into the hall, calling, "Mr. Massey! Come help us."

He went in and helped hold Ginnie.

"She's having a fit," the nurse said.

When Doc got there, he took one look at her and said, "She's just kidding. Let her go."

Gid had been holding her up in the air, her feet just off the floor, strong but not hurting her. He wouldn't hurt her. If they had laid a hand on her, he'd have struck them down. Mrs. Grant glanced at Gid's eyes, then looked again, wiser. Gid set Ginnie gently down. Her legs didn't buckle and she didn't run.

She turned to Gid and said, "I ate it. The whole thing."

Then they knew who had been writing to her, and they also knew that she hadn't been trying to protect him at all, simply defying them.

"If *we* had said 'eat it,' she'd have found a way to publish it on the front page of the *Enterprise*," Mrs. Grant said.

Ginnie said, "This isn't Russia. I don't have to stay here."

The three o'clock bell rang. "I'm walking," she told them. "I'm sixteen."

"Are you dropping out?" Doc asked, grabbing her arm.

"Some of it's up to us, not Ginnie," the principal reminded him.

"We must get to the bottom of this," Mrs. Grant said.

Gid stood there, watching them talk fast.

"That man is dangerous," Mrs. Grant said, pointing. Gid stepped back, but he didn't relax till Doc released Ginnie; his fingers left marks on her arm.

"We'll just talk it through," the principal said, bringing in another chair. To Gid he said, "You may go." Behind Gid's back, he mouthed to Mrs. Grant, "Fired."

Ginnie saw. She took the principal's desk chair, tipping it back as she unraveled the thread from her finger. The bloodless white skin pinked and plumped with each heartbeat.

"Why do you like trouble?" Mrs. Grant wondered.

Gid didn't shut the door as he went out. In the halls, there was the afternoon chaos of lockers slamming and bus lines and laughter and scraps of song, the roar of normalcy.

"First of all . . ." the principal said, closing the door on all that.

It was a lengthy conference.

Ginnie rode out a three-day suspension and then was back in class. She didn't see Gid for a long time afterward, but he was watching her. After he lost his job at school, he found work at a sawmill. He stayed gone from Deerfield during the week, but he was back in town on Saturdays. That's whose boots left the tracks in the driveway by their mailbox, that's who left kindling on their porch. It was Gid who waited in the woods behind the Baptist Church and watched Ginnie smoking a last cigarette before services, her Sunday shoes flashing like glass, her legs still summer-tan under her choir robe, her hair caught tidy in enameled combs. He saved her cigarette butts, her lips printed on the filter in Frosted Plum.

When she started going with Dean Teague, Gid watched more closely. Some weeks she left church with other boys from school; it wasn't always Dean. They went to dinner at Pizza Hut and sometimes Gid followed them, on his bicycle. He never came close.

Ginnie was popular.

Her mother said, "Baby, now don't give these little old boys heart failure. Don't play them off one against the other."

Meaning what? Fickle? Ginnie just laughed: "Mama, you know anybody but a baby can eat two french fries at once."

At Christmas Ginnie got a card from Gid, a big satiny

one proclaiming HAPPY CHRISTMAS BIRTHDAY TO A WONDER-FUL DAUGHTER. He had bought it — the most expensive card in the store — from Ginnie's father himself. Gid counted the sawmill dollars into Doc's clean palm, laid the exact change for tax on top, and didn't understand why Doc asked him, twice, "You know what this says?" and read it to him, like Gid couldn't read.

Gid didn't get mad. He thought Doc meant, "Are your intentions serious?"

He liked the card. He knew it was Jesus' birthday, so that was the birthday part of it. And he liked the red satin, like a valentine, and the gold shining on it — that was the Christmas part of it. And he knew Ginnie was a wonderful daughter, and Doc must be so proud to be her father. "Good," he told Doc. "Happy."

Doc rang up the sale. He was uneasy with Gid so near the cash drawer stuffed with holiday money. Doc got the pistol and laid it on the counter in plain sight. "Anything else?" he asked, businesslike. "Card like that takes extra stamps."

Gid shook his head, no, no. "Take," he said, taking. He smiled.

Ginnie saw his boot tracks and knew, even before she opened the mailbox and found the card. She was furious as she read what he had written inside:

ALAWAYS LOVE YOU HAPPY DAY YOU LOVE GID.

It wasn't funny any more. When it was happening at school, there had been an audience. Now it was boring. It was nothing. What was she getting out of it? And yet sometimes she thought of how he had lifted her in his arms in the principal's office. That had been interesting. And how he had taken her side, had stood for her and by her. Strong as that, he could be trained, broken. He could serve. "There's

72

something good worth getting at in any soul," her mother always said. Ginnie wanted to get at it if she could; maybe he would be harder to solve than most, but that made it more of a challenge. Once she had seen a man on TV take down a whole round factory chimney by chipping the mortar from the bricks, one course at a time, row on row. When the chimney fell, it swooned in slow motion, ending in rubble. The man was famous for it. He had stood there, just beyond reach of the topmost fallen bricks and rising dust, smiling.

So she went from wishing Gid would get lost forever to watching for him on the road or in town. She went from wanting everyone to see them together — so that they could laugh behind his trusting back — to not wanting to see him at all again, and then, finally, to wanting to see him alone. He wasn't hard to find, once she made up her mind. Everyone knew Gid.

After New Year's, she drove to where they said he lived. She had never been by there before and was just going to look, not stop. But she decided to stop — why not? — and parked behind an old barn, a field over, prying off a hubcap and tossing it into the briars at the turn, in case she needed an alibi. She was always losing hubcaps.

Gid was living as a squatter in an abandoned houseboat, atilt in a cornfield gone to sedge and scrub oak. She had to be careful where she stepped; there were tires and junk everywhere. She could see where his garden had been, outlined in stones, his scarecrow slumped in a broken lawn chair. He'd staked his beans on a bedspring. Everywhere were aluminum cans he'd salvaged from the ditches for scrap. The doghouse was made of sawmill slabs, and the ax he cut kindling with was deep in a stump. His small dog didn't scare her.

The snow had about melted; only the roots of the trees

wore little rinds of it. She made a snowball around a rock and threw it at his window. It missed, thudding softly against the houseboat's siding. Gid couldn't hear well, she knew, but she wouldn't shout. She was sure he was in there, so she kicked on the crumpled pontoon, kicked and kicked, till he finally felt it and opened the door. He looked down, not knowing what to do, not even saying hello.

"Come out or ask me in," she told him. He read her lips, puzzled, then jumped to the ground — there were no steps — and they stood in the sunlight while the dog barked and leaped.

"I don't know what you want with me," she said, suddenly wanting to kick Gid instead of the boat. She talked too fast for him to catch it all. She beat at him with her fists and he let her.

She had all his notes in her coat pockets. She took them out and flung them. Then she tore his big red Christmas card into pieces and scattered it on the wind. When a car drove by on the high road, she turned her back and raised her hood over her hair. She wasn't afraid, and she wasn't being discreet; she just didn't want to be stopped.

"Invite me in, dammit!" She didn't wait for him to help her; she planted her boot on the sill and drew herself up by the door frame, strong.

"Oh, God," she said, when she saw how he had painted everything red, barn red. "Massacre," she said.

He had nailed the ceiling over with raw boards. The quilts were folded across the foot of his neat bed. Things looked clean. He even had a few books, missing their covers, that looked as if he had found them in the ditches as he hunted cans. An oil lamp stood on his table, nothing special. He had framed a picture of her, from the newspaper. She shook her head.

He chunked more wood into the fire and latched the

stove door, taking his time adjusting the draft. Then he looked at her with those trusting-dog eyes. "Trouble?" he guessed. *"Tubba"* was how it sounded.

Ginnie laughed. "No trouble at all," she told him. He was slow-blooded, like a lizard in winter. She knew it would be up to her to warm him to living speed. Funny how he acted, standing there looking proud.

"You love this dump, don't you?" she said, checking the old Coleman icebox for beer. No beer. She'd bring some next time.

As she drew him down, down with her cool hands, she warned, "No future, and my terms."

"Friend," he said. It sounded like *fend.*

"All human beings are is animals who can talk," she told him, peeling the watchcap from his big furry skull. "And you can't even talk."

She teased him till he was crazy, till he barked, till he sweated, crawling after her on all fours. She rode him bareback. "Lady Godiva," she called herself. He was "Tennessee Stud." She sang it to him, till he knew the tune. He couldn't sing, but he could keep time. She tied him to the table. She learned him by heart. They played like that for hours, till the sun headed down. She wasn't afraid of a knock on the door. She wasn't afraid of anything. If anyone had come to that grounded boat then, she'd have answered the door herself, wild as God made her.

"As God made me," she asked Gid, "how'd he do?"

"Howdy do," Gid said.

They ate canned soup afterward — she had interrupted his lunch — and she drove home by dark. She warned him again, as she left: "No future, my terms."

Gid couldn't hear her.

* * *

75

Ginnie wasn't crazy about Dean Teague. She could make him do some things, but sometimes he wouldn't. It took her a little time to figure out whether he meant no for now or no forever. Not about sex, but about dope. And not because his father was the police chief, but because he ran on the track team. It would have been something to get him to smoke, or some other thing, to have him beg her for a light or a line. She couldn't make him, though. She liked him better when she couldn't make him, till she figured out she never would be able to. Then he wasn't much fun any more, and she told him so.

She told Jeff Davis about him too. "He's just no fun," she said.

"Why is that?" Jeff asked. He was like a little pony you train on a course to take each jump with a mere flick of the whip. He wanted to know why so he wouldn't make the same mistake. But Ginnie wouldn't say. That was better for business.

She ran Jeff ragged. She called him "Reb," and made him feel special, and called him "Manny," and let her hands rove as they were driving up to Hammermill to the basketball tournament. She rode so close to him she could feel him heating up. It was going to be almost too easy.

Excited, Jeff drove wild. He wasn't used to dope, and he ran them into the ditch, lightheaded. He was almost crying to get out of there, before his father found out. He went all around the car checking on the paint. All he needed was a wrecker, but he beat his hands on the roof of the car, and cursed his luck, and cried.

He even made her put the Miller in the woods, out of sight in case the law should happen by. "I'm not drunk," he said, over and over. She would have had time to finish the grass, but he knocked the roach out of her hand into the mud and stomped it out of sight. He wasn't thinking party any more.

The first one to stop by was Buck Gilbert. Ginnie told Jeff farewell, and she and Buck drove off for help.

At the first house Buck slowed. "What're you doing?" she said.

"Telephone," Buck said.

"Let the little jerk sweat," Ginnie said. "He's already wasted enough of my precious time."

Buck put the big-footed four-wheeler in gear and gunned the truck on by. Ginnie liked the way it wallowed on the curves as though it might roll over, but Buck knew how to drive it. He laid it around in the gravel, full circle, twice — no accident the first time, more fun the second. She wanted to try it. He let her. She sat in his lap, the way she had learned to drive in her mother's own lap. She had the hang of it soon.

She wasn't drunk and she wasn't high. She was willing. "Let's go back," she said. "See if he's still sitting in the mud."

They wheeled around and headed back. The ditch was empty, though, and the mud tracks headed south. "Home to his daddy," Ginnie said. She got out and ran into the woods and found the beer she'd stashed.

Buck had the 4x4 turned around, nosing back toward the north.

"Well all right," she yelled. "Party time!"

"Satisfactory," he said, finishing off one of the ponies and tossing the bottle. It shattered into smoke on the road behind them.

Buck knew where to find others in a party mood, so they never made it to the tournament. They hung out at the video arcade for an hour or two — nobody was watching the clock. Then, in a convoy, they headed down to the thousand acres where the off-road vehicles churned up the mud on weekends.

They had picked up Johnny Bates and Chris Olds. "Love makes room," Ginnie said. She sat across their laps, her back against the door, washing down Chris's pills with Johnny's vodka. Buck was tailgating the Trans-Am ahead of them. "Kiss it! Kiss it!" Ginnie urged, bracing herself for the collision, but the 4x4 was too tall; Buck ran right over the car's trunk, and they had to stop — the whole convoy — and discuss it. The other driver was too stoned to walk straight; when Buck pushed him down, he crawled on the road, trying to get up. "Like a spider," Ginnie said. "Step on him." She stomped, just at his fingertips. He rolled away and staggered to his feet, as she climbed into the 4x4 and revved the engine. "Where's your balls?" she called, backing the truck off the Trans-Am. Buck and Johnny and Chris jumped on board, laughing. The boy in the road didn't step out of the way. The 4x4 grazed him, and he grabbed on to the hood, trying to haul himself up. "Bull-fighting!" Ginnie said, jerking the wheel sharply left, then right. He slid away into the dark. Everybody was laughing. Ginnie drove on, leading the pack now.

They prowled on down to the landing, where there was moon enough to party. Ginnie felt the light hit her arms like blows as the shadows of the pines laddered over her flesh. "I *feel* it!" she said, jumping from the truck, spinning, savoring. She fell in the sand and sat, looking around. She didn't even get up when the headlights of another truck swung across the sky and headed toward her. The other truck's radio was on the same station as theirs. Full blast.

They danced, then, Ginnie and the others. She didn't know quite who they were, but she liked them. She wanted to take off her clothes and dance on the dock in the moon-light. She wanted to swim all the way to Thompson Beach. She was the only one. It was still winter.

When the fight started, Ginnie pitched right in. She didn't like the other girl and began tearing at her face and clothes and calling her "slut" and "whore" and kicking sand and cursing. She found a pine limb and wielded it like a bat, trying for serious damage. The girl was screaming and crying loud enough to turn the lights on in the windows across the cove. They could hear sirens far off, nearing.

Buck and Chris got Ginnie into the truck and got out of there — not waiting for Johnny, who had disappeared as soon as the fight started. They pulled into a side road, lights off, till the deputies had passed.

Ginnie didn't want to go home. She thought of Gid's houseboat. It wasn't far.

"Let's stop here," she dared.

She knew Gid wasn't there except on weekends. He boarded up at Dixon now, since it was too far to commute weekdays on his bicycle. Too cold.

"It's abandoned," Ginnie said, crawling up inside. She lit the lamp and turned to give a hand to Chris.

He climbed up, looked around, and whistled. "I know this guy," Chris said. "He —"

"He's dandruff on the shoulders of life," Ginnie said.

Buck was wild enough for anything, and Ginnie was ready, but Chris edged toward the door, saying, "I need air."

"Did you say prayer?" Ginnie asked, her scorn so sud-den and hot it made her want to kill him. He was the one she wanted right then — Chris. She'd make him.

She stood blocking the open door, all the night behind her, dark, nothing to break her fall. "Say the word," she

79

teased. She didn't lay a hand on him, just waited for him to try to get past. She could change anybody's mind.

"What're you doing these days, Ginnie?" Chris asked, as if they were meeting on the street at noon. "Found one that fits yet?"

She looked at their faces as they laughed at her, Buck laughing louder.

"Y'all just get out!" she screamed, kicking at them wildly. "Out!" She was still raging and cursing as the 4x4 roared away.

After they had gone, she trashed Gid's houseboat, broke and tore and spattered and fouled it from bow to stern. Then she made a fire in the stove, stoking it till the flue glowed red, and left the place to find its own fate. It would look like an accident. She knew Chris and Buck wouldn't tell. If they did, what could they prove?

She cut across the sedge fields toward home. It was miles, and she had blisters the size of silver dollars on both heels by the time she got there, sober and vomit-hollowed, her hair tangled with burs. She chewed some Dentyne and thought fast. There was a light on. She began crying.

Her mother met her at the door and cried too.

Ginnie told her, "I've walked miles. I made them let me out. They weren't Christians, Mama. They weren't good boys at all."

"Did they hurt you, baby?"

"I'd die first," she said.

Doc didn't do anything except turn out the yard light, lock the door, and listen. He knew Ginnie well enough not to swear out warrants. He knew where the birth control pills missing from his inventory were going. He never challenged her, just went on pretending she was who she thought they thought she was. "We all ought to be in bed," he said.

"Let her talk it out," Ginnie's mother said. "Talk it out, honey." She drew Ginnie to her, shoulder to shoulder, so alike that time was the only thing that made the difference: Before and After, Doc thought, clicking the three-way bulb to low.

Ginnie said, "I just want to put it behind me, you know? Like, it's over." She bent to pry off her boots and look at her heels.

"Vitamin E," Mrs. Daniels said, going to the cabinet to get a capsule. She believed in *Prevention;* she kept a stack of the magazines by her bed, and could rattle off the names of vitamins and minerals and their uses the way some people name saints and their miracles. She might question Doc about some vitamin controversy, but she believed in miller's bran, aloe vera, and D-alpha tocopherol with the same blind faith she put in Ginnie: a wholesomeness never to be doubted, and possibilities worth any expense. If Doc was a realist, and hated talking things out, just getting on with it instead, his wife had a softer eye and heart. Maybe she didn't really know her daughter. She didn't worry; she trusted. Not to trust seemed dishonorable; when doubt shaded in, and chilled her, she turned her mind's channel to another station, just like she did the TV. She kept herself busy, living in a world of her own making, putting her own crazy captions to the pictures in the news, watching TV for hours with the sound off. When they were driving along and passed a road-killed animal, she said, "Probably just playing possum," even if you could *smell* it. Doc always said, "Goddamn!" and laughed. "What'll it take to convince you?" he wondered.

Mrs. Daniels came back with the vitamin E. "There won't be any scars, if you'll just start this early." She knelt and helped smear the oil on Ginnie's wounded heels.

Ginnie laid her hand on her mother's head. "Mama,"

she said. "Did you save the receipt for these boots? They're going back."

"Tomorrow," her mother said. "First thing."

"It's already tomorrow," Doc said.

Mrs. Daniels stood and wiped her hands. "It may already be tomorrow, but it's never too late." She headed for the kitchen to cook them something special for breakfast.

"I bet you didn't sleep a wink all night," Ginnie said to Doc. She tossed her ruined boots over by the hearth and sat down in Doc's recliner, shoving it all the way back. She looked up at him. "Your bags have bags." Doc had been about to yawn, but he forced it into a smile.

"Slept great. Your mother got me up when you came home."

Doc never slept great. Sometimes he woke in the night and felt like breaking things, or shooting up the whole world, every lying thieving cheat in it. He'd been burglarized again, and often, and not always petty thefts: they knew what they wanted, what was worth anything. He had changed his whole antitheft system after the Bland boy broke in and stole the drugs that killed him. He'd installed alarm systems connected to the police direct by radio signal, and new deadbolts and wires on the windows. From time to time he bought another gun and registered it. What more could a man do? All that trouble and expense at work, and at home, Ginnie and her mother would be unruffled, calmly paging through their catalogues for custom curtains, brass bedsteads, Fair Isle sweaters, Hummel figurines . . .

"What do you say, Daddy?" Ginnie sounded serious. Doc hadn't been listening. He tried to catch up, then decided against asking her flat out. She had something to say? He waited to hear more.

"I'm going to graduate next year," she vowed. "I'm going

to settle down and study and make me some A's. What do you say?"

Her mother, in the kitchen making banana waffles from scratch, always a big deal out of something, deliverance this time, hummed "Come Thou Fount of Many Blessings," beating eggs in time.

"This is the turning point of my *life*," Ginnie told him. "You hear me?"

"I'm listening," Doc said. The anniversary clock chimed six-thirty.

"What do you say to Beta Club and some A's and all that Glee Club stuff and a diploma and graduation with my class and all that?"

Doc bent and picked a section of briar from the toe of Ginnie's boot.

"How much will it cost me?"

Ginnie didn't even open her eyes.

"Have you seen the new T-roof-Z's?"

He flung the bit of briar in the fireplace. "No way," he said. He laughed. "Not for straight A's and perfect attendance." He took off his glasses and polished them, settling them back on his face again, giving the room a clear hard look. "You should have started sooner."

"I'm starting now," she said.

"No sale," he told her. "Besides, I thought you were dropping out. Going to cosmetology school or something."

"You say that like it was worm-farming, Daddy," Ginnie said. "People change."

In the first light, she looked like herself at ten, scolded too hard, afraid to raise her face to their anger and disappointment. He didn't really believe in evil, born in, unchangeable. People could change. We all start off even, her mother was always saying. Some of us learn a little slower and whose fault is that?

The recliner snapped upright and Ginnie sat staring at her hands.

"Shit!" She held her hand out for him to see. "I broke my fingernail getting off those damn boots."

Doc didn't move and Ginnie glanced up. Then he reached over to the cat's scratching post and handed it to her. "Here," he said.

She couldn't believe her eyes and ears. She looked at him as at a stranger. He *was!*

"Daddy?"

She was gifted, he knew, by all her test scores. Genius. *"Underchallenged,"* they had told him and his wife. "Keep her busy," they had said. "Keep her motivated." He resumed himself. "T-roof-Z?" he said, thinking it over.

To help him calculate, she asked, "Can you stroke it? Are you good for it?"

"I'll tell you the truth," he said. "I don't think *you* are."

Ginnie reclined her chair again, smiling. "I guess it's up to me."

She was asleep at breakfast time. Her mother called, then came to see. She laid an afghan over Ginnie and tiptoed back to the kitchen to serve Doc. "Sleeping like a baby, like an angel." She moved around to Doc's chair and poured his coffee. She set the pot down and hugged him, rocked him to her, and let him go.

"She's going to straighten up," she told Doc. "This time she's on her way. I pray it for her all the time: something good for Ginnie."

Doc said, "It's her deal, and she knows it."

"I'm happy, *happy!* Thank you, Doc. Thank you, God," she said, and then sat down and cried. She was still crying, and Ginnie was still asleep, when Doc left for work.

* * *

84

Ginnie didn't see Gid much any more. After his boat burned — it went down as accidental — he took a permanent place at Dixon and didn't even come back on weekends. He was saving his money, had an account in the bank — one of the mill workers helped him open it — and he was careful of his pay. He planned to marry Ginnie. She had plans of her own.

She quit dating. Quit partying. Dropped out of sight except for school and church. In the afternoons, twice a week, Jordan Kilgore came to the house to tutor her in geometry. This was Doc's idea. Jordan was fifteen, sprouting his first manly bristles and nervous around Ginnie, who was a little older and beyond wild hope. Jordan lived with his grandfather, who owned the yacht club across the lake, but he didn't go to school at Deerfield. He went to Atlanta to special classes for the gifted. He was already taking college courses twice a week. Those were the afternoons he had free to help Ginnie. He was a virgin, Ginnie could tell — as much fun as a newborn kitten. She played little games all through the lessons; he never even suspected. She'd let the top button on her blouse gape, and then button it quick, shy. She wore scent on her hands so when he went home, her flavor was on his books. She didn't have anything in mind, just to drive him crazy a little and pass off time. On lesson days she wore her daintiest clothes, no leather, no make-up, no angora, no jeans. She wore dresses or full skirts and eyelet and never said "damn." When his cat died, she cried and came down to the lesson with her eyes red and swollen.

On her birthday in March he gave her a silver cross set with aquamarines, for studying so hard.

She kissed it and said, "I'll wear it always, when I marry, forever, I'll never take it off!" She let him clasp it, his hands clumsy and slow, tangling in the stray curls she had left out as she pinned her hair up. When it was fastened, she had him kiss it too, and she dropped it down her blouse, out of sight, but known.

"You look like a valentine," he said.

She looked down at the tucks and laces and white white shirtfront and bit her lip. "Thank you," she said.

"Ginnie," he said, hurting. They were alone.

She shook her head. "Let's pray," she said. But it was too much, too strong. They embraced, and she let him — soft lips! untrained shy questing shy lips — kiss her. He quivered like a horse wearing its first saddle. She was almost bored, but not quite. She drew away, and stood, tucking her blouse in and smoothing her hair. "We mustn't."

"I have wicked thoughts," she said, as he looked away. "But we have just an hour, and it's for geometry."

"You — you're making progress," he agreed. He turned to the lesson.

"I think about you all the time!" she said, just as his mind had gotten fixed on the matter at hand. Ginnie was having trouble proving triangles. "I dream about you," she said. She checked the clock. Her mother was at a luncheon.

He drew a triangle. "I dream about you too," he said.

He could smell her shampoo. He leaned into the fragrance, inhaling, all the time drawing another triangle inside the first triangle, and numbering from one to ten.

"Tell me," she whispered, stopping his pencil with her fingertip.

He leaned away.

"What do you dream?" She got up and went to the window and looked out. "What did you do with those magazines I gave you?"

"They — I burned them."

"Daddy has more. New ones. He keeps them under the counter. You have to ask, people always ask."

"They're trash," he said.

"Slime," Ginnie agreed. "Filth. Don't think about them!" She watched as his color burned higher. "Do you dream about them? Things like that?"

Her mother's car was turning in the driveway. Ginnie slapped her book closed. "We ought to burn them all! It could be" — she drew a breath — *"noble,* like Jesus running the moneychangers out of the temple." He gathered his papers and books. They hadn't done a thing for the hour except those two triangles, one inside the other.

"Don't tell!" she cautioned him, and ran outside to meet her mother. He passed them in the drive as they were picking daffodils. He was on his ten-speed, bent forward, his bookbag strapped across his back, his legs strong on the hill.

Ginnie's mother worried what he'd do when it rained. Ginnie said, "With an uncle who's a bishop and a granddaddy who's got a wad on his hip the size of Stone Mountain, he could have a Porsche if he wanted it, if he knew how to ask."

Doc was paying Jordan five dollars an hour for the tutoring. Sometimes Ginnie borrowed a little of it, just a few dollars now and then. "I'll pay you back," she always promised. "Somehow."

"He's a darling boy," Ginnie's mother agreed.

All through Lent she tormented him like that, till she left the note in his book. Unsigned. Who could prove a thing if it went wrong? "Tonight, back door at Doc's, midnight, god's sake don't leave your bike in plain view." She typed it at school, in a spare moment.

He'll never show, Ginnie thought. And if he did, she'd think of something.

She left her car at the roller rink, and walked back to

town. Two, three blocks, no street lights till the post office, where the sidewalk began.

Anne Summerday, charge nurse for the 11-to-7 shift at Tri-County Hospital, saw Ginnie walking along the road toward town, all in white. Anne pulled alongside the girl, thinking she might be a nurse in some kind of trouble. When she saw it was Ginnie, dressed like a bride in a dream, vacant-eyed, ghostly, she knew better. "Anything the matter?"

Ginnie said, "One of your headlights is out."

"I meant with you — need any help? Anything?"

"Nothing radical," Ginnie said. "Just airing it out, y'know?" She played with the ribbons at her waist. "Massive weather, hunh?" She blew a gum bubble, perfected it, inhaled it whole, and popped it with a blink of her eyes. Then started over.

"Take care of yourself," Anne told her.

"Not going far," Ginnie assured her.

"It's dark as an egg's inside," Ginnie complained as Jordan came in. She had opened the door at his third tap. She groped over to the partition between the storeroom and the pharmacy, pulling open the golden plastic curtains that served for a door. An eerie light, green as the aurora, streamed through the gap she made.

"I can't stay," Jordan said.

Her eyes glinted alien in the strange light that pulsed from a cosmetic display in the front of the store.

"Why did you come?"

"I shouldn't be here."

She shoved him away toward the door. "That one-eyed granddaddy of yours, I bet, calling frog and you hop." She covered her eye with her hand and tilted her head at him, saying in a mocking mannish voice, "Jordan, boy, you better love Jesus, my Jesus yes!" She had smoked a roach on the way. He couldn't ever catch up with her.

"I do!"

"I do!" she mocked. "Is this a wedding?"

She slipped into the store and brought back a hairbrush and handed it to him. "Do me," she said.

He began stroking her hair, too lightly, tangling as he went, then smoother, firmer, from her crown to her waist.

"How I like it," she said, leaning into the stroke.

"You smell like clover," he noticed.

She spit out her bubble gum and stuck it under a shelf. "Sweet Honesty," she said. "Avon. I don't sell it any more. Daddy says it's competition for the store." She took the hairbrush from him and threw it over a pile of cartons in the corner. It scuttered out of sight.

"Everything in this store is *mine*," she told Jordan. "I can help myself. What would you like to have?"

"I have to go now," he said.

"You ought to teach your folks a lesson," she told him.

"How?" Like a man in a dream, he kept on walking toward the cavemouth, his heart pounding.

"Make them afraid. Afraid you'll die. Afraid you'll run away." She turned to face him and got close. "You scared of me?"

"No."

She laughed. "Miles to go to mean it," she said. She drew the cross he had given her up from her blouse, saying, "Feel, it's as warm as I am."

He touched it but didn't touch her.

"I could wash your feet and dry them with my hair," she suggested. "I think as highly of you as I do of Jesus." She said, "Take off your shoes."

She didn't figure he would. There was a slight film of sweat on his face.

"Do you really believe God made me out of your ribs?" She put her hand out and touched his chest. "I just want to see the scar," she said.

He thought he heard something.

"What could you hear?" she said. "Your heart?" She leaned her ear and listened.

Ginnie heard something else.

"Did you lock the door?" she wondered.

"I —"

"Did you?"

"I —"

A flashlight beam prowled across the ceiling over their heads. They ducked to the floor. "Night watchman!" he whispered.

"No," Ginnie said. "There isn't one. It's somebody breaking in!" She almost laughed aloud. Luck! She couldn't think fast enough. She was excited and almost danced. Which way? Which way? "In here," she decided, and they crept around behind the curtains into the store and waited. Ginnie leaned around to look.

"Get behind me," Jordan said.

"You! In there! I hear you!"

"Daddy!" Ginnie breathed. "Oh shit!"

Doc kicked the door open and yelled, "Freeze!" just as Jordan stepped forward, his hands out in the dark. "It's all right, sir," he began to say.

Doc fired, both barrels.

The impact knocked Jordan backward, the ribs Ginnie had touched a moment ago gone like the plastic curtain in their faces, and then Jordan fell. There was nothing between Ginnie and Doc but that spilled blood.

Ginnie didn't scream but once, then she bent there, trying

90

to pull her skirt out of Jordan's grip. Doc stood looking down.

"Goddamn mess," he said.

Jordan tried to say something, but he couldn't remember what. He rested. When the sirens neared, he asked, "Who's hurt?"

When Ginnie said, "This didn't happen," he asked, "Who is it?" already forgetting, with each emptying pulse, time running backward as it ran down.

"You're hurt," Doc told him, facing facts. The emergency unit arrived.

"I'm not afraid," Jordan said. The technician stripped back Jordan's sleeve to start plasma.

"Take it easy, son," the attendant said. "Stay with us." They lifted him up and even then Jordan was awake, gripping Ginnie's skirt. She rode beside him in the ambulance.

"Notify trauma," they radioed ahead.

Ginnie said, "I need to wash my hands," and someone gave her a towelette. There were bits of the curtain in her hair. They kept drifting randomly down.

Doc said, mile after mile after mile, "It was self-defense."

In emergency, they all waited together. Jordan's grandfather was there, his sports coat pulled on over his pajamas, no socks on his pale feet, the elastic to his eye patch lost in a rumple of white hair under the yachting cap. Doc sat in the corner on a straight chair. Ginnie stood at the window, looking down at traffic. She had washed her face and arms. All of the blood was Jordan's. She hadn't got even one pellet, she was that lucky.

Jordan's grandfather said, "Seven units of blood already."

A policeman was standing in the doorway, filling out reports. Doc answered most of the questions. Ginnie moved back and forth in front of the windows, like a fox in a cage. Finally she sat. She drew another chair over and propped her feet on it.

From the hall, footsteps brought them all to attention. A woman looked in at them, waiting. Her left hand was cupped to catch her cigarette ash, her eyes witness to some unspeakable anxiety. She looked at them all, one by one, then studied the policeman's insignia, the flag on his sleeve, his badge. She shook her head, lost in her own anguish, tears brimming. "Mine's not a police matter," she said, going on by, down the hall, out of sight.

Jordan's grandfather said, "Sonofabitch!" and pounded his fist into his thigh. He passed his hands over his face, and blinked at Doc.

"I thought he was reaching for a gun," Doc said.

At the door, the policeman cleared his throat.

They looked at him, for news. He said, "I was just clearing my throat."

"They ought to have a TV in here," Ginnie said.

"I could see them moving around — the silhouettes, you know?" Doc spoke to the deputy. "I did what I thought right at the time."

Jordan's grandfather said, "He was born right here in this hospital."

Doc said, "She was too."

Jordan's grandfather said, "The night you made her, you should have shot it in the sink instead."

Ginnie laughed.

Doc didn't. He jumped up so fast his chair turned over. The two men kept hitting each other, and sobbing, till the orderlies and the officer pulled them apart. The old man sat down, still crisp with anger, and pressed his handkerchief to his lip. A nurse brought Doc a plastic glove filled with ice for his eye.

Doc blew his nose.

Ginnie shook out her dress and sat again. "This was a Laura Ashley," she explained. She looked down inside the blouse, then stood and shook her skirt. The cross didn't fall out. It was gone. "And I lost my necklace too," she said. She started looking for it on the floor.

"Sit down and shut up," Doc told her.

It was another hour before the surgeon came in. He was as bloody as Ginnie. He paused a moment, then said, "Kilgore?" and the old man stood, slowly but tall.

"Alive," the doctor said. "I came to let you know we've had a look around. It's bad, couldn't have been much worse. Spine's not hurt, but the bleeding has to be stopped. We do that, he's got a chance. I don't kid you, abdominal's second only to head for tricky. We're layered, not toys. And he's a mess. We have to stop the leaks first. Then we might have a chance," he said. "A chance."

"I'll be here," his grandfather said, in a different voice, and not as tall.

"It'll be hours. There's a snack bar down the hall; we'll keep you posted." At the door he turned back and said, "Good luck."

"And to you the same," the old man said.

When the surgeon had gone, he told Doc, "I don't want you here, none of y'all. I don't want to see you." He looked at Ginnie. "I don't want to *smell* you."

Doc said to Ginnie, low as prayer, "Not a word."

They walked with the lawman to their car. Doc wasn't under arrest; charges pending. "But you'll both have to answer some more questions," the officer told them.

"I'm not going anywhere," Doc said.

Afterward, as they drove home, Ginnie said, "I guess this cooks it about the Datsun for graduation, doesn't it."

"Could you cry for that?" Doc wondered. "Could you?"

The bright moon stared down at itself in the river as they crossed. It was almost dawn.

"This'll put your mother back at Brawner's," Doc said. "If they sue, we're looking at chapter-seven bankruptcy."

Ginnie clicked on the radio. Doc cut it off instantly. "For God's sake!"

Not that she was listening for news. There wouldn't be any, not for three days. Jordan lived three days. No lawsuits.

Gid didn't die until the next summer, and Ginnie didn't know anything about it at the time. Doc had double-mortgaged to send her away to finish high school at Tallulah, and then she spent the summer at a mountain camp, lifeguarding.

She heard about Gid casually, soon after returning home, and she didn't ask any questions. She went to the library and read about it on microfilm. He had been riding a lumber truck, atop the piled wood. He was leaning against the cab, not watching where he was going, just looking back at the road he had already traveled; they went under a low railroad bridge and he was killed instantly. It made her feel funny, reading about it like that. She hadn't thought of him in a long time.

Home again, she went to her room and got her majorette boots out of their box, dumping the newspaper stuffing on the bed. There wasn't much to sort through. She didn't even have to hide her pills any more.

She found the matchbox crammed in the left toe, filled

to roundness with cotton. In the center of that cotton was the ring. It wasn't worth anything. All its pawnable worth had fallen from it the day it arrived in the mail. She had carried the little package upstairs to open it and had dropped it on the bathroom floor. The laid-on stone, turquoise paste, had crumbled off. The silver was so thin the brass showed through. It had a coppery smell, like blood. Its flashiness was plated on, and inside, engraved within its tarnished perfect greening circle was "REMEBER GIDEON." He'd paid for that. It still made her laugh. She said it: "Remeber." Had the engraver made the mistake, or Gid? When she stepped on the broken blue stone from the ring, it had powdered to dust. She had cleaned it off the floor with a tissue and flushed it away.

She had never worn the ring and had never seen Gid again. A week later she had gone away to school. Now she tried it on, and it fit so tight it frightened her. She had to work it off with soapy water.

She put it back in the box and headed downstairs, with the box in her pocket. As she went by her mother's door, her mother called, over the top of her latest Harlequin, "Seat belt!"

The Datsun was backed into the garage. She opened the door and drove out, leaving rubber on the concrete. That was for her mother, listening upstairs. She tapped the horn at the end of the drive. That was for the dogs. They jumped in and rode with her, nosing out the T-roof, taking the air.

It was a fine day, a late autumn day. The lake wasn't busy — a few sails on the far channel, a bass boat on the west cove, and no skiers. She let the dogs out to run; they drank from the lake and chased each other clumsily along the muddy shore, turning over rocks, sniffing at debris.

Ginnie stood at the car a moment watching them. She left the door open, sliding the keys on their jailer's bracelet onto her wrist, walking easily down to the water and along the littered and slippery beach. She stepped over the cable anchoring someone's dock to the shore. The "Private" sign nailed to the dock stuck up just enough so she could clean the mud off her boots on its sharp edge. The wood was so sun-warm she could feel it through her soles. A kingfisher buzzed her, and flew past, settling on the reef-warning, looking this way, then that, at the green reflection of the pines in the water. Out in the channel the lake was blue as the sky. The dock dipped under Ginnie's feet, slow, drowsy, on the lapping rim of the lake.

She shaded her eyes and looked as far as she could, claiming it all. She felt as free and right as she did in her own home. The untrammeling world was widening in ripples around her, and she was the stone at the center that set things moving. She took out the box from her pocket and shook the ring out of its cotton, like a seed. The cotton blew away, and the lake took it, dragged it down slowly. She held the ring on her palm in the sun till it burned hot, hotter than her blood. Then she tossed it as far as she could, out past the low-water reef. It skipped once — plook! — and vanished. The dogs chewed up the matchbox, playing on past her, barking off on trails into the woods. Ginnie stood there a moment in that impersonal vantage and solitude, breathing deep.

She reached high over her head and clawed the sky, then folded up, right at the edge of the dock, which tipped a little with her hundred pounds. Her hands smelled brassy. She dipped them in the lake, troubling the clear water, then drew them up, splashing her cheeks with the cool. Refreshed, she looked up, as though something on the horizon had caught her attention. She stood, flinging the last drops from her hands, drying them on her skirt. She walked back to the car, whistling the dogs in, and churned the car slowly uphill through that sand onto the lane between the windbreak pines, heading toward the main road in no particular hurry. It wasn't life or death.

Moths

IT HAD TAKEN since Easter to cut this much. It would be another two weeks till they had pulped all the way back through the thousand acres to the lake. They worked hard, from early breakfast till late supper, as the year turned toward summer. It was just the three of them, Cheney and two green kids, cutting and loading onto Mr. Anderson's old truck.

Mr. Anderson wanted the oaks left standing, but he had said Cheney could have the sweet gums and poplars for his own woodpile — just don't cut firewood on wages. That meant Cheney had to come back in the evenings to gather it. Every night he would fill his pickup truck bed with the day's rounds and haul them home. He would split them later, when some of the sap had dried out. The days were getting longer, but it was always dark night when he gave the last log a kick and it rolled from the truck. Sometimes he sat on the steps, too tired to wash, or eat, or sleep.

Mr. Anderson wanted the pines cut no lower than waist

high to leave the dozers something to push against. They were going to tear the stumps out and grade the acres into lots. They had already begun piling the pinetops, limbs, deadfall, and stumps to burn. The smoke rose high in the dry, still air. The light had a strange yellow look to it, and the flames and heat cast their own shadows.

They were going to clear the land and build houses — not Cheney and the boys who worked with him, but another crew. Mr. Anderson had plans. He and the surveyors stood by his fine car, talking, looking at blueprints, pointing, nodding. Mr. Anderson was the boss now, but he had started out just like Cheney and the boys, harvesting pines for someone else.

When they had stacked the truck with the morning's cutting and chained the logs down, it was almost time for lunch. They would take the load to the pulpyard and on the way back, get something to eat. The boys always stopped at Mama Red's for lunch. Cheney told them they were wasting their time working so hard if all they did was spend the money on food. "Besides, all that grease'll kill you before you're twenty," Cheney warned.

"You're getting old," they ragged him.

"I'll die rich," he said.

He brought his lunch from home — a mayonnaise jar of tea and rattling ice, corn bread and a sweet potato, slab meat in a biscuit. While the boys drove the truck to the pulpyard and stopped by the hamburger joint, Cheney stayed behind. After he had eaten, after he had sharpened the saw-chain for the afternoon work, he would lie down in the shade and sleep till they got back.

Once when Cheney had slept past their return, the boys woke him by dropping peanut hulls on his face. So today when the crunching noise woke him, he thought it was the boys sneaking up on him to play a trick. He opened his eyes and sat up, quick. There was no one around. The truck wasn't back yet.

Again he heard it, that slow crunch, crunch, like dry cornflakes being broken one by one. A squirrel? Cheney yawned. He couldn't see any squirrel. The sun was directly overhead. He squinted up at the limbs above him, listening. When he put his hands to his mouth and gave a squirrel call, no squirrel sassed back. The crunching noise came again, not up in the tree, but on the ground.

"Something's getting itself ate like corn on the cob," he said. He took up his file and gave the saw a last lick, tightened the chain on the bar, checked the oil and gas. He was ready to work. If the boys didn't get back soon, he was going to start without them. As he knelt to crank the saw, he heard the crunching again and noticed the dry leaves move.

With the file he flipped the leaves over. He thought he would see a mouse — or a snake — or something . . . He didn't see anything. There was no hole. Nothing had escaped, yet nothing was there.

"I don't care," Cheney said. He didn't like tricks. He didn't like not knowing what. He was going to kick the leaves around, just stomp whatever it was out of business and be done with it, when he noticed the moth on last year's dead goldenrod. The wings were silver-green, like two dogwood leaves. Cheney leaned low to look, and his laughing breath made the weed sway. The moth held still.

So that was it — he had been right about it being a trick. The noise was probably some little gadget the boys bought at Bully's Store, something rigged up with fishing line and a spoon lure, wired to the paper moth, then wired to the twig. The paper legs looked like chocolate. Cheney knelt closer. The feelers were two dusty little feathers of angel gold, and the wings were outlined in pink.

But when Cheney reached for it, it flew — it was real, not paper! It left green chalk on his fingers. It flew low, as if he had hurt it, as if it were about to crash. Gliding more than flying, it didn't go far. When it lit on the next weed, it crawled out on a twig and hung itself straight flat open, like wash on a line.

Now Cheney reckoned it wasn't a joke unless it was a wonderful one, and this time when he reached for it, it shuddered away from him. It kited off in that same heavy-tailed way back to the first weed and clung, motionless. Cheney went to get his tea jar. He was going to clamp the moth inside. It was a quart jar and the moth would about fit. When he bent over to pick up the jar, though, he saw something trembling in the dry leaves with that same crunching noise that had waked him. It was papery, brown, no bigger than a cigar stub. Cheney took it in his hand and watched as one little gold feathery feeler stuck itself out the hole. It looked just like the feeler on the green moth.

The case was crumpled on one side as though it had been stepped on. Maybe the truck had run over it. Cheney shook it. Inside, the moth struggled. He could feel it. The moth butted at the frayed end of the case, trying to be born. It had worn a hole with its head, trying to escape. One strand blocked the exit, caught the moth across the head, between the feelers, tangling the one already free in the air. Cheney took out his knife, but before he could make the hole larger, the moth stuck out the other feeler and began pushing its way out into the day. Its eyes were rubbed dull, and there was white dust where the moth had scrubbed itself bald trying to escape the crumpled case. The hole wasn't large enough, but the moth wouldn't wait. It freed itself in stops and goes, and each struggle brought more of it to light. The wings were tiny and folded, like young pea leaves. The body was soft and covered in white plush, which the hard labor was scouring off.

When the moth was all the way out of the case, it was bigger than Cheney's thumb, bigger than the case itself, as though it fattened on sunshine and free air. It walked all around on Cheney's hand, always climbing upward. When Cheney touched it, to feel that soft plush, it squirted mud water on him, the color of the raw land being cleared. "You little beau gator!" Cheney said, almost slinging the moth away in surprise. It was more active now.

It climbed up Cheney's arm, across his sleeve, onto his shirtfront, up his chest. When it tickled Cheney's throat, he lifted it off, more gently this time, and let it start all over again, climbing up his arm. It seemed to be seeking. Cheney told it, "Settle," the way he would speak to his own baby.

He held up his arm, and the moth climbed as far as it could and hung from Cheney's busted thumb. Hung motionless like the one already unfurled on the goldenrod. Cheney was still holding his arm up, watching for the moth's wings to fill out, when the boys got back.

He showed them. They had never seen anything like either the flat moth or the crumpled one. Cheney thought he could see the little wings begin to grow — if he looked away, then looked back, he thought they seemed a little larger.

Nobody knew how long it took. Cheney fingered the moth onto a gum sapling. It clung to the bark of the trunk, hanging straight, the crumpled wings slightly raised. It didn't look to be busy doing much of anything. Neither did the other one. Donnie said, poking at the freshly hatched one with a pine needle, "Maybe he's dead." The moth raised a feisty foreleg. "Huh, nope." He kept tracing it with the pine needle to watch it make those little warning lifts of this leg, of that leg, but still it held its place.

Cheney said, "Now y'all leave my pets alone," and they laughed.

Ward said, "Something's wrong with him, he ain't never gonna be right," and Donnie said, "You mean Cheney?" and after that, they went back to work.

Cheney could gauge as well as any woodswalker how many trees to cut for a load. He'd been at it long enough, but it was more than experience. There was pride in it too, not to leave too much timber lying cut at the end of the day, making it easy for poachers.

Cheney was the one who cut. He didn't like felling timber too near another saw. But once the trees were down, Ward took the second saw and helped limb and top and walk off the lengths. Donnie stood on the truck, running the hoist.

When lunch wore off, when the afternoon began to cool and everyone was glad the day was about over, they took a break. Cheney and Ward smoked. Donnie washed his candy bar down with Pepsi left over from lunch. They had forgotten the moths. Cheney remembered.

Even now, hours later, the crumpled one was clinging to the sweet gum, its wings still stunted. The other moth hung straight on its weed.

"I bet they's a book about them, telling their name and everwhat else about them," Cheney said.

"What's to tell?" Donnie asked. "They just hang around." He stripped off his T-shirt, dried his chest and under his arms, and turned his back on the sun, hugging himself, enjoying his rest. His feet kept time to an inner radio.

Ward said, "Mama Red asked about you."

Cheney lit another cigarette. "Me?"

"Said why didn't our good-looking boss stop by."

"I ain't no boss," Cheney said, pleased. "Musta meant Mr. Anderson." He lay back on the ground.

Donnie said, "Didn't say 'boss' — said 'the old man' . . ."

That was when Cheney caught on — they had made it up to tease him. He sat up. "Tell Mama Red I got me a good cook at home. I don't have to hire it."

"Whoooeee!" Donnie said.

Ward kept on. "I told her that. And you know what she said? Said you was the first married man she knew who enjoyed it."

"What'd you say?" Cheney studied his cigarette.

"Said you enjoyed it a couple times a month — rest of the time you too tired."

Donnie gave his great huh-huh laugh.

"Check this," Cheney said. He dusted himself off, ran to the truck, and swung lightly up. On the crane he chinned himself, again and again. Ward kept count aloud, then lost interest.

Donnie said, "Any monkey can do that," and tossed a pine cone at him. Cheney ducked. He stood rubbing his palms on his jeans.

Ward climbed up. He wanted to try. He wasn't very good. Cheney said, "Your laigs'll get you wherever you need to go, but your arms'll make your fortune, boys. Them and knowing what five A.M. looks like every day but Sunday." He jumped to the ground and said, "Let's get this one finished. Two hours more ought to do it right."

Just that little break gave them energy. They started back to work, cheerful. Ward was whistling. Not thirty minutes later the hoist chain snapped as they loaded the truck, and the whiplash laid open Ward's scalp and took out his front teeth.

Donnie yelled, "No!" and jumped down, crying, "Jeez oh Jeez, Cheney!" Cheney was already there.

"It looks worse than it is," he said. That's the first thing he said when anything went wrong. He pulled the younger boy back. But Donnie swung around on him, wild.

"That's my brother! You fix it!"

Cheney said, "Son, you can help. Find the teeth."

The boy stood staring. Cheney said, *"Find the teeth."* The boy dropped to the ground, patting the dirt. Cheney said, "They can put them back. I saw it on TV. He don't have to go courting looking like me."

Ward's eyes flickered. He looked around. "God, I hope not," he tried to say. He turned his head to spit. "Blood," he said.

Cheney had taken off his shirt and was tying it around Ward's head. "You ain't pretty right now, that's a hundred percent sure." All the time he kept fixing the bandage. "Nurses going to drop dead right and left at the sight of you."

"That bad?" Ward coughed.

Donnie was crawling around under the truck, trying to find the teeth. "I got three. How many more?"

"Smile," Cheney said, trying to count Ward's gaps.

"You look like Halloween," Donnie said, helping count. He was red-eyed and sniffing, but he managed a huh-huh, and was steadier now.

"Aw, hell." Ward sat up. "I'm okay. Let's go back to work."

Cheney said, "First time I ever heard you say that. It must be the blow to your head." He and Donnie got Ward up and into the cab of the truck, and then they tightened down the load they had. The chains were rusty. Donnie rubbed that off his hands as if it was Ward's blood. They rode toward Deerfield, Ward between them. Donnie held Ward steady with one hand. In his other hand he still had the three teeth, all he ever found.

Cheney said, driving fast, "They can put them back in."

Donnie wanted them to go faster. "Put your hassle lights on and lean on it — he's my brother, man."

Cheney clicked on the emergency lights, but he didn't use the horn. The road was all theirs. He took the curves down the ridge in the middle, letting the loaded truck drift, then easing it back in bounds. He would get them there.

Deerfield was nine miles. When you got there, there wasn't much to it — one block of stores facing the railroad. But it was closer than anywhere else. And there was a dentist. He had a big plastic tooth for a sign, and a billboard at the city limits, needing a coat of paint.

"Dentist first," Ward mumbled. "I'd rather bleed to death than live looking like Cheney. Damn! I caint even whistle up my dogs."

But at the dentist's, the nurse, seeing they were strangers, said, "All emergencies are cash," and left them to talk it over. Cheney rang the bell again. They had eleven dollars among them. He held out the teeth and showed her. "They can fix this."

She said, "I'll ask the doctor." She didn't touch the teeth. While she was gone, the other patients looked at Cheney and the boys. When she came back, the nurse said, "If you have *proof* of insurance, of course we'll take that. Otherwise, cash." She smiled. "That's our policy for nonappointment emergencies. It's posted," she added, pointing. She wouldn't look at Ward, who sat forward so he wouldn't bloody the wall. He kept his handkerchief to his mouth, from time to time spitting into it.

Cheney said, "It was on TV, how they can put a man's

teeth back, so he don't have to gum along empty." The nurse swung her chair to the typewriter and began to work. There was music coming down from the ceiling. Donnie was hunkered in front of the fish tank, looking at the deep-sea diver.

Ward pushed up from his chair and said through his stained handkerchief, "C'mon." He went out.

On the steps, Cheney said, "Maybe there's another dentist."

"Not this end of the county. Forget it. C'mon."

But Cheney went back in. He told the nurse, who looked frightened now, "My boss is Mr. Anderson . . . He'll pay. You call him?"

"We close in five minutes," she said.

"You could just call him — it's not long distance."

"Look," she said, but that was all.

The waiting room was empty now. There was a yellow umbrella hanging on the hat rack. It hadn't rained in weeks. Cheney could hear water running. He could hear voices and the mosquito noise of the drill. The fish tank's filter hummed and the treasure chest's lid bubbled open and shut, open and shut. Cheney left.

Donnie said, "I think he needs stitches."

Cheney looked. "Yeah, I guess."

"Aw, hell, they'll shave my head." Ward sounded weak.

"He paid thirty dollars for those curls," Donnie said.

"They'll only shear half of that wool," Cheney said.

Donnie didn't want Ward to hear. He said, "You reckon they'll take us at the hospital?"

Cheney shrugged. "If they don't, my old lady'll do it with spool thread and a darning needle."

"Momma's gonna have a fit," Donnie said.

The hospital was across the tracks. Cheney had to ease

the truck over the rails. The side road was washed out. Donnie looked back, worried, but the load didn't shift. "That's all we need," he said.

It wasn't much of a hospital. Private, hardly larger than the dental clinic. "Maybe they're dog doctors," Ward said.

"An idea," Cheney said. "If they don't take you here, we'll drop you off at the pound. They'll feed you for a couple of days, and if nobody wants you, they'll put you out of your misery." They got him to the door, up the ramp, sagging between them. He was leaning hard when Cheney told the nurse at the desk, "My buddy here's been hurt. Got his skull busted open. We got eleven dollars. Maybe we can give blood or something for the difference." The nurse looked at them.

She rolled a wheelchair over and helped get Ward settled. "There'll be a way," she said.

Cheney stopped at the pay phone while they went on to Emergency. He found Mr. Anderson's card in his wallet and thumb-flicked the grime off the Atlanta number and dropped the quarter in. After he dialed, he could hear the faraway noises as his signal crossed the exchange boundary at the river. A long time later it began to ring. Mr. Anderson didn't answer. Nobody answered. Cheney tried again, to be sure. Then he went to find the boys.

They were asking Ward how long he had been knocked out. He didn't know. Cheney told them two minutes, maybe. Not long. Maybe less than that. The doctor wanted to take an x-ray of Ward's skull, just in case. Then they'd stitch up his scalp. It wasn't serious, they said, looking at Ward's eyes with a light. The bleeding had about stopped. They told him he was lucky. One of the nurses had filled a rubber glove with ice to hold on Ward's mouth. He wanted a cigarette — Cheney was out, and Ward's were lost. Cheney said, "I'm going to the drugstore, okay?" and left Donnie in charge of waiting. They rolled Ward down the hall to take pictures.

Cheney walked back to town.

Traffic on the state road was heavy. He finally took a chance and dodged across. On the sidewalk, he stopped at the phone and tried to reach Mr. Anderson again. He didn't know how much x-rays would cost. Mr. Anderson always said, "Do what you have to," if the truck needed a tire, or something done to the engine. Whatever it was, do it, and get on with the job. So Cheney thought it was all right about the x-rays, but he would like to talk to him to be sure. Mr. Anderson still didn't answer.

Cheney bought two packs of cigarettes — one for him and one for Ward. He headed back up the street toward the hospital road. Next to the Rexall there was an empty store, and then a dry goods store. In the window of the dry goods store were all sorts of things for spring: cardboard rabbits, little girl dresses like lamp shades, and a basket filled with plastic eggs. They hadn't gotten around to changing the window display, though Easter was past. The patent leather shoes looked dusty. The plastic tulips had faded. One of the wings was broken off the paper butterfly. That made Cheney think of the moths, and when he went past the last building on the block, on the corner, where the bank had been, he stopped and read FARMERS AND MERCHANTS carved in the stone of the fake front. It wasn't a bank now; it was a library. Cheney walked by, then went back. He stood another minute finishing his smoke, and then he went inside.

He was going to look up the green moths. He hadn't counted on there being so many books. He didn't remember from school days where to look. He just stood there. He didn't see anyone, but in back, between high shelves, he could hear quick footsteps coming his way. The door had a cowbell on it — that was what gave the alarm. When the woman saw him, she stopped. She had a watering can in her hands, and it dripped a little.

"Yes?" She came up and stood between him and the books. "And you want?" She was as clean as Sunday. Her hands were white enough to make bread.

Cheney didn't know. He wished he didn't have so much of Ward's blood on his undershirt. He wished he didn't have so much rosin on his jeans. He wished that he had washed his hands. He put his hat back on. "I come in the wrong store," he said. "Reckon I just didn't notice where I was." He went out.

He looked back as he crossed the street. She was already pulling the shades down, and locking up for the night. It was going-home time for everybody. He didn't worry about his wife, even though he might be going to be late. She was used to just about anything. Some days it took him a little longer, and she knew to keep the supper warm. When he was going to be very late, he'd call her sister, and she'd run the message by home.

Cheney figured they'd let Ward go as soon as they had stitched him up. Then Cheney would drop him and Donnie by their momma's house, and head on to the pulpyard. After that, he could go home.

When he got back, they had finished with Ward. He was sitting on the porch, and Donnie was sitting beside him. They looked okay. Cheney tossed Ward his cigarettes. He had a pack of crackers for Donnie.

Cheney went inside to tell them about the billing. They took down Mr. Anderson's name and phone number. It would be all right, they said. Cheney said, "Much obliged."

Ward and Donnie were already in the truck. Ward was feeling better. He still held the ice to his mouth, but he didn't have to spit so much. The bandage on his head wasn't that bad. The place they had sheared off the curls looked like where Rural Electric had clearcut for the powerline right-of-way through deep woods. Donnie said it again, "Momma's gonna have a fit."

Ward said, "Doc says for me not to do much for a couple of days, but I'll be ready tomorrow. I'll be ready." He talked fast. His tongue didn't know what to do with the gaps. He was talking funny from the shot they had given him.

"I'll find me somebody," Cheney said, "for the rest of this week."

"Don't give my job away."

"You know me," Cheney said. "I don't give nothing away worth anything." He handed Ward his teeth. "Put these under your pillow," he said.

After that, he went on to the woodyard. They didn't say anything much about the short load. It was sundown when Cheney got home. The kids ran down to meet him, riding on the running boards, yelling in the windows at him. Cheney went slow, the truck wallowing up the rutty drive. When his wife came out, with the baby, he said, "Just don't ask me about where's my shirt. You'd a lot rather I lost it than to have to wash Ward's blood out of it, anyhow."

She looked at his undershirt and said, "Bad hurt?"

"He knows what a rusty chain tastes like. He'll be ordering soup for a while."

The baby was fretting. Cheney took the child in his arms and talked to her. "Got any new teeth yet?" He checked. "Looks about like Ward." The baby began to cry. "Ssshh now," he said.

His wife said, "She won't."

A redbird chuck-chucked and flew across the clearing, with food for its mate. Cheney said, "It ought to be like that, him taking care of her, her doing her part, everybody working to make things go." The birds were almost black in the twilight.

"You going back after supper?" she asked, taking the baby.

"Let me think," he said.

They headed on up to the double-wide. She had been planting flower seeds near the porch. The ground was all dug up and there was a hoe lying there. She was outlining the flowerbed in rocks. On the way past she picked up the hoe. "Put this up," she told the nearest boy. He rode it over to the shed, straddling it like a horse.

"Y'all already ate?" Cheney said.

"We waited . . . You hungry?"

"I could take nourishment," he said.

While they were eating, his wife asked again, "You going back tonight?"

"Every stick I cut now when it's cool'll save me some sweat in July."

"We'll come too."

"Baby's sick, ain't she?"

His wife laid a hand on the child's forehead. "Teething fever's all it is. You know how they fret. We won't hinder."

"I didn't think you would. I don't want you lifting a twig, though. You know what the doctor said."

"I'm better," she said. "I been digging like a field hand all day . . . The boys can help you."

"I wouldn't mind the company," he said.

They worked in the wedge of the truck's headlights. Cheney had a lantern, too. He set it on the stump and told the kids to leave it alone, and they mostly did. The boys helped him load. The baby chewed on the corner of a washcloth, watching them work. She started to fret and cry every time Cheney's wife tried to lay her down on the quilt.

His wife was willing to let the baby cry it out, but Cheney said, "Put something in that child's mouth." It got on his nerves to think the baby was unhappy.

"One thing she wants," his wife said.

"Everwhat it takes," Cheney said.

His wife took the baby to the truck and sat nursing her in the cab.

The day's wood was mostly sweet gum. None of the trees was very big. The boys could carry two rounds across their arms each trip. The truck bed slowly filled. Cheney would have cut some more stove-lengths, but the baby was finally asleep — the saw would wake her for sure. She lay on the seat of the truck, but she still held to her mother's shirt hem. His wife shrugged and smiled. Cheney said, "She been like that all day?" His wife looked tired.

She said, "It's harder on her than on me."

Cheney pulled his wife's shirttail out of the baby's fist, and the baby didn't wake. "Come here," he said. He took the lantern and walked over to the sweet-gum tree where he had left the green moth. It was still there. They both were there, on that tree. Cheney told his sons, "Don't mess with them."

The crippled moth was still shriveled, but the perfect one had found it. One of the perfect wings was broken now, as though there had been a fight.

"They's like a cup and saucer," his wife said, and pressed her right fist against her left palm, in a cup and saucer gesture.

The moths were completely still. They were joined at

right angles, end to end. The boys said, "What is it?" and Cheney said, "It's a moth." He puffed the lantern out after lighting his cigarette from it. "It's hot," he warned, handing it to the boys. "Put it in the truck, safe, and both of you get in back, go on."

His wife told them, "Don't y'all wake her!"

In the beam of the headlights, dimmer and more faraway than the lantern's glare, the moths seemed to be one living thing, not two. Cheney's wife bent to see better. The moths were so still. "So that's how," she said.

Her shadow didn't disturb them. Nothing did. "You reckon they dead, Cheney?" She took a straw, the way Donnie had, earlier that day, and touched the one with crippled wings. The little dark leg lifted, warning. She stepped back. "Looks like a spider leg," she said. She shook her head.

The flat, perfect one was belly-up, but Cheney could remember how it looked topside. "It's got red around the edge. All around. And brown. And a sort of eye-looking thing on each wing," Cheney told her. Right then, before she could stoop to see the moth's back, they parted. The perfect one flew low and rested on some broken branches on the ground, then flew again.

Cheney could tell the other one wouldn't fly, couldn't fly. "Maybe it don't need," he said. "Maybe it just don't need to." He waited to see.

"We don't go soon, the battery's gonna run down." His wife looked around at the truck. The headlights were yellow and dim.

"Cut the lights off," Cheney called, and the boys wrestled to be the one to hit the switch. They flicked them back on again, playing. Cheney said, "Boys?" and then it got dark.

There was a little air stirring. The pines on tomorrow's cutting were tall against the first stars. Up toward Hammermill the sky was lighter. Cheney could see, after his eyes got sharper, the glint of the mayonnaise jar he had brought his tea in for lunch. He had forgotten it when they left to take care of Ward. He picked it up. The lid was missing. Cheney tossed it — it hit on something and smashed. "I'm so goddamn tired of being poor," he said.

The smoke from the day's burning stumps drifted toward them across the acres. They walked back to the truck in the dark. The baby was still sleeping and the boys had settled down in back, tired out, crouched on the logs, quiet, almost asleep.

Cheney steered home easy. The Ford rode low in the back from the load, the headlights striking high on the passing trees and signs. There was all that wood to unload when they got home. His wife mentioned that.

"It looks worse than it is," Cheney said.

The baby was sleeping good — she liked to ride along. The boys used to be that way, sleeping till they got home, and he'd lift one under each arm like groceries, carry them up the steps into the house to their bunks. But they were too big for that now. They were growing fast.

The Goodwife Hawkins

HE HADN'T thrown her a word or a look since he'd refused breakfast — some whole days passed like that — but as soon as she touched Hawk's cold shoulder she knew he was good and dead, not sulking. She hauled the drapes back, raised the blackout shades, cranked open the jalousies, shoved the patio door wide on its reluctant track, and ran his musty old pointer, Shelah, out into the fresh air. These were her first free acts. Then Vinnie and the dog just stood on the terrace disoriented, shivering in the surprise of being alive in the tender sun while acorns fell randomly around them, pinging on the rusty boathouse, skipping down the roof tiles into the clogged gutters, tapping to earth like those last huge drops of rain. A pair of flickers whirred up as the dog threaded through the sparkling hedge. She had worn a trail toward the evening sun. She'd limp back by dark; she'd never missed supper yet.

It had been drizzling all day, but now was fairing. The storm was over. A chill wind herded the clouds along, nagging Vinnie into buttoning her sweater as she surveyed the damage. The yard looked bad, the hard-won lawn rain-trampled, its bright rye gone under the autumn's castings. A section of fence had broken and the whole lot was littered like a schoolroom after a paper fight. Vinnie preferred things tidy.

She went back into the house for her galoshes. Without glancing at the bed or shutting the patio door — the room was already damp and cool — she headed down the wheelchair ramp with its new unpainted boards they had just installed and never needed, and headed out across the drying flagstones to the pumphouse where the tools hung. She took down the spring rake to begin setting the yard to rights. She was still listening for him — it would be a long habit to break — harking for that vigorous cough or her name fired at her like a gun or the imperious thump of his cane on the floor, summoning her once more up those stairs from the laundry room. From time to time their doctor would listen to her chest and report, "You have the heart of a child," and just as well. Hawk had put her through it.

The week-long storm had strewn downed limbs everywhere. Vinnie pulled at them as if she were a mule in harness, dragging them over to the pile for Yubo to clear away with his chain saw and chipper. The ringing phone drew her back indoors. Breathless, she explained to one of her quilting cronies, "I'm expecting unexpected company just now," and didn't talk long or mention Hawk at all. She knew she ought to make the necessary phone calls, but she postponed for a few more minutes. She had the front walk swept, the slick, leathery leaves piled to the side before Yubo arrived. She phoned only Yubo and the emergency medical service ambulance, not her children, not her friends. Yubo had arthritis and sciatica and hated to work in the damp, his blood pressure medicine had made him feel washed out, and as always he preferred to be paid in cash. Other than that, he made no demands, and was willing. He was the first one to arrive. He got there ten minutes ahead of the sirens. Vinnie had told the dispatcher that there was no hurry, but they came on as though there was life to be saved . . .

Yubo had drawn his hand back, quick, from Hawk's jaw — no pulse — and the chill of that flesh stayed on Yubo's palm till he bent to scrub it on the blanket. "Done dead," he said. "Colder than kraut." He looked toward Vinnie, who never in her life had said, I told you so. She sat on the chair she had eased onto as they came into the room, as though she had turned faint, yet even in weakness, she held fast, straight-backed from those years of wearing the brace, her lotion-scented hands lying quiet on her proper lap.

"You need you some Co-Cola?" he wondered.

"No."

"You look done in," Yubo said.

"He kept me up all night. When he finally slept, I let him."

"Too much for one little bitty woman to handle," Yubo agreed.

They could hear the sirens — the first responder's, and the sheriff's patrol too, his blue light flashing as the car turned in. Vinnie had given precise directions. She had an orderly mind, had been praised for it on many occasions, serving on charitable committees, a good wife to Hawk Hawkins, keeping his payroll straight all those years, raising his sons, never too tired for any of the other things he'd volunteered her to do, cooking all night for the game and fish suppers, taking blue ribbons for her quilts and India relish year on year, a boxful of prizes, plaques, clippings, and snapshots filed modestly away on the basement shelf. "Hawk's the one," she'd say.

Their den walls had filled and overflowed into the foyer with his hunting trophies, citations of civic and humane excellence, glossy photographs — noble or comic — signed "Your buddy," "Your pal," "Fraternally yours," and framed items from newspapers and magazines. Hawk was a justice of the peace, a former mayor, a Mason, a Shriner, a Legionnaire. He'd played a season of Triple-A baseball on a championship team. His was a documented life. Every room celebrated it somehow, and the dining room, mirrored like Versailles, with seating for twenty — all that needlepoint stitched by Vinnie's own hands — had the two corner hutches shining with loving cups and other engraved silver tributes. It was a long way through the empty rooms to admit the medical technicians. "Thank you for coming," she told them, leading the way back to the bedroom.

While they worked, Yubo scratched with the rake outside, within earshot. "You need me," he said, peering in through the jalousies, "you just holler."

Vinnie had sat in her chair again, at attention. She didn't answer Yubo, or say anything at all. The ambulance driver drew the drapes and clicked on the light. The other attendant drew back the covers. Though Vinnie knew Hawk — who better? — and had been his lover, his wife, and his nurse, she now averted her eyes. His soulless husk looked somehow obscene. She started up from her chair, to escape, but sat again as the driver said with a sigh, apologetic, "Fill us in." The deputy went out to the radio to summon the coroner.

"You'll have to ask questions," Vinnie said, suddenly at

a loss. She thought, They wonder why I'm not crying.

Yubo was telling the neighbors who had begun to convene, drawn by the sirens and flashing lights, "Hasn't hit her yet, is all."

The first time Hawk raised his cane and blacked her eye, he assumed she'd keep it a secret, as though the shame were *hers,* but Vinnie fought back on her own terms, calling his bullying bluff. She had marched into church, the bold bruises on her face unmitigated by make-up. When the choir asked her, "What did you *do* to yourself?" Vinnie had said, looking right at him, "Hawk hit me."

Her plan backfired. They took it as a joke. They knew him; they knew better. They said, "No, seriously," and Hawk — his back to the wall, one hand gripping the cane, the other in his pocket jingling the keys to his new Mark VI — laughed, saying, "Well, if she told you she walked into a door, would you believe her?"

After that they greeted him in Sunday school, on the street, at the bank, in board meetings, at the lodge, or the club, or work, "Yo, Hawk, still beating your wife?"

Things hadn't always been like that between Hawk and Vinnie, or only rarely so. The real troubles came after they were already grandparents, their sons grown, married, scattered, when Hawk's Chrysler crossed the center line and struck the cattle truck head-on. This was on Derby Day, and they had been to several parties. Hawk loved juleps; he lost count. The driver of the truck had only minor injuries, but two of the cattle had to be killed. Several vertebrae broke in Vinnie's back, and she had to wear a brace from then on, but it was Hawk who would truly never be the same, something gone wrong in his brain. The surgeons drilled and repaired, and had him back on his feet even before Vinnie molted from her body cast, but Hawk — though he looked the same except for the drag to his left foot — had changed, his inhibitions gone forever, so that even sober, he was as graceless as he used to be when drunk. He might say or do anything in public. It got harder and harder for Vinnie to keep their secrets.

Little things ticked him off into fierce tempers and retributions. Sometimes she spoke up to him, talked back before she learned better, before she knew what it might cost. When he wrote out checks — five hundred dollars — to enclose in each of Vinnie's ritual letters to their sons, inviting them for Thanksgiving, Vinnie objected. "Don't you think they'd come, without it?" What was it but a bribe, a tip, as though he had to pay them to show up? But that's how he'd raised them, five dollars for every book they read in grade school, fifty dollars for every A in college, always spreading his money around, to make himself feel good. Now their sons called rarely, always collect, and never wrote — their wives signing the yearly cycle of greeting cards, enclosing snapshots, clippings from the newspapers, annual reports, hints of colors and sizes for Christmas shopping. All three had not been home at the same time in five years.

"A real reunion," Hawk said, ignoring Vinnie's objections. "They can come or not, but they can cash it either way."

"If they were real men they'd tear the checks in half and send them back," Vinnie said. "They've got their own lives, good jobs, don't they say so?"

"If I wanted to make sure they showed up," Hawk said, "I'd tear a five-hundred-dollar bill in two and send half, and tell them they'd have to pick up the rest of it in person. This is for *expenses*," he said, "that's all."

He had financed a condo for one, an auto parts franchise for another, and law school for the third. He wasn't about to stop now. He went on writing out the checks, signing each with that lifelong illegible flair, heavy pressure and a broad flourish — the signature of an important man with no doubts and no patience to waste on details.

"Will that be enough, then?" Vinnie asked. "No son of Hawk Hawkins will settle for breaking even . . ." Which could have been taken as a compliment, but wasn't meant so, and he knew it.

"Mama," he said, shutting his checkbook ledger and capping his pen, "you're getting into some ugly little mouth habits. What do you suppose? Change of life? You think you could go twenty-four hours without saying something stupid?"

She knew better, but she didn't stop. She had never fought with anything but words. He outweighed her by a hundred pounds and the only blows she'd ever struck had been verbal. If she hadn't drunk wine with her dinner, she might not have spoken at all. But she heard herself saying, "Living with you is an inspiration, I guess." And it was the last thing she said, except "Hawk! Please don't —" till noon the next day, because Hawk taped her mouth shut with two-inch-wide adhesive and stood her against the refrigerator door, at attention, while he sat at the dinette table, pouring whiskey into his coffee and aiming the pistol at her good heart.

Something in her wouldn't satisfy him by crying or begging or slumping. She kept her head up, her chin level, and her eyes stern. She knew he meant it, about the gun. He'd shoot if he wanted to. Hadn't he lain in wait for the dogs that overturned their trash cans, his deer rifle propped on the picket fence, night on night, till finally he blew a neighbor's Siamese cat to rags, a house cat out on a midnight stroll to relieve itself, a collared and tagged pet, its mistress waiting on the side porch at home, calling "Kitty? Kitty?" into the dark? Vinnie was the one who shoveled it up, handed the collar over, and expressed their deepest regrets. Nobody slept *that* night, either.

Hawk paid, of course. Fifteen hundred dollars, settling out of court. "No use in things going that far," he said. "I'm a justice of the peace."

Now he sat, weary, his freckles standing out stark against his pallor. When he had drunk all the coffee, he hit the whiskey straight. The dog lay by his knee, her tail tump-tumping on the tile; no question about her loyalties.

His making Vinnie stand like that wasn't new, but the tape over her mouth was. And he'd never made her stand there so long, usually only an hour or two, till the phone rang, or the dog needed feeding, or a neighbor stopped by. He called it Posture Drill, holding her at attention like that.

The week of Thanksgiving, that first autumn after the wreck, he called Posture Drill so often he made a joke. It was Wednesday night, and the turkey was already roasting. Over the dark roads, through the black skies, their children were coming home for the holidays. Hawk let Vinnie relax every hour, long enough to baste the bird. He spent the break whetting the carving knife to perfection; he took pride in his ability to carve.

"We keep this up," he said as he motioned Vinnie back in place against the refrigerator, "you won't need that brace any more."

When Vinnie had mentioned Hawk's moodiness — that's how she described it — to his doctor, she asked, "Have you noticed anything? Might it be his blood pressure? Some side effect to his medication? Alzheimer's? Something?" The doctor, one of Hawk's lifelong friends and fishing buddies, had spent the previous Sunday morning on the lake with him. He cocked his head and asked, "For instance?"

"He gets upset, turns almost purple. The cords in his neck stick out like thumbs. He runs at me yelling." Vinnie willed her hands to unclasp, to lie quiet in her lap. "I forgot and started the dishwasher while he was in the shower."

The doctor looked at her.

"Our plumbing's inadequate. There's not much pressure during peak demand."

"Can't stand the competition?" the doctor said, nodding.

At first Vinnie thought he meant Hawk, not the plumbing, how he criticized her and her cultural evenings — bus jaunts with the churchwomen to the High Museum or the Academy Theater — or the quilting bees, the afternoon phone calls, auxiliary teas, committee work, bake sales. She thought the doctor meant how she had learned to bake two identical items, or else to make something Hawk didn't like, so he wouldn't object to her giving it away, and at the same time to make something he liked very much, so he would be appeased, and not try to spoil her day. He had taught her that in one quick lesson. "For a good cause? I'll show you a good cause," he said. "Feed the birds!" And he had thrown a pound cake still warm from the oven right out the back door. He couldn't have pound cake, because of cholesterol . . .

"Our plumbing's like that too," the doctor said, "and nothing makes me madder than having the hot water poop out halfway through a shower. Listen, Vinnie," he said, leaning across to look right into her eyes, "Hawk's got a lot of adjusting to do. This year's been hell for him. For you too, of course. He needs you now. He needs a buffer. Someone to let down with."

Vinnie listened.

"All marriages have their rough spots. Sometimes Fran and I . . ." he was saying.

Yes, but do you run through the house cursing, or go out in the yard naked, covered with soap, and haul your wife indoors by the hair of her head because she was watering her flowers? Do you drag her into the bathroom and shove her into the shower and turn it on COLD till she shivers, then HOT till she's scalded? Do you make her strip and crawl? Do you ignore her for days? Or make her sleep on the pallet on the floor while the dog sleeps on your wife's pillow?

She held out her arm for the blood pressure cuff, warning herself not to talk crazy.

"Heart like a child," the doctor said again. He wrote out a prescription for Valium. She wanted to ask, For me, or Hawk? She wanted to ask, Have you ever raped your wife?

Hawk had three business supply yards; one on the north side, one on the south side, and the central office, on the L&N spur. Vinnie had been Hawk's bookkeeper for years, since the time he had tax trouble, which the IRS agreed looked more like carelessness than intentional deceit. Vinnie got things organized in no time, and now she only had to ride in to work with him three days a week, supervising payroll, running down special orders, handling complaints. When they went to computers, Vinnie took a course and handled that, too. She was as good at ballpark-figuring materials and costs as anyone on the lot, and since Hawk had slowed down some, she did more of the legwork, checking up on deliveries, showing the contractors around, giving and taking advice and chances. Hawk sat in his office, staring out the window at the trains shunting cars off onto their spur, the front-end loaders scooping gypsum out, the white dust of it blowing like smoke. Sometimes he lost sight of Vinnie. Then he'd go out on the steps of the office and yell for her. The longer it took her to get back, the madder he was.

One day, as the wind was whipping the bright dust between the sheds, rattling the corrugated roofing on its old nails, fluttering the Day-Glo pennants over the retail parking lot, she made apology to her clients, and headed back, almost trotting, wondering what had gone wrong in that three-phone bedlam of the office this time. Hawk hated to answer phones.

She took a short cut behind the mill building, and in the alley, tripped. She didn't hurt herself, but she got sawdust on her clothes, and Hawk started right in on that.

"Where the hell have you been? Wallowing around like a bitch in heat with the yard hands . . ."

Papers — all her neat files! all the computer records! — lay strewn where he had tossed them as he cleaned out every drawer and shelf. "What's missing?" she asked, getting as usual right to the heart.

"Coffee filters," he said.

"The filter's built in."

"Since when?" He spun around to challenge her.

The warning light flickered on in Vinnie's brain. She answered carefully. Hawk was between her and the door. Maybe it was a trick question, and the truth wouldn't make a dent, but she couldn't lie, she never had. All she could tell him was the truth. "We got it Christmas of 1982 and it's been perking every business day since."

"You're a goddamn liar," he said, "and I don't need

your 1982. You're out of here. You're fired!" He was always firing people, rehiring the next day, if they could be persuaded to come back.

She pointed to the sign over her desk: YOU CAN'T FIRE ME; SLAVES HAVE TO BE SOLD. Usually when she appealed to that sign, he'd laugh. In better days, he'd even taped one up over his own workspace: WHEN I WANT YOUR OPINION, I'LL BEAT IT OUT OF YOU. But he wasn't laughing it off today. He kicked a chair over and shoved it under the doorknob. "I don't have to buy or sell you," he said. It was plain enough what he meant. Fury had, as usual, its aphrodisiac effect: the madder he got, the harder. Sex had become for him an emergency procedure. Vinnie gave a little cry at her own lack of foresight, but this had never happened at work before. "If you've got the down, I've got the up," he said. *No* wasn't an option.

There was no back door and the curtainless windows were pinned, storm-glazed, and burglarproof. She prayed the phone would ring, or that a customer would arrive and pound on the door, anything to short-circuit Hawk's mood; Vinnie couldn't, but any outsider could. Hawk was all charm when he wanted to sell something.

Then she prayed, as he slung her into the wall and her head hit and she slid to the floor, that no one would drive up now, to witness this, for it was too late to stop it. The floor was cold and they struggled in the grit and spent cigarettes of the overturned ashtray.

"Jesus," he said, when he finished with her and hooked the chair away from the door, "this place is a sty." He went out whistling. He didn't even take his cane. She watched his public posture return to him, a few grooming gestures, and then ready for business as usual. She thought of the mallards in the cove at home, how the drake suddenly would steam after the hen, catch her neck in his bill as he mounted, and hold her fast, almost drowning her, then slip off, circling her, then swim away . . .

Two contractors had driven up. Hawk stood tall between their trucks, greeting them as they got out, slapping them on the arm, telling one of his jokes. She could hear their laughter as they walked off toward the warehouses.

She left the door wide open, propped with a two-by-four. The March winds came right in, scuttling around, stirring up papers. She gathered everything willy-nilly into a cardboard box. It would take her a week to put the files in order, but she could have coffee ready in nine minutes. She was pouring her second cup when the warehouseman came rumbling over the lot at full speed on the forklift to bring the news: Hawk had had some kind of attack and needed an ambulance. At the end of the yard a cluster of men stood looking down.

Vinnie dialed from memory, as in a dream, her hand steady. It took three tries on a dead line before she realized that Hawk had torn the phone cord from the wall in his tantrum. That caused a delay in getting help, but the doctors said speed wouldn't have made all that much difference; the damage was done.

His friends said it was a great pity to see a go-getter like Hawk coasting — he was only fifty-nine — but he had to take early retirement. They put the business up for sale, and before the summer was out they had a buyer. Vinnie had power of attorney by then, but Hawk made his own mark on the papers. Their sons took it hard; they weren't told till after things had been settled. They flew back to explain what kind of shelter they wanted for their share.

"If any," Hawk said, never the sort to break anything

gently. But since they were all there, he didn't mind deciding right then. Their sons wanted it all up front, ahead of time. "What time?" Hawk said, getting madder.

"You know how moody he is," they said to Vinnie. "He could do *anything* about his will. We're just thinking of our kids' future."

Vinnie left them, walking out of the lawyer's office. Even down the hall she could hear their raised voices, Hawk's as usual leading the pack. He'd lost speed but not volume, and once he got warmed up past his new stammer, he could bluster and sling spit like always. "I'm not dead yet," he was saying. "I'm present and accounted for. Talk *to* me, not about me. The lawyer's on my payroll; he writes what I say, and what I say is: read it and weep."

Nobody had said, "Vinnie, stay." She told the parking lot attendant, "I'll be back to pick up the pieces in an hour." She drove anywhere, nowhere, just around. Hawk had donated acreage and the steel and concrete for a new Legion Hall. Two hundred and fifty thousand dollars out of capital gains. That's what their sons were yelling about. There'd be a little left for Hawk and Vinnie, a cushion against catastrophe, and a couple of thousand for each of the sons; if they wanted it now, they'd get it now, without interest. Hawk had, as usual, pleased himself, and it was too late to argue it. They were already swinging steel at the building site.

Vinnie slowed as she drove by. The sign announcing "Future Home of . . ." stood in the scraped field that would be the baseball diamond. Hawk intended for them to have lights, too. "It's time for a little progress around here," he said. "Time for the phoenix to rise." The Legion had been meeting in a trailer since the first hall burned three years back. "I want this one to look like something," Hawk told the architect. "This is my pyramid." The golden shovels broke ground the September after Hawk retired. It was a front-page story. Hawk looked good.

At least twice a week since, Vinnie drove Hawk over to the site; it was good for him to get out. He shaved on those days, took pains with how he dressed, slapped on a little extra cologne, had a better appetite, and sounder sleep after. The foreman would show him the blueprints as though Hawk could still read, and when he had done looking, he'd swing back up the hill on his crutches with a smile on half his face. Easing into the car — Vinnie was in the driver's seat now — he'd sigh. "Mama," he'd say, adjusting himself, patting his wallet, "let's go for steaks."

He wasn't supposed to have red meat. Vinnie knew better than to bring that up. "What do they know?" Hawk would say, stripping the cellophane off another cigar and puffing it alight. "They said I might live to be eighty years old."

Or die tomorrow, Vinnie thought. As though he'd read her mind, he'd say, "Either way: *my* way . . ."

When they wanted him to throw out the first baseball for the dedication game of Hawkins Park — the new Legion field — Hawk said no. He'd had pneumonia at Christmas, and it had dragged on. Vinnie had bought all new clothes for him, and even so, his collars were too loose again. He moved around the house on a walker, and he didn't go anywhere else. Whatever happened to him now happened at home. They even brought the barber over, when Yubo and Vinnie could no longer talk him into riding to town. He wouldn't see his friends. They'd drop by, but Hawk would go to his room and not come out. Vinnie would stand in the hallway, calling to him through the door —

he'd lock it — and if Hawk growled "No!" that was the only thing he'd say. Sometimes he didn't say a word. Vinnie would come back, her eyes tear-bright, shaking her head.

Once when the committee had stopped in to try to talk Hawk into attending that opening game, he wouldn't unlock his door even after they had gone. She heard him smashing things. She got an ice pick and forced the lock. "It's my room, too!" she was saying, as the door flew open. "I live here too. Where do you get off —"

Hawk sat on the edge of the bed. He had cast away his pajama top, trying to get dressed. A fresh shirt lay tangled on the floor where he had thrown it, when he gave up trying to unbutton it. The mirror lay in shards; he had shattered it with his walker. His feet were bleeding; he was bloody all over, front and back, as though he had rolled in the glass, not just fallen. She began cleaning him up, cautious, ready to jump back if he were still in a fighting mood. The cuts weren't too bad. She kept saying, more to herself than to him, "You're all right now." His skin had a sallow look and his breasts sagged like an old woman's. Most of his freckles were gone. She made up her mind to help him get out in the sun — or to buy him a lamp — but what she said was, "What's going on here? What did you mean by this?"

Hawk turned away from her, lay with his knees drawn up to his chest, his back to her.

He shook so hard she thought he was having a chill. "I don't want them to see me like this," he said. She realized he was crying.

They listened to the first game on the radio. The lights from the playing field — half a mile away — lit up the eastern sky like dawn. "Look," Vinnie said, pulling the drapes open, turning off the lamp. Hawk turned the radio down and they sat in the dark, listening. They were too far away to hear the cheers.

After that it was all downhill. Hawk could still turn the charm on for the nurses on his clinic visits, or in the hospital, but all Vinnie got from him were complaints and cunning. His cursed her nonstop some days — her voice, her looks, her very breath an offense to him. Other times he ignored her; he'd sit in his chair all day, the shades drawn, the TV jabbering, and he wouldn't touch the trays of food she brought him. If she talked on the phone too long to suit him, he'd break the connection, or shout fierce and ugly words for Vinnie to have to explain. When he tried to strangle her with his robe sash — and later, with his bare hands — she began sleeping in the den on the day bed. Hawk didn't ask her back. He whistled for Shelah, and she came padding in and took Vinnie's place.

The walls, carpet, and furniture wore various stains from the struggle over mealtime. If he ordered chili, and she brought it — any hour, day or night, if he had appetite she tried to find something to please him — and it was too hot, or too late, or too spicy, he'd fling it at her head. Anything he didn't like he threw back in her face, whether food or conversation. Vinnie began pouring herself a little wine with her meals, and before bedtime, another tumbler.

Hawk could have one shot of whiskey a day; he generally managed more, if he could find where Vinnie hid it. She had begun taking the bottle out to the car and locking it in the trunk, and when he found it, she consoled herself that at least he had gotten out of the house a little; the exercise might be doing him good if the whiskey wasn't. She always knew when he'd been looking for it; his walker left holes in the lawn. Finally, when the bad weather came, Vinnie quit hiding it. She stood the bottle on the kitchen counter in plain sight. "Honor system," she told him. When she ran out of wine, she'd mix bourbon with the juice from Hawk's canned peaches; she learned to hold it down. Medicine, she told herself.

When he found her pouring one afternoon, Hawk said, "You may amount to something yet." He held out his glass. He was still wearing the identification bracelet from his last hospital stay; that had been a week, maybe two weeks ago. Yubo always clipped it and put it with the others; had Hawk not had a bath in that long? She made a mental note: call Yubo to get Hawk into the shower. He'd take things from Yubo he'd never put up with from Vinnie.

It was such a relief when they got him clean and shaved and into fresh clothes. Vinnie ran the washer and dryer every day. There were always so many linens. "That's what keeps my heart strong," she said, taking the soiled things from Yubo later that day. "Going up and down those stairs."

Hawk always seemed to need her the minute she started the laundry. She'd hear that cane thumping on the floor, lashing the wall. He'd call her name over and over, or sometimes only once, like something you hear in a dream that wakes you from it. Sometimes she thought she heard him and when she got there, he'd say no. Was she hearing things? Was he lying? Sometimes when she came running, he said, "Too late," which meant more laundry. He needed her help to get up from his chair; after that, he could manage on his own. He hates to ask me, that's why he's like this, she told herself. As soon as she went back downstairs again, she'd hear him calling.

She began to keep a bottle of sherry downstairs, to pick her up. At times it seemed as if Hawk wasn't using her strength to pull himself up by, but was instead dragging her down. Sometimes Vinnie was afraid.

For Hawk's birthday, Vinnie invited several of his old cronies over. Open house, dessert and coffee. She didn't tell Hawk; it was a surprise. She ordered the cake from the deli; she was afraid if she baked one, he'd suspect. If Hawk had time to think about it, he might try some meanness, or just vanish behind his door and not come out or say a word. Yubo had been over that morning to get Hawk cleaned up, and they had him out on the terrace, in his chair but tossing a ball for Shelah, when the guests arrived. He didn't have time to get to his feet and flee. He just sat there, like a king on his throne, and shook their hands and laughed.

Then the guests went home, and Hawk said, "You invited six; interviewing pallbearers?" Vinnie was cleaning off the table and as she reached across for a dirty plate, Hawk brought the serving knife down on her wrist. It went in deep; Vinnie needed stitches. She wrapped her arm in a towel and drove herself to the emergency room. She told them it was an accident. When she drove home, she found that Hawk had wrecked the house. He had cleared the tea table for her, by tipping it over. The patio candles had rolled off the terrace and into the grass, but the fires had gone out before they could do any damage. Inside the house, he had ripped the plaques and photographs off the walls and smashed them. He had broken the china hutches and emptied them. What he could break he broke; what wouldn't break he used to smash something that would. There were holes in the plaster walls, and the lights on the chandelier lay scattered like hail. She almost turned around and went out again, but made herself go on, till she found him. He was in his chair, watching TV; when he didn't respond to her, she jerked the plug from the wall — she wouldn't risk turning her back, within kicking range.

"Hawk," she said, "are you sick, or just pretending? Why are you too weak to bathe yourself but strong enough to wreck our home? Could you manage on your own? Do you want to? Am I why?"

He ignored her, just kept on staring at the now dark TV screen.

"I won't ask you again. This'll be the last speech I make. I just want to know where I stand, that's all."

"Get lost," he growled.

"They have retirement apartments, with nursing care. I could visit you."

"You want out? You got it," he said. "I don't need you at all."

"We could sell this place in a heartbeat; it's in pretty good shape except for what you did tonight. Yubo'll help us fix it up."

"The captain goes down with his ship," he said.

"Is that what you want?" she said. She remembered to plug the TV back in; that saved her a trip and a cursing. She was in the kitchen, loading the dishwasher, when he called her back. "Mama!" Just once, as for some urgent thing. She ran.

"Bring me that bottle," was all he had to say. "I've still got some ice."

When Vinnie wrecked the Lincoln, they suspected it was D.U.I. They took her to the hospital for blood tests and when the doctor had talked it over with Vinnie, he persuaded the police that she had had a medication reaction. He told Vinnie, "You're damn lucky. Valium and alcohol can kill you."

"Don't tell my husband," she pleaded.

The next time she wrecked, she didn't get written up because she didn't stop. She drove off the road into a ditch and flattened a highway sign, grazed a cherry tree and drove back up out again, onto the road. "Jesus, help me," Vinnie murmured. She kept on going. Most of the damage was to the right side of the car, easy enough to hide from Hawk; she just parked the car close to the garage wall on that side.

She shopped for ordinary things at odd hours. She used the liquor store's drive-in window most of the time; kept her motor running. Anyone who'd call to her on the street, "Hey, Vinnie," she'd wave to and hurry past, saying, "I've got to get organized." They'd say, "You've got so much on you right now; find some time for yourself, make a little room . . ." She hadn't been to church in months. She didn't even keep track any more of which day was Sunday. She shopped late hours at the All-Nite Market, and even so, at midnight or later, there might be someone who'd know her, and want to chat. She began to be furtive; she checked the mirrors over the meat counter, hardly recognizing herself any more, just a gray-haired woman with her chin down, pushing a shopping cart along. Her shoes were split on the sides and her sweater pockets bulged with lists and resolutions and saving stamps.

At home, when the phone rang, she dreaded to answer. If it was an acquaintance asking how she and Hawk were doing, she could still remember how to sound, to make them believe it: "Oh, we're holding our own . . ." but if they invited her somewhere, she could never think of how to say no without their asking why. She'd just hang up the phone, whispering, "I'm sorry."

Her prized Norfolk Island pine drooped and thirsted and bent toward the light. All those years Vinnie had given it a quarter turn every week to keep it growing straight; now it was an event if she remembered to water it. It was Yubo who drove over the night of the first frost and dragged it in, or it would have perished like the hanging baskets of ferns along the front porch. Vinnie no longer noticed.

Every day Hawk seemed weaker. Planning for what might be next, she had Yubo build the wheelchair ramp. He measured the doorways in the house with a retractable tape measure almost the same yellow as Hawk's skin. She watched the tape slowly vanish into Yubo's fist; he couldn't control its retraction. He had no finesse about anything. He was all for tearing into the woodwork right then, with a hatchet and a chisel. "Moldings'll have to come off, to get his chair through," Yubo said, but Vinnie said, "Wait. We'll wait and see." Hawk hated the wheelchair; so far he wouldn't use it. "It won't come to that," he vowed.

They took Hawk to the hospital that afternoon. He had never looked so thin; Vinnie thought he was dying. In a week, though, he was back in his own bed, up to his old tricks, sticking out his cane to trip her, or grabbing her arm, to try to swing her around. Calling her to come help him, then saying he hadn't. Not calling when he should. Throwing food. Breaking things. Keeping her awake all night and on her feet all day with his endless variations on "Pleased or Displeased." Once he shoved her with his foot as she bent to pick up his remote control for the TV; she hit her head on the bureau and lay unconscious for several minutes.

Another time when he got himself out to the kitchen for the whiskey — she had warned him not to try using the walker with something in his hands — he slipped and fell. The bottle skittered across the tiles and broke against the dinette table. She left him lying there. "How do you like it?" she asked him, stepping around him; she took a bath, made herself some supper, watched TV — her own choice of programs this time — and went to bed. For hours he called to her to come help him, that he was hungry, cold, hurting. All his old tricks.

"Liar! Liar! Liar!" she screamed. "I can't hear you."

The next morning, she discovered that he had dragged himself back to his own bed; he couldn't pull himself up onto the mattress, so he drew the blanket down and slept on the floor. Shelah lay beside him, on guard, anxious, reproachful.

Vinnie was sorry. She was sorry in a way that had nothing to do with having to clean the carpet where Hawk had soiled it. It was sorrow that swept her clean, a true repentance. She never let him see her cry, but now she didn't think of that. She helped him to bed, cleaned him, brought him breakfast, begged him to forgive her. She made a vow to God that she'd never again touch spirits, and the next time Hawk needed consoling, *she,* not Shelah, would lie beside him on the floor. All that day she tried to make him understand, but Hawk wouldn't hear. He didn't talk, either. Or eat; she brought him trays and snacks, and after an hour or so, carried them away. Three days passed like that. He wouldn't call on her for anything; he managed. When she had left the kitchen, he'd thump-drag, thump-drag in on his walker, and find crackers and milk, bananas. If he fixed himself some cereal, he cleaned up afterward. He left his dishes rinsed in the sink, and the counter top wiped with his sleeve. Three days they lived like that; the fourth day was the day he died.

Before the coroner arrived, Vinnie had time to plan. The death would be headlines, local and statewide. She and Hawk had talked, long back, about where and how: burial at the National Cemetery in Marietta, certainly. She thought of those massive death-fed oaks and hickories and elms. Each Memorial Day the scouts placed a fresh little flag at the head of each grave; Vinnie and Hawk's own sons had done that for merit badges, years ago. She had always looked away from those neat rows of markers . . .

"Taps," she said. She didn't know she had spoken aloud till the technicians and the coroner turned to her. She shook her head.

"It'll be all right if you go out now," the coroner said. She realized that was an invitation; she did not want to stay and see. While they were still making out their reports, Vinnie walked through the house; the front door stood wide open so anyone — caring or merely curious — could see in. Vinnie pulled it shut behind her. There they all stood, in the yard, facing her, like carolers in the twilight, Yubo to the one side, their director.

They stood just beyond the arc of porchlight. Except for the static on the police radios, there was absolute silence, which Shelah broke, padding proudly back from her sundown run. She brought a gift — a bunny — which she laid at Vinnie's feet; it was done for, its eye already glazed, its shoulder fur damp from Shelah's mouth. The dog stood gazing up at her with that "waiting for" look the neighbors wore.

The gravel driveway, ruled off like writing paper by the tines of the rake, had nothing on it but the dog's tracks, diagonally, leading to Vinnie's feet. Vinnie squatted stiff-backed to pick up the rabbit. It hung limp in her hand. "Ah, God," she said to Shelah, who stood nosing the dark fur. Vinnie shuddered.

"Bury that thing," she said, disgusted. She slung it over the hedge into the vacant lot. It landed softly in the dark. Everyone watched it go.

Desire Call of the Wild Hen

FROM THE MIDNIGHT she was born and the doctor slapped her, again, and she still didn't cry, Candy had been figuring out life by how the world could hit her and then hold its breath over her. An only child, and the first girl-child in three generations, she kept them busy praising her. The only thing she remembered one of her grandfathers saying was, "Pretty as a spotted pup," which she took — at age four — to be an insult, and resented noisily until he had purchased her affections again with a little red Mexican rocking chair and two pairs of ruffled socks.

She stayed involved, from grade school on, in scouting, band, sports, and Sunday school. She stood out in a crowd, even in uniform, at long distance, and especially up close.

She wore her swimsuit without self-consciousness, and from the beginning had a presence to her, a poise, that made anyone studying a group photograph point at her face and say, "This one's special." The years of ballet, jazz, tap, and orthodontia had paid off in straight spine and teeth. Modeling and charm school had taught her how to pose. Most of the time, though, she stayed in motion.

She perfected her skiing and her tan when she was fifteen, the year her parents died in the crash of her father's Lear jet. Insurance paid well enough that several aunts and uncles were willing to adopt her. She chose her grandmother's unmarried sister in DeSoto County, Florida, because she was right on the Peace River and U.S. 17, the closest any of her kin lived to Lake Eloise.

Racing across the rumpled surface of river or lake on her skis, she forgot her troubles. As her skills increased, and she began to flip, spin, and swivel, strong as her teacher, she could afford to let her concentration waver, to turn for a moment and appreciate the bathers on shore watching her cutting joyously through wind and spray, her sun-whitened hair whipping.

When she was sixteen, her aunt let her sign up to work at Cypress Gardens — not in the show as an aquamaid, she applied too late for that — but working concessions, waiting tables, biding her time, learning fast. She loved to ski in the moonlight, never too tired.

Each summer she got better, and at eighteen, she had the strength, experience, and confidence that endowed every move she made with authority. She was a champion. She planned to look this good all her life, recognizing herself — who she'd always be — in the quick check of her eye make-up in her compact mirror, or the impression her lips made on Kleenex, a perfect kiss, or as she readied herself, with one final pirouette before the glass in the dressing room, giving the spangles on her costume a settling shake. She was already a star. Yet even as she rode the broad warm shoulders of her partner behind the ski boat, his back braced against the pull of the towrope, her head just above his, their smiles and honed gestures twinned, she balanced there, emptily, waiting for the final thing that must happen, which they had prophesied for her in the school yearbook below her senior picture: *Candace Marie Taylor:* "By the power of gravity, she falls — in love."

She was nineteen when she met Phil Johnson. He was in Florida on vacation. In his regard for her she found the full-length image she had been seeking in every looking glass all her life. How she was was how she'd stay. "From now on," she told her best friend in the ski show, "it's a matter of maintenance."

Phil was from Atlanta, a few years older, already established in a career in construction, divorced. He had money to burn, and she was one of his flames. He flew her to Georgia in his Cessna, took her to the Braves games, the steeplechase, Limelight. He'd drop out of her life for weeks at a time, then phone, wanting to see her, keyed up from his high-pressure business trips.

He'd bring her gifts, expensive things. She moved from her aunt's house, enrolled at Florida Southern in a liberal arts course, then dropped out to go hunting with Phil in the Bighorn Mountains. She knew when to be quiet, how to see what she was looking for, but she never learned to shoot straight. Neither of them worried much about it. They'd ride all day, and she proved herself a good sport. By the campfire one night he told her, "I'm going to be a millionaire in three years."

"I don't care," she said. It was the truth, but he wanted her to care. "I'd love you if you were a bum."

"What incentive is that?" he said, plus a few more things. It was their first argument. It didn't spoil their trip. Nothing could.

On the plane home, he talked her into moving to Atlanta, letting him set her up in an efficiency on the north side. "Nonexclusive, no strings," he said.

She said, "Let me think," but she was already shopping for a winter coat and a vocational school to teach her dental assisting. She took aerobics classes, and eventually taught, at Fantastik Fitness. She tried out for Falcon cheerleader, but when Phil objected, she dropped out of the finals. They didn't always see eye to eye, and traveled together less frequently — she had her own life — but he'd still call when he was away, interstate or overseas all the same to him, just to hear her voice, and ask, "Who's that with you?" She sounded like a little girl when she was sleepy. Her soft, startled laugh passed through the telephone longlines like a germ, infecting him completely. How could he cure himself but by sickening of her, totally surfeited? She wanted to marry. She didn't say so, just waited without wasting any time, playing the game, and finally winning. One Friday night they drove to Ringgold to get married — "You didn't trap me, I *want* the baby," he protested — and spent the weekend in Chattanooga. She had a job, and needed to be back at work on Monday. He wanted her to quit. They discussed it as they drove back to Atlanta.

She said, "I hate to quit now, two jobs in one year . . ." referring to the ski show in Florida, which she had left because he didn't want her "showing off" any more. She wasn't complaining, or hinting, but on the way home he stopped at Bald Ridge and bought her a ski boat. Just like that.

They fixed up a cottage on Lake Lanier. She could ski every good day he was able to spare enough time to drive the boat for her. She hated what pregnancy was doing to her figure, but by being active, and skipping meals, she only gained fifteen pounds.

They had a good year, and built on a paneled room for his hunting trophies. His business didn't fail till the third year. They sold the ski boat, the Hobie, her car, the trail bikes, the pontoon, the camper, and his pool table. It wasn't enough. They dropped out of their clubs and he went back to work for his father, a ten-hour day, plus the grinding commute, and only two weeks vacation a year.

He drank a little all the time, crutching along Monday through Friday, limping toward the deeper oblivion of Saturday. They stayed home. He went from middleweight to heavyweight, though she wasn't much of a cook. For a while he took an interest in racing pigeons, and when they died off, he turned their coop into a chicken run, fancy birds; he took a few blue ribbons at the fairs, and had letters now and then from interested buyers. Candy thought of this as his "gentleman farmer" phase.

He laid off rows and planted a garden, and Candy stayed busy weeding and spraying for bugs, canning and freezing. "Phil hates vegetables," Candy said. "This is unreal."

Phil took one week of his vacation at Thanksgiving, and the other at Easter, hunting. Candy bought a slow-cooker for the venison and a Kamado smoker for the turkey and fish, and at Christmas tied red velvet bows on the deer racks that lined the den walls. One was a thirteen-pointer. "But that was before I met you," he said, as though Candy had changed his luck. He had moods.

She kept out of his way, when that would help, but if he wanted her she was always within reach, like the bottle. When they quarreled they made up later, and if you had asked Candy she'd have said they were happy. She was not disappointed in her life or her choice.

"I love you, baby," she never tired of saying, even when she knew he'd only reply "Yeah," with that look in his eyes like a glutted steer in a feedlot. They got through eight anniversaries like that, and there were always birthday cakes and Christmas trees and picnics in fine weather. Normalcy. He hunted whitetail in autumn, turkeys in spring. She gave her share of Tupperware and Stanley parties, and attended them in return. Her Tiara glassware collection grew. She signed their daughter up for soccer and scouts — though the girl was a disappointment in sports, too dreamy, frail, uncompetitive — and Candy took her fair turn in the car- pool. She and Phil were talking about repainting the house inside and out, and he also gestured at the back yard, spoke of putting in a swimming pool. "I'll help you dig," Candy told him, game for anything. She didn't point out that the lake was right there, for swimming, fishing, or boating. He didn't enjoy it much any more, but still some days he'd get up early and fish from the dock. He missed his boat. "As soon as we get back on our feet," they had said, when they sold it to help pay their debts, but they never had replaced it. He had always fished alone. If she forgot and came along, he'd remind her.

That was why Candy was happy to hear the talk about fixing up the house. She looked forward to working along- side him again, to laughing like old friends over the little things that went wrong. He'd slide his hands on her legs as he helped her down the ladder and it still went very well with them in bed, so it hit her hard when he called her and Melanie into the living room one Sunday night in April and announced, "Melanie, I love you and your mama, but I love Valerie more." He didn't look at Candy, who subsided slowly onto the couch, braiding and unbraiding the fringe on the afghan, wondering who Valerie was. She found her voice only to command softly, "Melanie, run play."

Melanie had moved around the room in shock, unresponsive, touching things, writing her name in the ashy fallout from the fireplace, stalling, finally — when Candy told her again, "Run play" — darting wordlessly out the patio door into the twilight, to knock the almost-spent tulips from their pencil stems with her majorette's baton. She loitered near the open doors, crouching under the window shrubs with her head on her knees, humming, while above her Phil and Candy argued and disavowed.

"Is it because," Candy asked in a crushed voice that carried, like a stage whisper, far into the dark, "because Melanie wasn't a boy?"

From that night Melanie had the habit — like a nervous cough, a symptom — of humming, or talking to herself. Dr. Bowen said she'd outgrow it maybe. He was their dentist, had been Candy's boss before she married Phil. "Nothing wrong with her teeth," was all Dr. Bowen could say. He thought Candy ought to consult their minister, or a counselor. "Or something."

Candy wouldn't. "There's never been a divorce in my family." She seemed to think that put heredity on her side. "Of course, we die young," she added, with that wonderful smile. She kept her morale high by reading inspirational magazine articles on coping, and stepped up her Stresstabs dosage.

With Phil's first support check, Candy had bought a trampoline. "Melanie needs some fun," she said. But she had spent as much time on it as the girl, perfecting back flips and dives and arabesques. When she finally wore down, she'd spread a towel and lie there on it, sunbathing, topless. She rigged a bell on the gate so she'd have plenty of warning to get decent if anyone dropped by. She kept herself in shape, as fit and firm and tan as when Phil had fallen in love with her in the ski show. "Looking good is the best revenge," she said to the clerk as she shopped for a rowing machine.

She called Phil from time to time, when the furnace failed, and the other household emergencies arose. Sometimes he'd drive back, from where he and Valerie were living near Stone Mountain, and fix whatever it was. She never begged, but he was welcome to stay overnight.

"It'll mess up the decree," he said, driving off. One day, toward the end of that year before the decree became final, she called him only to find his number had been unlisted. His lawyer wouldn't tell her where to reach him. She sounded so young, he thought it was Phil's daughter. "Your daddy will be in touch," was all he'd say. "He loved you, honey, don't take this personally."

When the day came that the divorce was final, Candy left off jogging and sunbathing. She kept her drapes drawn twenty-four hours a day. Melanie, with no school to occupy her, spent the summer riding her bicycle up and down the road, singing and talking to herself, scolding herself up the hills with a "Tough it out!" — standing on the pedals, then flying downgrade, triumphant, murmuring, "You gotta believe!"

Sometimes Melanie paced the porch instead, forlorn as a bewitched damsel in a tower, wearing her nightgown all day. When her interested neighbors asked her how Candy was doing, Melanie would call softly down from her parapet, "Mama's sleeping."

Summer passed, the lawn weathering into meadow and the fence roses falling to blackspot, undefended. One morning toward Labor Day — gunshots. One, and in a moment, another, followed by intermittent keening. The neighbors called the law.

The house was still shrouded when the deputy arrived and knocked. Candy took a little time to answer. When she opened the door, she wore a towel turbaned around her freshly conditioned hair. She had on a model's coat over a pair of baby dolls. She buttoned slowly up.

"What?" She sounded drowsy. She still had most of her enviable tan.

"There's been a report of commotion . . . shots fired."

"I missed," Candy said. "Both damn barrels."

Melanie came and stood by her mother. "Dogs was after our chickens."

"Peruvians and silkies," Candy explained. "Show birds."

A forlorn hen high-stepped through the grass and crossed the driveway, aimless, crooning.

"Report said there was a child crying."

"Not me," Melanie said. She had a milk mustache and sleep sand in her eyes. She picked at a scab on her arm, then laid the limp Band-Aid back over it.

"It's an Araucana chicken," Candy explained, leaning around the doorframe to point to the lone surviving bird. "Listen."

It stopped pecking and looked at them.

"My daddy's hobby," Melanie said. "But he's — "

"Run play," Candy told her. Melanie disappeared into the dark house.

Candy found her sandals and walked with the deputy out to the chicken yard to show him the devastation. There were feathers blowing around, and the weathered gate hung by one hinge. "That's how the dogs got in," the deputy said. He waded through the knee-high Johnson grass. Candy ran to him and took his arm when he mentioned snakes and rats.

"I'm divorced," she told him.

They passed the trampoline lost in the ascendant weeds.

In the overgrown woodlot, the ax stood rusted deep in the stump.

"Y'all been having trouble?"

"Well, I can't get the lawn mower cranked," Candy said.

The deputy looked at his watch. "Let me give it a try."

"We'd appreciate that so much," Candy said.

He came back that evening to finish the side yard, and stayed. Not forever, just for a season. He was the first.

Before she married Phil, Candy had worked for Dr. Bowen, the dentist. The white uniform — she graduated as an assistant and took pride in her professionalism — showed off her tan to advantage. It pleased her to hold a real job, not part-time like clerking at Zayre's, or entertaining, like the ski show. Phil was jealous, though. He didn't want her skiing behind any boat but his, so to speak, and he kept the towrope short. She wanted Phil to value her, to ask her to marry him, and part of her art was in apparent independent moves. They had quarreled more than once about her flirting with the patients. She said she couldn't help it if she felt most like a woman when there was a man around. "It's human nature," she explained. Phil wasn't the kind to put up with that sort of thing long. And of course she wanted, above all, to please him.

She was already carrying Melanie when they married, but Candy wanted to work on for a few more months. As trim as she was, she wouldn't "show." Phil kept on being sour with her till she finally gave Dr. Bowen notice and hung up her uniforms for the duration. She stayed around home, washing windows, wallpapering, complaining about not being able to sleep on her stomach any more, and in general marking the days off to delivery as a prisoner might scratch off a jail term. Melanie was late.

In desperation, Candy had Phil ride her around on his motorcycle on the back roads, hoping to induce labor. When that failed, she jumped on their mattress, jumped and jumped till she was sobbing with exhaustion, breathless and hiccupping.

Candy was at Dunaway's Rexall buying nail polish and Clairol toner when labor pains finally began. She asked the alarmed clerk, "How long does this take? Two, three days? You might know it would be a weekend . . ."

Phil didn't want any more children, and after what Candy had gone through delivering Melanie, she was easy to persuade.

"I had myself spaded," she told Dr. Bowen, who came to see her in the hospital.

The dapper old dentist turned his fedora around and around its rim, looking down at it for some clue. Candy could always tease him, but he wasn't as good at thinking up replies. "Reversible?" he hoped.

"Ain't nothin' *reversed*," she said. "It's clean gone." She laughed, but her eyes were hard. "I'll never be sorry," she said.

"I hope you will always be happy," he told her. "If there's anything I can do —"

"Talk Phil into letting me go back to work," she said.

But he couldn't.

Now that Phil had cleared out, there was more room in Candy's closet for the uniforms. She had never parted with them. A little Snowy Bleach and they were as good as new. They still fit. So, in the fall after the divorce Candy went back to dental assisting. Dr. Bowen welcomed her, two days a week at first, then full-time. She had a way with the patients, and strong hands. Melanie wore her own key to the house and only killed an hour or two alone most days before Candy came home.

"I'm not afraid," Melanie said.

When Candy and Larry began dating, two years after Phil left, things got better for Melanie. Larry had a daughter about Melanie's age and they became friends. Melanie would ride the school bus over to Larry's and wait till Candy came to pick her up. Candy knew a good deal when she saw one. His mother brought supper over and babysat till Larry got home from the quarry at Marblehill, about forty miles, none of it four lane. No matter how delayed he might be on the crooked mountain roads, Candy generally managed to arrive later, not driving in till Larry was home and his mother had gone. Sometimes Candy had to circle the block, or park and wait down the hill. She liked his mother's cooking, but not her questions and suggestions, or the gift subscription to *The Upper Room* or articles clipped from magazines on sewing for little girls.

"I'm not much of a seamstress," Candy told her once and for all. "I only know curtains and crotches." On the days when Candy managed to avoid Larry's mother, things worked out fine for everyone.

From the first, Larry's daughter and Melanie got along. The two girls were of a size and might have been twins. No need to pack clothes when they stayed over at each other's house: everything fit, even the shoes. Melanie was two years older, but she seemed to have stopped growing when Phil left. It was as though time had stopped. Sometimes it seemed as though she didn't intend to grow. Her teacher had recommended that she stay back a year, repeat third grade, and Candy said all right about that. "She just needs time to get over it," she told the teacher. "Soon as Phil and I work things out, she'll be fine."

When Candy and Melanie planned to stay at Larry's overnight, Melanie would pack her toothbrush and pajamas in her doll's suitcase; that's all she'd take. Plus the doll, under her arm. Candy left a toothbrush hanging in Phil's rack, and she didn't have to pack a thing.

Larry was one of Dr. Bowen's new patients. That was how he and Candy had met. Larry had been grieving his wife's death for three years that September. "I keep waiting for something," he told her. "Like her car to come driving in, late. I see things I want to tell her. Perfect little stuff, jokes, songs." Candy said, "I know what you mean." Larry was the sort who would stop and help you change a tire, if you had a flat. Or offer to jump-start your battery off his . . . There were so many things that needed attention around her house, Candy called him for advice all along. Larry was more than willing to help. From the first, he talked of marriage, but Candy always laughed it off. "My way or no way," she told him every time. "No more paperwork."

At Thanksgiving, as he was moving in with Candy — her idea — he had his house up for rent. "You'll be rolling in it, better than a Christmas club account," Candy pointed out. Larry's mother asked him, "What happens to you if her ex drops by?" but Larry said, "Don't tell me anything secondhand; I don't want to hear it." The girls shared Melanie's room.

"It's just not *home* without a man around for Christmas," Candy said, when Dr. Bowen stood considering the personalized stockings Candy had bought on her lunch hour for Larry and his daughter, not exactly like the ones she and Phil and Melanie had always hung, but close. Melanie was insisting on hanging Phil's sock this year too. There would be five red socks in a row, just above the fire. "What do you think?" Candy said, taking them back from the dentist. "Will these do?" Dr. Bowen went to wash the glitter off his hands.

"I don't know," he said, afraid to say too much. "Are you sure you should —"

"What's two more nail holes?" Candy decided.

Once Larry started hammering, he could see any number of things that needed improvement, and he was handy. Right away he persuaded her to install glass doors on the fireplace, safer and more efficient. He did the work himself, and the check he wrote for the parts was drawn on his own account. "This isn't your Christmas present," he assured her. He knew what she liked, how she distinguished between things being bought for the house and things being given just to her. Twice she told him the joke about a man who forgot his anniversary and was in *big trouble*. "Because he didn't think of it till after all the hardware stores had closed . . ." Larry laughed. He was a good listener.

He held the ladder steady as Candy set the angel atop the tree. "What *is* my present?" she asked, looking down at him.

Melanie was in the den with Larry's daughter, wrapping presents, singing along to the Chipmunks.

"Is it big or little?" Candy asked. "Hard or soft?"

"Why won't you marry me?" He wouldn't let her wriggle past him. He wouldn't let her tease him. He held her still. She had to stand there and look in his eyes.

"Why?" he insisted.

"Some people buy, Larry. Others rent." That's all she'd say. Finally he let her go.

Later, at the yacht club, she kept on till she got wild drunk. It was the first time Larry had seen her like that, haggardly vivacious. She never did eat right, worried she'd lose her lure. She had dieted right down to her nerves on Herbalife, and was so loose in her jewelry she danced out of her wedding ring, which she still wore, guarded by diamonds. She didn't miss her rings right away, but when she did, she had the whole party crawling around, patting the carpets, ransacking the sofa cushions, feeling under the furniture, sorting the garbage.

When she finally got them back, she kissed them and headed for the bathroom for tape to wrap them so they'd fit tight. "Till I can get them cut down," she said. She got the party rolling again after that, making up for lost time. She set a plastic holly wreath on her head like a crown and danced with them all.

Larry stood aside, leaning against the wall, not looking. Toward eleven o'clock, he said, "That's enough, and more," collecting her into the rabbit jacket he'd given her. On the way home she was sick, spoiling the fur coat, and then she cried.

They didn't argue about it. They never even discussed it at all, but for New Year's they didn't party. They stayed home, watching on TV. Drinking 7-Up, Candy's midnight toast was, "Who knows?"

If that got Larry's hopes up, it wasn't for long. In mid-January, Candy asked him to move out. They were "getting too serious, too fast." She needed "space and time." Melanie still spent an occasional night over at Larry's — his renters left mid-month — and sometimes Candy stayed over too. His tenants had caused some damage, and he killed a couple of the first endless weekends on his own again plastering and painting. While he was at it, though, he offered to touch up the wall in Candy's kitchen where Melanie had let the french fries catch fire and scorch the paint. It took a couple of tries to match the color. He came over one Saturday to finish the trim work.

Melanie was home alone. She didn't know where her mama and the man had gone. "Some man," Melanie said. Larry didn't ask where they went, but Melanie told him anyway, "They didn't say."

Larry heated some soup for his daughter and Melanie. He made sandwiches and said, "Remind me to buy you some milk." While the girls ate, he split firewood into kindling.

When Candy wasn't back by sundown, Larry had Melanie write a note.

"I'm at Larry's with them," she said. She posted it on the liquor cabinet.

Candy didn't call Larry till around midnight. Larry answered the phone. He hadn't been asleep.

"That was so sweet," Candy said, "but Melanie knows how to manage. She would've been all right."

Larry didn't say anything.

"The firewood's wonderful," Candy said. "It was dry enough we didn't even need kindling. Feels so good." Someone in the room with her said something and she laid the phone down to answer. Larry could hear her voice, far off, and the man laughing.

Larry was about to hang up when Candy said, "You still on the line, babe?"

"Yeah."

"Melanie might as well stay over with you, hadn't she? Just this once?"

"Yeah," Larry said. He said a lot of things, fair enough, coming out with a little force from pressurized storage. Candy laid the phone so gently back on its hook Larry didn't even notice at first the connection had been severed.

When Larry drove Melanie home on Sunday morning, he stopped to let her out at the back gate; he didn't turn in. There was a car parked in the driveway, its roof covered with frost. The license plate was from Bibb County.

"Daddy!" Melanie cried, jumping out to run see.

She knew better! Larry called back, tapping the horn once, lightly, and leaning across his daughter to roll her window down and say so.

"It could be!" Melanie said, sullen now, with that defiant little head toss, like her mama. Faking confidence. She didn't meet Larry's eyes. When she lied, she put her chin up, daring reality to sock her.

Larry studied the house, all its windows dark, the curtains closed. "Hey, I forgot to buy the milk. Let's go pick up a quart."

The cold had pinched Melanie's face into womanhood. She looked old. "I don't need milk," she said. "I'm weaned."

"I thought you didn't know *where* your daddy was," Larry's daughter said.

Larry said, "Hush!"

"Hey, okay," Melanie said, fiercely. "It's somebody's car. Who cares? I live here too."

Larry said, "I think maybe you should come on back with us. We'll stop at Mrs. Winner's, get some biscuits . . ."

"I'm not hungry," Melanie said, fishing up the key on its ribbon around her neck. She walked back to the car to reassure him. "It doesn't matter," she explained. "I'll play."

Her steps left black holes in the frost. She waved as they drove off. She set her doll down to use both hands unlocking the door. Humming under her breath, she fitted the key into the lock's secrets and turned. "Hey, okay," she said, walking into the dark.

She left her doll on the porch, forgotten. Candy saw it and brought it in when she took the ashes out around noon.

By then the guest had gone, and they were alone together. Candy scolded, "This doll's got *papers*. You're too young to appreciate her. Do you know what I paid?"

Melanie had thought Santa Claus brought the doll, but that had been a year ago. She knew better now. She said, "I'll be glad when I'm grown and have a real baby and don't have to do anything."

Candy slapped her crooked across the face, not even waiting to take good aim. "You watch your mouth!" she said. "You think it's easy?"

Melanie spent the next hour in her room, on orders. She came back from exile to get the doll and announce, "Larry wanted you to call him sometime."

"Then sometime I will," Candy said.

When she did, he wasn't home. He had gone to Vermont on a business trip for the marble company. He returned bringing maple syrup and news. Georgia Marble wanted him to relocate, for at least two years. He wanted Candy with him. "This is our chance," he said. "Everything brand new, nothing but future."

They could fly north together. Larry had one more interview, and they could spend the rest of the time skiing. "I've never been to Vermont," Candy said, thinking it over. "All right."

Larry's mother kept the girls. Candy slept on the plane, hoping to be strong enough to enjoy the snow. She had been sick with a cough that forced her into a rib brace and left her run down, and she didn't like being sick, or missing work — or anything. On Valentine's Day Larry had brought her a ring — "Not a diamond," Candy hoped, opening the box — and some roses. Larry knew her well enough to know a diamond would scare her. He had chosen a ruby instead, and promised her matching earrings for her birthday in July. "I ought to say no," she said. Larry laughed. "Just don't get serious," Candy had warned him, slipping the ring onto her right hand. Even so, she let him wonder up until the last moment whether she would fly with him to Vermont. "Are you waiting for a better offer?" he had asked. Candy didn't answer.

"This is terrible," she said, the minute she stepped off the plane in Burlington and the wind cut through her thin blood. She took the climate personally.

"It'll require some getting used to," Larry agreed.

Candy slept in two pairs of socks and wore a sweater of Phil's over her flannel gown. Larry left her in bed, the electric blanket turned to HI, and went to his interview alone. When he returned that afternoon, Candy had dressed and was sitting downstairs, reading *Yankee* in the lobby of the inn, by the fire. She marked her place with a finger and looked up.

"It's all settled," he told her. His lips were cold from the wind. She flinched.

"A month more," she stalled. "Just give me a month more, to be sure." That was in March.

The April turkey hunt, with wives and children included, had become an annual event for Phil and his friends. They had built a shack and a tradition down on the Alcovy, one weekend every spring. When Easter fell late, as this year, the men took Good Friday too. They told their bosses, "religious reasons," loaded their 4x4's — with guns, family, sleeping bags, beer-stocked coolers — and headed for camp. Phil had never yet missed an Easter hunt, but since he and Candy had divorced, she and Melanie hadn't gone back to camp until last year. Women and children slept on one side of the cabin, men on the other. No problem about that, and Candy hadn't haunted Phil or made a play for any of the other men just to make Phil crazy, but still it had been awkward; the divorce seemed to frighten the other couples. It had not been a good camp. So when Candy tried to get in touch with Phil this year to say, "Are you going to be there? I'm not," she had to leave her message on his lawyer's answering machine. What she told him, at the sound of the beep, was, "I won't be going on the hunt this year. Enjoy." By Friday morning he hadn't called back, so Candy changed her mind. She more than half hoped Phil would show up in camp too — she would claim it was all a mix-up — and she'd have denied that she set it up, or even hoped for one last chance. Time was running out on that think-it-over month she had begged Larry to give her, about moving to Vermont. She didn't call Larry till early Friday, as she was throwing things in the car to go. When Larry asked, "Is Phil going to be there?" Candy said, "If it happens, it happens." Larry had never been to camp; he was no hunter. He was hoping Candy and Melanie would join him for sunrise services at Stone Mountain instead. Candy said, "Maybe your mom would like to go."

When Larry sounded upset, she told him, "For God's sake, be flexible. I am."

Candy and Melanie set off, southeast, not even taking time for breakfast. Candy drove fast and earnestly, as though catching up.

When she rolled into camp, unexpected, unescorted, and nosed the red VW bug into the gap between young pines, she got out, slammed the door, and announced, "Surprise, I changed my mind," looking around before adding, "Phil's not here yet?"

Melanie was singing, and suddenly, out of the car she

popped, like a jack from its box, her green-eyed adoption doll under her arm, the doll's suitcase in her other hand.

Candy smoked her cigarette down to the filter and toed the stub into the sand. "Go see what the other kids are up to," she told her daughter. "Run play." She counted, always, on the fostering of friends. "I'm not running for Mother of the Year," she'd said more than once. And when Melanie had brought home that third notice from PTA reminding her that she was the only holdout from 100 percent membership, she had finally said, "All right, I'll join, but I won't bake any more cupcakes!"

Now she headed for the cooler on the bench, the only one of the wives who drank, but then she wasn't a wife any more, either. That made a difference. She'd been running on pure nerve and more than occasional alcohol ever since the final decree. She never drank alone, and she preferred someone else to buy.

Candy lifted the lid on the beer cooler and looked in, stirring the ice around and shaking the crystals, bright as diamonds, from her fingers. There was still a white unpigmented stripe — like a scar, or a string reminder — where her wedding band had been. She had only recently stopped wearing it on her hand. When Larry bought her a gold chain, she threaded it onto the chain and wore it around her neck. She moved the diamond ring guard that Phil had bought for her to her right hand, with Larry's Valentine ruby. She said it fit better there.

Everyone said Larry was a patient man . . .

Dropping the cooler lid, Candy decided, "Liquor, not beer. Where's the bottle?" and headed into the lodge, seeking. The other wives and children were out in the yard; the women watched her go inside. Candy was saying something outrageous — each wife knew her own husband's laugh — in that clear, childlike voice of hers that was wickedly a disguise. Like a pepper that gives you sweet flavor first, and then, slow fire. A favorite, with her cheerleader stamina and party spirits. She came back out to the cooler, fished up a few chunks of ice to drop into her drink, and settled on the top step. She sighed.

"So, where's Larry?" one of the men asked.

"Separate vacations," Candy said, after due consideration.

"Shoot a monkey, I thought he was *it*."

"Who'd you ask?" Candy finished her drink and flung the ice out into the shadows, then crumpled the paper cup and tossed it after. Standing, she shouted toward the clear-raked area where the kids were jumping rope.

"Melanie? *Melanie!* Bring me my sweater from the car, sugar."

Melanie, whose turn it was to jump, her doll in her arms, ducked clear of the rope and ran to fetch. "Is Daddy coming?" she asked when she brought the sweater.

Candy rammed her fists into the sleeves and said, "Not this time." It was Phil's sweater, one he had left behind. Melanie wouldn't go; Melanie wouldn't quit. She burrowed her face into the sweaterstuff and said, "Smells like Daddy." She leaned back, her face upturned, empty, hoping for hope.

Candy said, "He's not coming."

"Ever? Ever again?"

Candy laid her cold hands over the child's hot eyes. "That's hopeful wishin'. Run play."

Melanie ran.

Candy shuddered. She buttoned up, right to the chin, and still she was shivering. "I need to circulate," she decided, like it was a party, not a hunting camp, where she stood. She walked around, stretching. She did a few jump-

ing jacks, wandered over to where the children were playing. Gauging her main chance, she scooted in, stole a turn,
just as the jump rope rose to its full height. She was good
at it, her sunny hair lifting and falling. As she jumped, she
faced north — east — south — west. Then she was back
where she started, and skipped out, laughing, that soft laugh,
those quiet yelps, turning heads. One of the hunters said,
"Desire call of the wild hen," and it is true that she sounded
like the record of turkey calls they practiced to. She blew
the men a kiss and ran back in on the rope and jumped
some more, since they were looking.

The men brought the table in from the yard, the lantern
balanced in the center, orbited by moths. "Deal me in,"
Candy said, helping to bring folding chairs. In the yard,
the women were finishing the dishes. The men were going
to play poker. The wives finished their work and came in,
standing around, keeping the children out of the way,
reading the cards over the hunched shoulders of the players. Candy had her back to the wall, facing the open door.
She was the first to see the headlights coming. Long before
she could have been sure she cried, "It's Larry!" and jumped
up. She fled to the other side of the tarp that divided the
sleeping quarters from the living area.
    "Well, durn," one of the wives called after her, "I thought
you loved him."
    "He said he wouldn't come here," Candy whispered,
crouching by her cot, fumbling her cigarettes from her
pocketbook, lighting, smoking fast.
    "You can't hide back here forever."
    "He wants to marry me," Candy accused. "He wants
me to migrate a thousand miles off up yonder and live."
She pointed wildly north.
    Outside, Larry was saying, "Tell her I'm here."

"Dammit!" Candy cried. She put her fingers in her ears and shut her eyes. Melanie poked her head around the tarp and announced:

"Mama? Larry wants to talk to you."

Candy rummaged in her pocketbook again, finding her brush, fluffing her bangs, pulling one long blond hair from the bristles, idly inspecting it. "I'm overprocessed," she noticed, stretching it till it snapped. She told Melanie, "Scat," but Melanie just stood there. Candy gave Melanie's backside a swat with the brush. "Run play and let me live my life," she said. Melanie went.

Candy said, "I'm not having much fun for the fun I'm having." She pushed the tarp back and walked to the liquor, poured and drank a shot, then went out. At the door she paused to tell the card players, the game suspended while Larry paced outside, "I'm going for a ride, don't wait up, and if y'all talk in your sleep, don't mention my name."

It was after two when Larry's station wagon eased back into camp. He didn't even cut the engine to let Candy out. She slammed the door without another word. Larry didn't stay.

The campfire was ashes now. Candy sat on the top step watching the coals wink out, chain-smoking the last of her cigarettes. The Easter moon was cold and far. When she finally let herself in, and crawled across the cots to her own place, one of the wives whispered, "Did I hear somebody's heart break tonight?"

Candy sat up in bed doing her bust exercises, smoothing cream on her elbows and hands, massaging her jawline. "I'll get over it," she predicted. She yawned and lay back. "I'm going to join that new spa," she decided. "Going to learn to play racquetball . . . It's the second most strenuous sport."

The other woman cleared her throat.

"Mountain climbing," Candy said.

For Melanie's birthday, Candy and she drove down to the Hallmark half-price sale and bought plates and napkins that almost matched. Candy had said Melanie could invite eight guests. "A real party." Melanie addressed the invitations herself. She addressed all eight to Phil. When Candy saw that she said, "I don't even want to consider it. You might as well drop them in the trash right now." But Melanie mailed them anyway, all eight. Like prayers.

Phil answered. He called. He said he didn't see why not. "Who else'll be there?" he asked.

Candy was listening on the other phone. "Just us," she said.

Phil said, "Maybe I'll bring a little something."

"Not a puppy," Candy said, before Melanie could get her hopes up. "Not unless you buy its food and pay the vet bills. You hear?"

Phil laughed.

The week before the party Candy and Melanie started getting the house ready. They painted over the wallpaper in Melanie's room. It took two coats to cover the nursery print.

"I'm past all that now," Melanie said. "I'm ten now. Double digits." She weeded through her toy box; there was a pile of culls to be hauled out: her little rocker with the broken arm, the gerbil hutch, a threadbare stuffed lion, and the cracked kiddy pool. She set her remaining dolls on the shelf in a tidy row, like a hobby.

"What happened to *your* dolls, Mama?" Melanie wondered.

Candy aimed the Kirby sweeper into the corner and

gathered up seasons of webs. "I wore them all out, except for the one Mama kept in the glass case for when I grew up and had you."

Melanie came running when she heard that. "Where is she?" She tripped over the vacuum cord and sprawled. Candy clicked off the machine and sat down on the floor beside her.

"She died," Candy said.

Melanie slowly sat up. "She died?"

"I meant Mama," Candy said. "The doll broke. Somebody dropped it, maybe me. The whole thing went to pieces, like a stack of plates. The eyes were blue, that's all I remember."

She went into the other room and poured a drink. "I'm pooped," she said. "Maybe we better pace ourselves. We've got a week."

It took it.

They clipped the holly hedge and planted a six-pack of marigolds by the walk. Candy line-dried her best blue-striped sheets in the sun and bought a new shower curtain and mat. They got the front windows washed and Melanie taped a WELCOME sign to the front door. Candy picked up the cake on Saturday morning. Everything was ready. They walked through the house and felt like company.

"This is my best birthday ever," Melanie said. She waited in the yard watching for him to arrive. He was only a couple of hours late.

As it turned out, the "little something" he was bringing was named Debbie, his co-worker. They arrived on a brand-new apple green Kawasaki, in identical jumpsuits and helmets. Melanie's birthday present was in the motorcycle's saddlebags. They let her dig it out: a Sony Walkman. Phil clipped the receiver to her belt and Debbie snugged the earphones over Melanie's ears. Melanie tuned to 96 Rock, and said "thank you," too loud, and wandered off to get her bicycle. She didn't even stay around for cake and ice cream. She was singing along, pedaling hard, going uphill. They watched her from the porch and then went inside.

"She likes it," Debbie said softly, as if it had been her idea. She wasn't talking to Candy.

"She's a kick, isn't she?" Phil said.

Candy said, "I got total custody."

Phil said, "I wasn't sure if she'd remember me, you know."

"It's only been fourteen months since you saw her," Candy said. "She was looking forward to —"

"She'll be back when her batteries run down," Debbie said confidently. She stood at the window watching. She turned to explain, "I come from a big family," and sat down next to Phil on the couch. Instantly their hands linked.

Candy said, "Remember the time we didn't have a dime for presents? I wrapped Melanie in funny papers and when you came downstairs on Father's Day, she said in that dinky little baby voice, 'Open me first!'"

Nobody said anything for a moment, then Phil said, "Debbie and I are getting married."

"I'll get some wine," Candy said. She headed for the refrigerator.

"Hey, no big deal," Debbie called after her. "Lemonade's fine."

Candy looked back around the door. "I've been drinking lemonade all day and I'm not getting anywhere."

Phil wandered out to the kitchen to ask Candy something. She was downing some pills with a tumbler of Chablis. He laughed. "I've reformed," he said. He was lean, back to the weight he had been when he and Candy married. No more beard, either. The gold chain she had given him had a new charm on it. "I'm off red meat and french fries, too," he said, folding his sunglasses, zipping them into his chest pocket, safe. "I didn't remember this place being so dark," he said, looking around. He helped Candy get the stemware off the top shelf.

"Listen," he said, "you don't need that smoker any more, do you? Maybe I could come by some day and pick it up in the truck. Debbie and I are really into mesquite broiling. It makes great fish, a handful of herbs, no salt."

Candy laughed, those soft yelps. "All yours," she pointed out.

"Great. I'll be by sometime."

Going back into the other room with the wine, she answered the anxious look on Debbie's face by saying, "This is what you call a friendly divorce."

Phil showed Debbie the house then, while Candy answered the phone. Melanie came back just as Debbie and Phil were leaving.

"Can't you stay?" Melanie hoped.

"It may rain, and we've got some miles," Phil said.

As Candy and Melanie cleaned up after the party, Melanie said, "They're getting married. To each other. Did he tell you?"

"She's not much older than you!" Candy said. "She still wears braces."

"She seemed nice," Melanie said, crumpling paper.

"Then *you* marry her."

Melanie stopped working, and sat, thinking it through. "I thought you liked her."

"I hope they run off a cliff, both of them."

"Not my daddy," Melanie said, swallowing. She tore the wrapping paper. Pieces feathered onto the carpet, as if she were plucking a bird.

"I was kidding," Candy said. "He's coming back sometime, he said so."

They swept the room clear of every bit of festivity. Not a ribbon remained. They took turns popping the balloons. "That cake cost me eight dollars," Candy said, licking the knife.

Melanie picked up an empty box from the trash. "I want to keep this," she said. "It'll do for burying my turtle when he dies."

"What next?" Candy wondered.

In July honey began dripping from behind the window air conditioner. It ran down the living room wall and Candy called a beeman. The ad in the *Market Bulletin* said he would repair all damage, too.

He did. He also helped Candy put together the steel walls of the swimming pool she bought at the Sears Liquidation Center. It wasn't a very big pool — she could swim across in two strokes — but she had to run the garden hose night and day to fill it because of a slow leak.

After Candy got her August water bill, she turned the hose off. The pool slowly emptied. The lawn around the pool was a marsh. Candy called the beeman, who had helped her put the pool together. He had moved back to south Georgia. Nobody else Candy asked about it had any ideas. Meanwhile the pool itself dried.

"I didn't get to use it a month!" Candy was saying to Dr. Bowen. She had seen a hand-written card on the community bulletin board at Kroger. A man advertised that he could repair vinyl liners and brace the buckling sides. "What do you think?" Candy wondered. "Is it too late in the year to mess with fixing it?"

Dr. Bowen didn't like the idea of hiring strangers like

that, no credentials, no background, complete strangers. "Maybe you ought to consult an expert," the dentist suggested. All summer Candy had been grasping at straws and holding on till her hands shook. "Maybe Sears will take it back, make some adjustment, even though it's surplus."

Candy decided, "I'm calling the man from Kroger. He says he's reasonable." Her laugh was a little wild and harsh. "Who knows, you know? He might be my future has-been."

But the pool was still dry the Friday before Labor Day when Phil drove up to collect his smoker-grill. "It was yours, anyway," Melanie reminded him, when he said, a little defensively, "I've got all new utensils and stuff."

It was a surprise visit; he hadn't called first. Melanie had come out at the sound of his horn at the back gate, to open it for him so he could drive right across the lawn. Candy was at work. Melanie helped him wrangle the grill onto the truck, up two planks, pushing hard. "Over the hump," Phil said. When they had got it tied down, Phil walked all around, kicking at trash in the weeds, standing for a time in the empty chicken yard, the gate completely off its hinges now, a year's grass growing up through its rusted wire. He rang, just to hear it, the bell on the back gate, and walked down to the pool and stared in. There was a maple leaf stuck on the bottom, scarlet, stark against the blue vinyl.

"Your mother probably lies in here without any clothes on," he said.

Melanie climbed the ladder and dropped from it into the pool, crouching right in the center. "Not really," she said. "She just comes out here at night sometimes and sits and screams. Nobody can see."

Melanie showed him how.

She climbed back out then. The maple leaf was stuck to her sneaker. She scuffed it off in the grass, tapped an anthill with her toe, peeled a little twig smooth as bone. "Mama'll be home soon," she told him. "We could cook hot dogs or something?"

But Phil didn't stay.

Finding the Chain

BEN WRAPPED a feed sack around the flat rock and hooked it onto the chains. There wasn't more than ten feet of sound hemp or baling wire on the whole farm and he'd used that to tie the dog out of trouble. Not that Shin would've run off; she wanted to run *in*, and she'd already fought a skunk and lost and come rushing back so fast nobody had the wit to grab her and drag her out before she ruined — "It's clean gone, you can just cut it up for stinking rags for all I care now," Cliffie raged — Grandma Gable's Storm at Sea quilt, which was still on the floor from where they had huddled to sleep the night before, cold, damp, and hungry.

By flashlight Ben had found the one can of tomato juice in the trunk of the car and had poured it over the dog, rubbing it into her coat, but there was no way, till he got the chimney swept of bats and birds' nests, to safely heat water to rinse her. She sat at rope's end, still reeking, griz-zled pink with tomato and whining with embarrassment. She never had been restrained in her life — it had been honor system all the way, and mutual trust — and now this.

They had arrived late, well past dark, and the first thing Ben had tried to do for them, when they had finally got into the log cabin, was make a fire. It hadn't seemed worth it to pay a deposit to have an electric meter installed for just a weekend, so they came prepared to camp, to cook over the fireplace, and draw water up from the well. Ben laid a good enough fire to get things going and cheerful, only before he could turn his back the house had filled with smoke, all of it coming into the rooms, none of it going up the chimney. They had doused the fire with water and waved damp towels to get the air clear, deciding not to mess with the chimney till daylight.

First thing Ben did in the morning was run Mary J and Drew out to look around, to find something long enough to use to clean the flue. There were snow chains, eaten up with fertilizer, and trace chains, not long enough in themselves, but linked to the swing chains, they were about right. Ben reached up and unhooked the swing, hardly stretching. He left the swing on the porch, flat, and scaled the old ladder to the roof, telling himself, "Easy, easy." The mossy shingles were rain-slick. "No time to be airborne," he said.

He was whistling a little as he dropped the bundled rock down the chimney's crooked throat. Before he could even draw up, on the first sweep, here came Cliffie boiling out of the house like a hornet from a lit nest, yelling *whoa* and cussing like a Christian.

"Are you out of your mind?" she screamed. The echo bounced off the barn. Mary J prissed over to stand by her momma under the umbrella. All Ben could see was spattered shoes and neon anklets from that angle. Everything looked different. He almost laughed, till Cliffie shoved the umbrella back and he saw her face.

"Did soot get all over the house?" he wondered. It might have been an apology, but after all, it wasn't his fault. He had told the boy to run in and help his momma cover the hearth and seal it off with newspapers and duct tape. He'd even tossed the boy his car keys, so he could get the tape from the toolbox in the trunk. Ben reckoned Drew had just skipped off, and not accidentally either. Cliffie said the boy had some adjusting to do, that was all, and she never came down hard on his "pranks." Ben eased over onto his other hip and stretched his bum leg. Bad weather reminded every bone of where it had broken and healed.

"I told him to tell you," Ben said. "Where is he?"

"Don't start on him," Cliffie said. She'd been saying it for over two years, ever since Ben and Cliffie's first date, when Ben had offered Drew his hand and the boy pocketed his fists and turned away, sour as sorrel.

"I'm through *starting* on him," Ben said. Loud enough for the boy to hear, if he were skulking in the barn loft or on the back porch or stretched across the back seat of the car, reading his comics. He knew the boy wouldn't be sorry, early or late, for messing up. He didn't look for Drew to poke his hard head up over the edge of the roof and say, "Sir?"

"I've got news for that little pecker," Ben boomed. "The paperwork's come through. I'm his old man now."

Cliffie looked hurt. "I wanted to tell him!" She leaned on the ladder and stared up, but she wouldn't climb, wouldn't meet Ben halfway. She cocked her head like she heard nothing but bad news from an angel. Tears of rain ran down her face. Ben wasn't fooled. He knew it was rain. She'd laugh it off, or fight it out, or sue, Cliffie would, but never cry. "Not my Cliffie," he said.

She had been about to pull the ladder away and strand him up there, but when he spoke as cheerfully as that, and him wet enough to wring rainwater from his shirttail, she moderated. She and Mary J headed back to the house without another word. "You just cover the fireplace and save me a round trip," he called after them. If Cliffie heard it, she didn't say so. He posted himself by the chimney, listening. He could hear Cliffie comforting the baby, and warning Mary J not to run the batteries down on the transistor . . . Because of the crook in the chimney he couldn't see the light, or if the fireplace had been covered, if they were ready. He called down to them — Cliffie had to hear it! — "Now?" and tried to sound like he was enjoying himself. "Say when," he hollered again.

Nothing.

"If you can stand it, so can I," he decided, and having given her time enough, and warning — "It be on your head" — he let the bundle fall, giving the chains a good twist and scour, hoping, maybe, for the worst below. That's what it had come to after only twenty-four hours away from the Jim Walter home-on-stilts he had built for her in South End, with a view of the docks and marsh.

When Ben stamped back across the porch and into the house with an armload of wet kindling, he reminded her, "I'm no goddamn pioneer."

Cliffie had been so sick after the baby came she made Ben promise if anything happened — "Now, honey, please, just listen to me" — he'd take her back to her homeplace, have the funeral there, and bury her in the mountains with her family. "Mama's got the prettiest stone, marble, and white as the winter moon. It says WILDROSE WOMAN / GOD LOVED / SORROWS ENDED . . ."

Ben didn't want to hear that kind of talk. He said, "You're going to get well and when you do, we'll all drive up there and see how the other half lives." He promised.

"You mean it?"

Of course he did. But when she got well, he acted as though she had taken advantage of him. It was two years before they finally got away and headed due north. By then, the last of the Gables had died out and Cliffie had been fretting all summer about what was happening to "the things" left in the abandoned cabin. She couldn't locate a cousin willing to go see, or find a tenant steady enough to keep the farm going. Taxes kept coming due, and Cliffie was settling it in her heart that she would have to sell. This would be the last trip. She would bring back with her all that she could not bear to part with, and make her peace about the rest. She wanted them to love the place as she did. She wanted them to know everything, all the little stories. She wanted everything to be perfect, and she was so excited the night before they left that she kept getting up to write down something else on her lists. Ben would turn over in bed, his back to the sudden light, and grumble for her to settle down.

"You could sleep through a war," she told him.

"Not the one I went to," he said.

She had them out of bed and spooning cold cereal toward their zombie faces by five o'clock the next morning. Even then, she was telling them how great things were going to be.

Ben warned her again as they left the last traffic light in Glynn County behind them, "It won't be like you remember it," as though he expected her to reconsider, admit it was a mistake, and tell him to turn around in the churchyard at Sterling and head back to the coast.

"I'm prepared," is what she said.

Ben had never been north of Lyons, where the sallow clay hills begin, except for a class trip to Macon when he was a kid — to see the circus — and his time in the army. He couldn't imagine what there was about red mud for Cliffie to love and miss. He liked the rich flat black sandy land, the rise and fall of the tides, the evergreen oaks . . .

He had to press the accelerator harder all the time now; every mile was uphill. Already his right knee felt stiff. The engine made a dry tapping sound, noisy as diesel, and he prayed the valves and lifters would behave themselves. He had packed extra quarts of oil and a can opener in his toolbox, but he wasn't like Cliffie, he couldn't plan ahead the way she did, for emergency and bad luck. He called it "borrowing trouble," but she'd had a lifetime to get good at it, no changing her ways now. The trunk of the car overflowed with things she had crammed in because they "just might need this up home." Besides the lunch she'd made for them, for the road, she had packed groceries, candles, matches, a hatchet, pillows, blankets, coal oil, and lanterns.

One suitcase contained the clothes they'd need if the weather stayed mild and another was stuffed with sweaters and warm hats and gloves in case it turned cold. "It can get mean in the mountains at Thanksgiving," Cliffie said.

She looked over the seat back to check on Mary J and Drew. They had set out perky enough, full of questions, jokes, quarrels, and fighting for place, but now had subsided into sleep, catching up on the dreams they'd lost in the early start. The dog, Shin, rode between them atop a pile of bedclothes that wouldn't fit in the trunk. She was a medium-sized dog, not young but alert, her hindquarters on the package tray, her front legs stretched out, her chin down, her ears up. She widened her grin into a sour yawn, but her eyes never left off for a moment searching the center line that came at them out of the dark.

"Dog is my copilot," Ben said, glancing in the rearview. Cliffie disapproved of dogs and blasphemy.

"We should've left her with Palma and them. They had room."

"They had room for Mary J and Drew too," Ben pointed out. He didn't want to leave the children behind, but he loved his dog. "She was my family, the same way Mary J and Drew were yours." He'd been wanting to say that for some time, waiting to see if she'd figure it out without having to be told.

The lights from the dashboard lit every hurt and hollow in her face with an eerie green. "We're all Stevensons now," he added, for once saying exactly the right thing whether she admitted it or not. "Little pitchers," she said, putting her long fingers over his mouth to hush him, adding, "Keep your eyes on the road." She sounded pleased.

It was false dawn. They were driving away from sunup. By the time it was true day, they had covered a hundred miles, had almost left the cypress lands behind. Jondi stirred and woke; Cliffie unharnessed him from his carseat and stood him on her lap to see out. "Look, baby boy, now we're getting somewhere."

When they stopped for a fill-up, Cliffie wrote down the mileage and the time and amount. She kept books on everything like that, had clipped coupons in case they had a chance to see some museums in Atlanta. "This isn't just another joy ride," she told them. When the kids wanted Cokes at the service station, she wouldn't let Ben shell out change for them. "We have our own cooler," she reminded them, "and pretty soon we'll be stopping for lunch." All along the way she pointed out things she thought they might not notice, and explained history and geography, and what the fall line was and why so many pines grew and how to preserve the indigo snake from extinction. She was always teaching, whether she was in her classroom or not. She had even brought along a library book on the historical markers, so they wouldn't lose time stopping to read them.

"There's not an hour in the world for every little thing," Cliffie said, "but it's good to know what you're missing."

Mary J and Drew argued and begged to take turns reading the book, but they got carsick — "I told you so," Cliffie said — and had to walk it off on the roadside between endless cotton fields. Another good reason to travel U.S. 341, not the Interstate. Plenty of stopping room. "If you want to race, go to Daytona," Cliffie said. "All you smell on a four-lane is exhaust fumes . . . I'd know this was cotton with my eyes shut." She breathed in, in a testing way. "Everything done by machine now," she said. "No more chopping. No more laying by. No more protracted meetings, muddy baptizings, no more one pair of new shoes in November having to last all year." They gathered along the fence — Shin, too — looking. Ben and the kids stretched across to pick a boll or two. "The rains have about ruined it," Cliffie said, as they drove away. Jondi, who had never seen any kind of the real thing, just cotton batting and angel hair and aerosol flakes, kept pointing out the window at the dotted fields and calling, "Snow!"

"I never picked cotton," Ben said.

"I'd rather pick rags," Cliffie said, so bitterly he let up on the gas for a moment. She'd had it hard, so hard he wondered again why she'd want to go back and remind herself of what she'd left behind.

Cliffie had been so sure of the roads, the turns, the old landmarks, but in the rain her memory failed. It had never been but the dimmest daylight all day, and they had driven in rain from Macon on. Cliffie sat right up at the windshield, rubbing it with her hand, trying to see past the headlights. "This isn't where," she realized, looking scared. "Am I losing my mind?" Ben didn't complain; he backed them around in a wide place and they tried again. Finally they stopped at a dark store and Cliffie beat and beat at the door till an old woman dragged open a window in the house and yelled, "They're out of business. What?" Cliffie stepped around a pile of coal, to stand in a puddle and talk. As she came splashing back to the car, she was smiling. "We're just not there yet. Two more miles to Wildrose."

When they drove around the curve and the white-washed church came into view, Cliffie said, "Of course," meaning *Here we are,* but Ben didn't understand, so he kept on driving, almost past, till Cliffie cried, "STOP!" He slammed on the brakes and they slid around in the mud. "I didn't say have a wreck," Cliffie said. "I didn't say break my nose." She had brought fresh-cut flowers from a florist. "Not artificial, not weeds. When will I ever have the chance again?" she explained, justifying those six red roses kept on ice in the cooler every mile of the way. The buds looked almost black now in the rain. That's how near nightfall it was.

Mary J got to steer the car when it slid off the road and stuck in the mud. Everybody but the dog and baby got out to push. Mary J liked the way her fingers curved around the wheel, and she was glad she still had polish on some of the nails and hadn't gnawed it all off. She had on so many coats of paint she could peel it off in one piece that tasted like banana oil. Kid stuff . . . She felt grown-up, driving, and she knew what she wanted for Christmas: a birthstone ring. "Aquamarine," she said, loving the sound of it, forgetting Jondi was listening. She wanted white gold, like her momma's. She could turn the stone under to her palm, and just let the gold show, like a wedding band. When she got married — didn't know yet *who,* but probably a fisherman, like Ben — she was going to live in a little house right on the marsh, and have a baby sweeter than Jondi, a little girl baby, and drive around in a boat the color of the sky. And if she didn't want to wash the supper dishes, she wouldn't. Her momma couldn't make her. And she wouldn't have to fold clothes or study books any more either. It might be another year or two, she didn't know just when she'd be a woman and could put her feet up and look at magazines and pin her curtains back with paper roses and have flowers everywhere, in a tire ring under the trees, and at the windows. "Window boxes, definitely," she said, sounding enough like her momma to make Jondi sit up and reach.

"Momma," she announced when everybody got back in the car and she slid over to let Ben drive again, "I'm not going to marry till I'm tall enough to see into the soup pot on the back eye. If a boy caint wait that long, he probably doesn't love me anyway. Right?"

Her momma felt her forehead. "I think this child has a fever," she decided. Jondi already had his ears filled with sweet oil and cotton, and coughed. "You next?" she asked. Mary J crawled over the seat back and lay in her corner and imagined what it would be like to be a nurse, like Aunt Palma. She would bring comfort and cheer to all her patients. She would wear a cape the color of midnight and walk quietly down the halls and carry a silver pen in her pocket to write important things on the chart . . .

As she brought luggage in from the car she imagined these were emergency Red Cross supplies. The next day as she carried Grandma Gable's red and gold candy jar from the hutch to set in the center of the table she imagined it was a bottle of blood. She held it to the light and said, "Plasma," and shivered. That wasn't why she dropped the jar. She didn't know why she dropped it. She couldn't believe she had dropped it. How could something that terrible happen? It didn't shatter, it broke in three shards, as if it had been meant to, and lay there empty as a shell. Her momma came running, picked up the perfect lid, kissed it.

"Not my bowl," she said. "Anything in this house but that bowl," she said. She knelt and picked up the pieces and tried fitting them together, like a puzzle. Ben came in and put his hand on Mary J's shoulder and said, "It's stopped raining. Why don't you and Drew take this grocery sack and hunt me some pine cones?" When she went out, he was telling her momma, "You going to have a funeral for it, or what? It ain't going to grow back. It ain't flesh and blood."

"You don't understand," her momma said. "I wouldn't expect you to."

Mary J handed Drew the bag. She went to the barn instead, and pulled the door shut behind her. It was so heavy.

Drew wasn't strong enough to drag the barn door open. He didn't want to play with Mary J anyway. She was too bossy. He looked around, his first chance to explore the farm in daylight, in good weather. It was Thanksgiving day, after noon. They weren't going to have a turkey this time. There was no stove to cook on. They heated soup over the fire. The smoke smelled nice when wind blew it down the roof of the house and swirled it around in the yard. His momma told him to watch the weathervane. She said, "This is the fairing-off shower," and, sure enough, the arrow backed from east to northwest and the rains finally drizzled to a stop. The cold wind was rolling fog over the gray flanks of the Blue Ridge and Drew's momma said she didn't care what the man on the radio had to allow, *she* smelled snow. Drew couldn't smell anything but smoke and skunk-scent the dog had brought back. The ruined quilt hung on the slack line between the barn and the cherry tree. "Crazy place for a clothesline," his momma had said and Mary J and Ben laughed along. Drew couldn't understand. He never understood anything. They'd tell a joke and laugh and he wouldn't get it. At school they called him "Dumbo" partly because he was slow and partly because of his ears. He pulled his cap down over them. He liked winter best, when he could wear a cap all the time. When he was grown up he was always going to wear his hat, never take it off except when they played the national anthem; he'd take it off then, if the other soldiers did. He was going to be in the army. He'd grow. He'd be tall enough. He'd lead the way. "I'm not afraid," he said. He ran in the tunnel the quilt made hanging over the line; he held his breath. When he came out the other side, he took in a chestful of frosty air. It burned. It was getting colder. When he breathed out, he made steam clouds. He found a stick and broke it to length and pretended it was a cigarette, puffing on it, exhaling. It really looked like smoke. He wished Mary J was spying. She'd snitch and then he'd get her back for once . . .

Jondi had an earache and couldn't play outside. He wasn't even supposed to go on the sleeping porch. "Right back in here this minute or I'm coming after you!" his momma said when he went. He was watching Drew play with the chain. Drew had the chain around his shoulder. He dragged it then wrapped it around him again, at the waist, like a belt. He held it in both hands like a snake. He was going away with it. Jondi couldn't see where. Momma came and picked him up and carried him back into the house and set him by the fire. "Don't get in the fire," she said. "Be an angel," she said. When she had gone he crawled over to the shelves. There were no picture books. There was a basket. There was a jar. He liked the jar. It took both hands to carry it back. He sat on the floor and dumped it out. Buttons rolled everywhere. He laughed and chased them. His momma came back angry. "You put them up, look at this floor, I asked you to be an angel."

He reached into the jar and put a handful back. He gathered up another handful and put them back. It was taking a long time.

"Every last one of them," she said. She went away again.

Jondi thought of something fun. He dropped a button down the knothole in the floorboard. It disappeared. He had a savings bank. This was like that. He kept on putting buttons down the hole. He used both hands. Some of the buttons were metal, some were bone. He didn't have to force any; they all went.

"Gone," he said, reaching into the empty jar.

"What have you done with Grandma's button collection?" Momma shouted when she came back. Jondi cried.

Ben said, "I'll crawl up under there and get 'em for you, no use in hearts busting over something I can fix."

When he came back, he set the buttons on the porch. "Blow the dust off and they'll be fine," he told Cliffie. "Good as new." He went whistling off to the barn. He had an idea for a Christmas present for Cliffie, and he hoped there was a shovel around.

* * *

193

Cliffie felt like the whole trip so far had been one long erosion. They didn't appreciate this old place or the things in it. And why should they? "It's just somewhere else they'll probably forget they've ever been." She picked up the jar of buttons and was turning to go back into the house when she noticed the swing still sitting flat on the porch, its chains gone.

Before she could holler *Where?* Mary J came running out of the barn yelling, "Fire!"

Drew heard her. He was in the field, swinging the chain. Turning in a circle holding the chain. Whirling faster and faster till the chain stood flat out from him and pulled at his arms in their sockets. When he couldn't hold the chain any longer, or whirl any faster, he'd let go and tumble backward and the chain would fly out from him and then drop in the sedge. He had invented the game on his own, and he liked it. His hands were stiff with cold. He didn't know where he had lost his gloves. He had let the chain pull him around in its circle all afternoon, and when he fell, he'd lie there and look up at the sky.

Clouds were coming fast. Low clouds, soft gray clouds. The sun struck through their gaps, casting golden shafts. Shadows raced. The mountains had vanished. Gusts of wind rattled the last soft downy seeds from the sedge and launched them across the pasture. When Mary J ran out of the barn and yelled, "Fire!" Drew was swinging the chain as hard as he could; he felt that this time he might be lifted from the earth and flung. He let go.

As soon as he scrambled to his feet he ran toward the barn. Shin stood at the end of her taut rope and barked. Momma came running down the steps, her hands over Jondi's ears to keep the wind off. "God help us, God help us," she was saying.

194

Ben had the shovel. He ran into the barn and Mary J and Momma were calling, "Come back! No! Don't!"

Drew ran past them. He ran in after Ben. He didn't know why. Maybe he just wanted to *see*. He didn't think. He just ran. He wasn't afraid. He darted around the door and crashed into Ben, who came laughing out of the barn. "False alarm," he said. "That board looks like it's cherry red," he said. "I'd have thought the same thing. Its rosin's catching the sun . . . You did the right thing." Mary J beamed.

"I remember that board," Momma said. "I remember that board so well."

Everybody went back to the house, everybody but Ben and Drew. Ben said, "You come with me." They went back into the barn to put up the shovel.

"I gave you my keys this morning," he said. "Remember?"

"In the car," Drew said. "I left them on the — the —"

"Well, you go find them, and you open that trunk for me, and you get back here warp speed, you hear me? I got a chore for you."

Drew started out.

"You owe me," Ben said. "If you're not back here in two minutes I'm coming to feed you to the hogs."

Drew said, "I ain't scared of nothing." Then he ran.

Ben was sitting on a crate when Drew came back. It was pretty dark in there. "You still here? Mister?"

It had been more than two years since Ben and Drew declared war. The boy never called him anything but *Mister*. "Here," Ben said.

"What you want me to do now?"

"Help me load this box in the car."

"Just old mud?"

"It's for your momma's Christmas," Ben told him. Maybe it was a crazy idea. "A surprise," he told Drew. "A little bit of here, for there."

"I hear you."

"I'm asking you to keep it a secret," Ben told him. "Man to man. You give your word and you keep it. You do that for me?"

"I'll do it for *Momma,*" Drew specified.

"No, you'll by Jesus do it for me," Ben said, "or you won't do it at all."

The boy's chin came up and his lips narrowed. He didn't promise, Ben thought. Goddamn little peckerhead, he thought. Where's the pay-off? He said, "Tell me something nice your daddy did for your momma. Just one nice thing."

Mary J asked Drew, "What do you mean 'crazy'?"

"He's giving her a box of dirt, the reddest dirt he can find, for Christmas."

Mary J wished she had thought of it. She decided right then to give her momma some rocks; she still had time before dark to find them, wrap them in a gunny sack, hide them in the car under the seat. She'd find the prettiest stones, to outline the flower beds.

Cliffie said, "All I want is that other chain. They were both right here this morning and they got no business being anywhere else tonight." Drew just stood there, looking at her. "And don't stare at me like a refugee," she said. "I know it isn't all your fault. If Ben hadn't taken the swing down, you couldn't have lost the chain off it." She glanced across the yard at the field beyond. She could smell it so plain: snow. No use in telling them that again, getting their hopes up for nothing. But she wanted that chain, and if it snowed, they'd never find it. It would lie out there all winter, forever maybe, if whoever bought the farm left the field fallow. She could remember the day that porch swing got hung. They called it a "courting swing." She was finally old enough to keep company. She went with her daddy to the feed merchant — it was her sixteenth birthday — and watched as the bright links of chain reeled off the spool. He had bought a better grade than just getting by. "We want it to last," he had said. "A hundred years from now, my grandchirren's grandchirren'll be sitting out here in the breeze saying, 'Thank you, Charley Gable.' " He had died the next year.

Cliffie got up and paced. "I'm just going to look some more," she said. "I feel like a mama cat that's lost one of her kittens."

They could see her in the field, passing back and forth, looking down. She came to the far line and just stood there staring north where the Blue Ridge earned its name in fair weather. It was getting on toward sundown now, and the sky was still full of those tumbled clouds, plum-colored and ragged. Far off, crows laughed, fighting the wind.

Mary J eased off her chair and pulled on her jacket. She put her soup bowl in the dish bucket and skipped out.

"Mary J'll probably find it too," Drew said. "She likes being the hero."

Ben said, "I hope she *does* find it. . . . This has been some day." He folded a piece of bread in half and ate it. Two bites.

"What if she doesn't? What if nobody finds it?"

"Your momma wanted to take the swing home with us."

"We still can. They sell chain."

"Some things in this world there's just one of, even when

you get something else just as good. Or better," Ben said. He and Drew studied each other, thinking it through.

"Work to do," Ben said, pushing back from the table. "You going to be here, you watch Jondi. Keep him out of the fire." He zipped his jacket and ducked out the door.

Drew said, "Easy when you tall." Meaning life in general. His daddy had been a featherweight Golden Gloves champ, five foot three. Everybody said Jondi was going to be big, big as Ben. "Look at those hands," they'd say. Drew pulled Jondi's hand away from the lantern and balanced the baby on his hip till he could get dressed for outdoors. He set the screen in front of the fire and slipped out the back way. He didn't want them to see him coming, as if he were tagging after.

Jondi jogged along in Drew's arms, asking *Why? Why? Why?* about everything he saw. Drew hoped Jondi wouldn't start crying when he saw their momma on the far side of the field. Drew just wanted to be by himself. He just wanted to find that chain.

But Jondi cried. He wouldn't toddle along, he wanted to be carried. When Drew set him down, Jondi grabbed to his leg like an anchor, and howled. Across the field their momma was calling instructions to him. Drew picked up Jondi and carried him to her.

Back of the house Shin was whining again. She ran as far as she could and then jerked over, held back by the rope.

Cliffie was saying, "Look!" She had found something. Not the chain. It was a little heap of trash, years old, in a ravine where they had brought the things they no longer wanted in the house or barn. A bedspring. A broken TV. Pickle jars. An old antenna. "Here's where they threw out," she said. "Look at this." She picked up the doorknob she had told them about. The white porcelain one that her great grandmother saved for the housewarming, from the other house, the one that burned. Cliffie had told them all about it. They had expected to see it on the front door instead of the deadbolt that had greeted them. They didn't have a key. They could see the key in the lock on the inside. They stood in the rain, locked out, and Ben went from window to window, trying each one. He managed to get the one in the kitchen open wide enough to slip Jondi through. Cliffie shined the flashlight from the porch toward him, calling him, and he had finally arrived at the front door and pulled the key from the lock inside and pushed it under the door so they could get in. All that because Cliffie didn't want to break a window . . .

The porcelain doorknob was chipped and the shaft wrung off. "I guess they knew what they were doing," Cliffie said. She turned her back, closed her eyes, and tossed it over her shoulder, refusing to look at where it fell. "The best way," she said. "I can't save every little thing."

Drew made sure no one was looking, especially not Mary J. He made it look as if he were just wasting time, prowling around in the weeds. Momma was saying, "Grandma always said a field that grows sedge is too sorry to plow." When they had gone on past, still hunting the chain, Drew stooped down and picked up that old white doorknob. It had rolled down the gully a little farther when his momma threw it. He didn't even take time to rub it off. He couldn't force it into his pocket, so he hid it in his sleeve. His heart was pounding. He felt so proud, as though he had saved a life. He ran with his arm up, so the knob wouldn't slip out of his jacket sleeve. He slowed down when he got back in the field. He walked along kicking at the tufts of sedge, trying to remember where he had been the last time he swung the chain. He wanted above all to find that chain. If Mary J found it, it would be all right, but if he found it, it would be exactly right. She was searching along the crumbly edge of the brook, so he turned upland, his arm raised, his eyes down. He didn't see Shin chew through the last threads of her rope.

They were never going to find the chain. All they were doing was wandering around in the last light, hoping. Shin ran back and forth over the soggy ground, greeting each of them, forgiving them. They had been walking the terraces away from the house, Mary J here, Drew there, Jondi and Shin everywhere, and now that they had come to the far fence row, scattering its sparrows, there was nothing to do but turn back. They were by chance or grace almost in unison now, apart from each other, absorbed, looking down, but moving, pausing, and keeping pace.

It had begun to snow, the first flakes they'd ever seen; only Cliffie had been in snow before. They'd have stopped to enjoy it, to catch the white cool feathers on their hands and tongues, but Cliffie moaned, "That's gonna do it. Amen. Y'all go on."

Ben said, "I wish I had a big magnet."

"Or a giant rake," Mary J said. They closed ranks against the coming dark, against the soft, random flurries, against the idea of giving up. Not touching, still at arm's length, but now shoulder by shoulder, like a chorus line, they swept across the field. Shin barked them along, and raced ahead and then padded back. Finally she took her sober place beside Ben, on the right flank. Drew, on the far left, stumbled, fell, and pushed himself to his knees. The doorknob had flung out of his sleeve and he was so intent on getting it back, on keeping his secret, that he didn't notice the chain. That was what had tripped him. It lay in a loose curve, muddy, and till he touched it, got it in his hands and lifted it, he couldn't believe it. He had seen it in his mind's eye all afternoon; he didn't believe it. Then he jumped up and hollered, "Ben! Momma! Over here!" and everyone swerved, everyone came clotting around him, reaching, touching. Holding on.

It was funny how they all held on. Even when they turned and headed for the house, its one window lit golden by the oil lamp, the smoke from the hearth fire beaten down flat from the chimney into the bare yard, the air between them and comfort filled with that confetti of feathers, they still held to the chain. It seemed so right. Ben wanted to say, "Don't nobody let go," but he didn't. Some things just have to happen.

And Venus Is Blue

Imagine a photograph album, with a bullet fired pointblank through it, every page with its scar. Murder attacks the future; suicide aims at the past.

Daybreak

IT WAS the phone ringing — not the dogs barking, not the
single gunshot that roused the dogs — that woke him; it
was the phone ringing. He lay a moment, dry-mouthed,
wondering how many times it had already rung. Would it
stop about the time he got to it and raised the receiver to
his pillow-warm ear? All his adrenaline surging for a wrong
number? Always a wrong number. But he was on his bony
feet now, stumbling toward the phone, and it kept ringing.

When he picked it up, Carol was breathing into the line,
"Webb? I need you, Webb."

He couldn't even ask, around his surprise, "What is it?"
because she was already panting again, softly, so softly,
"Webb . . . Webb . . . Come help me, it's James, it's bad."

And he was on his way, zipping his jeans as he ran. He
knew by her voice there was no time to find his boots. His
bare feet splashed dew as he cut across Miz Matrill's back
lot. He jumped her rabbit fence, thrashed through last fall's

goldenrod, cursing the sharp rocks and briars. He lurched across the brook into James's yard. The tool shed light drew him.

As fast as Webb ran, it took forever. As fast as he ran, there was no need, not for James, lying there in his own spilled thoughts. In the surprise of seeing that, Webb marveled then, *I didn't know this man,* and he rested, hands on his knees, catching his spent breath. Carol stood at the door, looking out at the morning coming.

Webb told her, "We have to call the law, you know."

But she just stood there. Webb was the one to walk back to the house in Carol's earlier tracks, and phone. She couldn't bear to leave James, but she couldn't look at him either. She stood guard at the door against anything else that could happen, that could matter — the lace on her sleeves spoiled with blood, her robe's hem, too, damp with death.

When Webb came back from phoning, he brought a blanket to cover what was left of the look on James's face. While he did that, Carol said calmly, "I'm the one who went from window to window all winter like a fox in a cage."

"Carol, don't."

"I'm the one who said, 'If you want to kill yourself, there's faster ways than cigarettes.' "

"Carol —"

She wasn't crying. "You called the law?" Her quiet was more terrible to Webb than wild tears. It was as though her warmth had all drained with James's, and they were both dead now. "I found him in the dark," she said, turning off the light. Webb took her cold hand and led her outside to wait.

"Electric bill ran fifty-three dollars last month," she said.

They sat shoulder to shoulder on the doorstep, brother

and sister, their bare, sibling feet chilling on the flagstones. They listened for sirens. Webb couldn't tell if it was Carol trembling, or himself.

She said, "You called the others."

"Nobody else."

It wasn't right — her calm — and it wouldn't last. He knew it would all break any time now, and she would be crazy, crazy when she let herself believe it. But now he was grateful for it, for that dreamy speech of hers. It kept him from jerking all to pieces. He was afraid of what he might do, once he let go. As long as she held up, he could. She'd always been the one that kept the lid on things. There was some gin in the house; he wished now that he'd drained the bottle while he was phoning.

"They'll have to hear it," she said. She took off her wedding ring and laid it on Webb's knee, then took it back again, staring through it at the sunrise. The first bird was singing.

"Red sky in the morning," she said. The sirens were close now. Webb put his arm around her and helped her stand. Lights were blinking on in houses up and down the street.

"Y'all supposed to deck and felt the Baker roof today."

"We won't," Webb realized, thinking, So this is what James meant yesterday when he said, "You can finish it yourself, every damn bit of it, you know that, don't you? You've got it all except my gray hair and leather liver . . . Soon enough . . ." Giving Webb that quick hard look, like he was hacked about something. Or like his gut was kicking up again. *Jesus Jesus.* James had taken his time. Had squatted with his back against a sweet-gum tree. Had let a handful of sand fall slow. "I'll tell you something, Webb," he'd said then. But he didn't. He didn't. He had opened his little knife to nudge splinters out of his palm. "Damn cedar," he had said.

Webb had thought he and James were in it for life. He had thought he'd grow up and grow old building houses for James. James had taught him how. . . .

Supposed to finish decking the roof on the lake house, pull out the gables and deck it over and get the felt tacked down so the roofers could do their thing on Thursday if it didn't rain. They had raised the rafters on Monday, starting early, with Bevel and Wild Billy and Red and Roy Boyd shouldering up the trusses, lining them on Webb's taut ridge string. Bracing. Joking. Taking and giving and making. Belonging. The good heft of the loaded aprons weighted with nails. The clean sweet pine. Mastery. That chorus of hammers, five men keeping different time, Bevel the newest, the slowest, always finishing last by three beats. The scream of the saw. The work drawing their sweat out, leaving them dry with a good thirst. The sun burning their shirts off their backs by noon, all of them getting looser as they got tireder, good tired, and keeping on, never mind it, strong and sure and tired.

Webb was thinking, *He knew yesterday,* and chewed back over it, every moment, to see if there were something, anything to the way James had driven in with the extra roll of felt, had hefted it onto his shoulder out of the truck, then dropped it in the shade, wedging it to a stop with his boot toe, never wasting a second to light the cigarette between his lips, just turning and running up the ladder to the next thing to be seen to, an invoice sticking out of his shirt pocket, a little tar on his hands and shoulder from the roofing felt, the sun blinding his digital watch, which was right then beeping noon, taking everything in without making a point of it, seeing how many of the men had showed up and how far they'd gotten, easy on everybody but himself, taking the delays in materials and setbacks from iffy weather out on his gut — so that while they spat tobacco, he spat blood — five different crews going full tilt, his shrewdness judging the men, juggling labor from site to site, shuttling back and forth tracking things down, on the road from dawn till midnight sometimes, and up again by six, phoning his diggers or roofers or painters or masons or bankers, saying, "A subdivision's like a race, like a gamble — it'll either go or it won't, all this huffin' and puffin' we're doing is just blowing on the dice," with that laugh of his, as when he reached the top of the ladder and cleared the edge of the roof in a low, one-armed vault, strong, natural, unthinking, just doing what it took to get where he wanted to be, calling, "Afternoon, boys. How's the old hammer hanging?" finally lighting his cigarette, looking around, pleased with their progress, squatting to eyeball the ridge, to check if things were truing-up, with that sixth sense of his that could judge by sight if work was square, with that uncanny skill at measurement that let him draw off a yard in builder's sand with the blunt toe of his boot, marking off feet and inches and not be out one-half inch in thirty-six, or estimate shingles for a multi-gable one-to-three pitch roof and come within a half-bundle, or by feel sense curve and angle in his fingertips so he could match moldings from memory after one touch, or figure compound cuts in plain air . . .

Bevel kept on, around that cheekful of Levi Garrett, whistling to Wild Billy's radio. They were running the Bronco's battery down again. Red was singing along, tuneless, low, his voice like his lame foot dragging a little behind. "No matta how hard I try, I'll never leave this woild alive . . ." James laughed, taking his slow, squaring look

209

along the ridge, peak to peak, then squat-running along the bare ribs of the roof as sure-footed as a fox, not even looking down to see where to jump next, just setting his pace to sixteen-inch centers and catting along.

When Webb had first tried to do that he had been nothing but a green, seventeen-year-old linthead dropout, nimble-handed from a year at the quick machines of the cotton mill, but stupid and soft for working wood. Webb had eased out on the rafters, willing, but when he first slipped and looked down at the ground two stories below, he had sweated and frozen. James had laughed. It happened like that more than once, and Webb had kept on trying, singing in that broken tenor of his, "Gimme weed, whites, and wine, I'm willin' . . .." trying to sound tough as the rest of them even while he trembled. What good was a carpenter afraid of heights? He practiced running up the ladder and across the roof in his dreams. He bought a pair of boots like the ones James wore. When James noticed, he said, "Son, it ain't in the leather, it's in the attitude. If you get it right, you got nothing to fret about, and if you get it wrong, why you just fly on down. For a little while, you're flying." He handed Webb the flask. It poured like water, but wasn't. Webb drank. Choked.

"That's *gin,* son," James told him, laughing. "It ain't courage but it's close." When Webb raised the flask again, James said, "Not *too* much, this ain't a funeral," and when Webb stood there, feeling it in his spine and belly, feeling stronger, James warned, "Yeah, but it don't last. Like leaning on the wind."

It was three hard years later before Webb moved up to James's crew chief, but from the first, they were close like that. From the beginning, really, if there had been a beginning. James loved Webb's sister. Webb chose James's daughter, Delia. There had been no beginning to that, it had been like always, like the sun. But Delia — *No* —

Webb had asked James what the doctor said that morning.

"Didn't go. Slipped my mind." Grinning, he swung over the roof and onto the catwalk, chinning himself, then dropping lightly to earth. He drew some tea from the Igloo cooler to wash down his medicine, a prescription he swore at every four hours. "Five hundred dollars, Webb, to keep those pills in my pocket. I'm out here pushin' roads and eatin' mud and sawdust and the sombitching specialist's tooling his Mercedes to the country club."

"What'll you tell Carol?" She had made the appointment for James to see the doctor about his three-Anacin headache every night, his five-hundred-dollar bellyache, his insomnia. Chain-smoking in the dark and thinking, for hours. "Just thinking." About what? *Oh God if they had just* —

"I'll tell her what he told me last time," James said. "What he tells me every time. It cost a hundred bucks then, I guess it's worth it now, and saves me a trip downtown. 'No caffeine, no nicotine, lay off the gin.'" James pronounced "gin" as though it were initials: G.N. "Hold off on chili — all like that . . ." Shaking his head, pokerfaced, lighting up from the stub of his last Lucky. Everybody busting out laughing.

Like the time Red asked, "Say, James, that a hymn you whistling?" and James fired back, "Damn right."

Of course James had ordered Mexican food for lunch. "It don't matter what you order, when you send Billy and Red, you get Mexican."

Bevel, refilling his apron from the nail box, left the ones he dropped for anyone's tires to find, bragging, "I don't pick up nothing but blondes, brunettes, and redheads." Then when Billy drove back in and dusted to a stop on the spilled nails, he drawled, "What the hay-ull," jumping out of the truck, solicitous, checking his traction treads as if he were solving a crime. He had the bags of food in both arms.

"Crissake, get your beard out of my lunch," Red grumbled, reaching to rescue his portion. A scuffle. Nothing serious. In a few minutes they got it all sorted out and quieted down, sitting wherever they could find a flat place, eating like wolves. A long time since breakfast.

"This time tomorrow you'll be flying high," Billy said to James.

James said, "Could be."

"What time's your plane leave?"

James pulled the tickets out of his wallet and looked at them. He shrugged. "Midmorning, I reckon." He was going to see Delia's baby. He and Carol were flying up. First vacation in years.

"I'll miss this," he said. *He said I'll miss this* — They started back to work now, scattering to their tools, a little stiff. "Miss sitting in the sun and scouring the skin off your ass and knees, pounding the sense out of your wrists and thumbs? Sure you will," said Bevel, flinging away the last of his ice, then heading over to the stack of plywood, taking his own good time, as usual, to hand a sheet up to the roof.

"Enough now," Red called down.

Bevel wasn't eager to climb up and start nailing in the sun. He squatted in a shady spot, resting. "I'll lissen fo' you to hollah, a'right? Huh 'bout it?" He drawled as slow as he worked. James laughed.

"You got the makings of an executive," he told Bevel. To the rest of the crew he said, "I'll remember you."

And Wild Billy said, "Shoo', where you going you won't think of us once!"

Oh God —

But James didn't drive off then. He sat in the truck hassling with his paperwork. Everybody gave it a little more, even Bevel, because James was there. There was that good feeling standing there on top of a month's work, every fair day's labor straight and square and true under them. James ran up the ladder again and took Webb's hammer from him. "This thing work left-handed?" Same joke he had pulled on Webb's first day, and Webb, just out of the mill, had no more sense than to head back to the toolbox for the special hammer . . . James belted on Webb's apron too. The others dogged it, slowing, then stopping, just to watch James work. It was always something special to see.

He started up at the ridge with his apron full and his hammer high, waiting while that something inside him got ready, as for a race. Then, suddenly, he was off, hammering his way down, hunching along behind the sinking nails, feeding them with his right hand, sinking them with three blows of his left, dead-on, fast as light, sure as God, straight as string, all the way down to the eaves and back up again, scooting, hands moving back and forth and up and down with the hammer, like a toy too-tight-wound, like a madman, like a machine, wild with some inner clock, beating that clock, beating everybody. They just stood idle, watching.

Finally, James had enough of it, dropped the hammer, shed the apron, flexed. "Rough on goats and old folks," he said, standing tall, listening, as if he heard something way far off. He cupped his hands around his ears, narrowing his focus on a spot in the sky. "Red-shouldered," he decided.

He looked up at the hawk. They all looked. It was high, circling the sun, its free cries drifting down dry through air thick with the scent of crabapple flowers. The blooms were almost gone now; the breeze that came and went shattered the last blossoms, scattering the petals like ashes. James caught one out of the air, barehanded, then let it fall. "Sometimes," he said. Then, "Just once," letting his breath out, long. He squatted on the ledge, cooling off. Webb followed him down, and they went over to the truck for the miter saw. The others started back to work, happy, because James had said, "If y'all get the felt down, maybe you'll be able to spare a couple of days off . . ."

But they didn't finish; James wanted the gables pulled out and planked, not decked with plywood, and he didn't get back with the lumber till late. And when the crew saw that they weren't going to get through, they were like children cheated by bad weather of some holiday or other. They lost interest and will. Slowed like a train coming to a station, losing steam. They knocked off on the dot of four. Somebody yelled, "Miller time!" and they all headed down the ladder as if it were a fire drill. Leaving behind the framing square, half a pack of cigarettes, the tape, and a hammer. One of them even left his hammer! Webb went around cleaning up after them. Even though he was youngest of the crew, he was their old man; they were like kids. *Somebody has to tell them.* Carol saying, *They'll have to hear it —*

James had brought the one-by-sixes just as they were leaving. "Just in the nick," Billy said, but not meaning that he'd help unload and stack, or work on; he just wanted to jump-start his Bronco off James's truck battery. Soon as he handed the cables back, he scratched off out of there, hollering, "If the creeks don't rise," and leaving dust in the

air behind him. They could hear those oversize tires singing and the boonka-boonka of his radio after he was clean
gone.

James saw the look on Webb's face. "Don't sweat it,"
James told him. "They don't see it as their job, so I guess
it's ours." They began to unload the planed pine.

"Nail drivers," Webb said. "That's all they'll ever be."

That was when James had said what he said about Webb
knowing how to finish it all, every damn bit. Sitting there
with his back against the tree, nudging splinters from his
palm.

"Nice day," Webb said, thinking back over it.

"About over," James said. He closed his knife and put it
in his pocket, then took it out and said, "Keep this." Handed
it to Webb, just like that. When Webb said he couldn't,
James shrugged it off. "It'd probably set the metal detector
off on that airplane." When he offered it the second time,
Webb took it.

"What about your keys?" Webb wondered.

"You've got a set," James said. "I'll leave mine on the
dresser." He went over the time sheets again — "Got it?" —
and Webb nodded.

Webb said, "If you was to fall dead, I know where the
plats are and how to break it to the bankers too." Laughing. James laughed too. They laughed!

Then James stood, tossed his cigarette, flicked it away
behind him as if he didn't care if the whole world burned
down. The butt fell safe in the sand, and Webb knew that
James had planned it like that. "If it rains on Thursday,
y'all work Greyridge. Drywall man's supposed to be there
next week. Get humpin'."

"Multiply anything he says by two," Webb said. They
laughed again. They walked all around the house, stepping

through walls and over window sills and out. "Pretty near done," James said. "Near enough to start bragging." He picked up the hatchet and cut a little pine about as tall as Delia had been at fourteen. He took it up the ladder to top out, nailing it to the crosspiece by the chimney frame. James liked to do that; had learned that as a steelworker years back. Webb ran up the ladder after him. It was nice on the roof. It had been a long time since Webb worried about height; he just wasn't afraid any more. Of anything.

The tallest poplars, in new leaf, stood gold-tipped in the sun. The dogwood trees and scrub were already in shadow. Blackbirds flocked over, flying north to their roost, hundreds, maybe thousands chuck-chucking above the treetops, guiding by the road. Webb slapped two blocks together to make a noise like a gunshot. When the birds heard it, they swooned, sideslipping in the air, almost falling, as though they had stumbled in unison, then flying on. "Look at them," Webb said. "They think they're dead but they keep on going."

"There'll always be blackbirds," James said, heading down the ladder. Webb stayed to cut the ridge string with James's knife. The string fell in slow motion, like writing on the air, unstretching after taut days in the sun. Webb followed it down, and coiled it. By the time he got back to the truck, James had two Budweisers side by side on the tailgate. Like it was Friday.

James said, "Webb, it's nice doing business with you," just like always. They were both looking up at the topping-out tree — a black-green silhouette against the deepening blue sky.

James invited, "Come to supper with us."

But Webb didn't. *Should have* — "Billy's bought him an appaloosa. I'm going to help him fix it up in the shed.

216

Going to cut a picture window in the stall so the damn horse won't get depressed."

They laughed about that, too.

"Maybe I'll see you later, then," James said. He got in his truck and backed out, first. He had Webb blocked in. He waited for Webb on the road, pulled up alongside, door to door, window to window. He gave Webb that look again, hard, hacked, like there was something needing to be settled, but all he called out was, "Keep the greasy side down." *The last thing he said* — And they laid drag, door to door, cab to cab, dead even on the blind curves, smoking all the way out to the county-maintained.

Webb kicked it the last quarter mile and won. This time he won. James dropped behind then, maybe six inches from Webb's back bumper. He was in Webb's rearview all the way to the four-way stop.

Webb peeled off east, toward Billy's, and James headed west, to check on the log house and secure it for the night, and after that, over to Greyridge, then home to Carol. Webb went with him sometimes, but not this time. It was the good hour of twilight, sundown but not dark, everything rushing to shelter, birds sweeping low across the clearings to their roosts, cats in the ditches turning up wild yellow eyes at the passing cars. Day things winding down, and night things waking. Even the winter-scalded roadsides looked better, the raw mud greening up with fescue and clover that camouflaged the litter. Dark enough for the neon signs at the Double Nickel to beckon friendly. *Maybe I'll see you later then* — Listening to the radio — *It'll be on the radio* — Billy's horse looking over the fence as Webb made the turn. *On the radio on Billy's radio on the Bronco's radio at lunch like it was anybody not James not James* — Billy looking up from where he knelt hammering a rusty

217

hinge flat. "Whattya know?" Carol saying, *They'll have to hear it* — Saying, *I'm the one who* — All the dogs barking. Sleeping warm while he — *No* — Waking — *Why why* — Waking sudden, warm, in the cold, all the dogs barking, the phone ringing, ringing, and James already — *No* — Working with Billy on into the dark, setting the window into the horse stall, toenailing it, framing the first stars. *I found him in the dark* — The look on what was left of his — *No* — On the back of the ticket envelope his stained, steady unendorsement, *It wasn't any one thing please* — The dark stain on Carol's hem. *You can finish it yourself you know that don't you?* Carol telling the sheriff, her words like ice rattling in a tall tumbler, "My husband," her calm breaking then, finally fracturing as she said once more, "My husband," counting him on her fingers, and again, and again, until the paramedic stopped her wild reckoning with a sedative and Webb and he led her to the house, away from all that heartsickening business of the law, her glazed look as she explained — her mind snagged on that like a bread sack on a barbed wire fence — "I'm his second wife," finally sleeping, persisting as she drifted away, "I'm his . . ."

Jesus somebody has to tell Delia

Dawn

DELIA, AGE TWO

THE SINGLE GUNSHOT woke the dogs, got the local dogs started up again just minutes after the silence finally fell with the passing of the freight, everybody's dogs barking fast to make up for the surprise of the single shot — a storm of yapping, deep woofing, howling — every mutt and cur in the mill town contributing to the frenzy. And then, when no second shot came, a suspense — a listening truce along the lanes and lots and alleys. Finally the ear-witnesses sank back into silent roaming or sleep. But it was their barking, that sudden outbreak of the dogs in rejoinder — to what event? — that people later recalled as having disturbed their peace, not the gunshot.

It was still night. You couldn't see the dawn. You knew it was coming but you couldn't see it. You had to trust a while longer. In the bushes the sleeping birds shook themselves and resettled without opening their throats or their eyes. If you were sleeping soundly enough, or unsuspecting, you might not have heard any of it. Delia was sleeping like that.

When Delia woke, later, the robin was singing that treedley-oop pip pip rain-clean April song. She heard it. She lay listening. She lay sorting out all the sounds. Her eyes were still shut. She knew all the sounds of the house. She knew the creak of each door, how the hall floor groaned over the sagging joist by the furnace. She knew the particular click of each light switch in every room, could tell which cabinet was opened just by the distinct voice of its latch. She knew her family's footfalls — slippered, booted, barefoot. She could tell which dog it was by the unique clatter of toenails — the poodle's were high-pitched, the old feist's had the same sound, but slower paced. Delia could tell the difference between workday and Sunday even without the bell at the mill ringing. She could tell by the different tempo of traffic and by the smell of shoe polish.

She had learned a great many noises in her two years, but there was one she didn't know; she focused on it now and frowned. Her eyes opened as she puzzled it out. Her mama was making the sound!

Delia got up to go see what. There was no one in the big bed. She went next to the room where they ate breakfast together, their one meal together every day, since Delia ate early supper in the kitchen and lunch at Miz Matrill's. She didn't find her mama anywhere in the house, not in the bathroom, not in the front room. Delia crossed the soft rug to the window where the old geranium leaned toward the sun. The sound was coming from out in the yard . . .

Delia pushed at the door on the left side. Nothing. She pushed at the door on the right side. Open! Cool steps on her bare feet. She turned and backed down, high-rumping it, easing her weight from hands to feet, crawling carefully down backward, listening for that sound — her mama's new sound — caught up now among other sounds but not diluted in any way. Delia stood listening, sorting out — her mama's sound . . . a man's voice . . . company? . . . somebody and somebody else . . . man legs . . . white car . . . brown car . . . red car making a noise coming sparkling . . . her mama's sound . . .

There. Where the washing machine was. And the hedge tool. And the mower. One step up. Hands on the wood floor, then right knee up then left knee and pulling herself upright in the open door to stare into the cool dark, breathing open-mouthed, taking in the scents of grass and soap and men and dust and oil.

Her eyes traveled over the dim shapes of the tools, the stacked cans and bottles, the arrayed brushes, the skew rake tangled in the snakey hose. Her mama's sound and legs . . . a man's legs . . . somebody's . . .

Her daddy's shoes? Her daddy's legs? Her daddy going night-night in the spilled paint?

Squeezing through between somebody and somebody, to see.

Daddy?

Jesus Cries Catcher

Game?

Delia stood a moment wondering. She didn't know that voice. She didn't know the game. The paint had spilled on her daddy's face.

No Delia — Man reaching over to grab her.

Somebody crying, *Come heah sugah* — False voice. Stranger's voice.

Somebody — *Sweet Jesus Cries Stopper* — as she edged nearer her daddy lying in the spilled, pretty paint. Pretty red paint.

Her mama, *No don't touch* —

Deciding it was a game. Game!

No Delia —

Good game. Touching. Touching her daddy. Touching and running. Dodging. Good game!

All of them reaching and chasing and calling her and Delia running and hiding. Running behind things. Running between things. Running along things. Running under. Running into. Into! Sharp hurting. Hurting . . . No more game . . . Wanting her mama. Crying for her mama because of the sharp hurting, duller hurting now, but wanting her mama!

Mama?

The others, somebody and somebody reaching down, reaching under to pull her, drag her out . . . Swinging her over to her mama.

Angry?

Her mama's face and arms — *Baby oh baby —*

Her mama's arms and smell.

Baby —

Both of them sobbing, making that sound. Her mama holding her.

Somebody angry. *Gettemouttahe —*

Lifting Delia up and swinging her out into the sky and sun and trees. Holding her arms up, her mama catching her close, her mama's hair between her and somebody angry shouting, *gettemoutta* — Holding her mama . . .

Baby oh baby —

Holding. Holding.

The robin kept singing treedley-oop pip pip pip in this tree, in that tree. Delia thought of something.

"Daddy?" she asked, listening.

Morning

DELIA LISTENED. Old Miz Matrill lay resting in her pushed-back chair, fully reclined, her talc-foxed Mary Janes side by side on the sticky footrest. She lay staring up at the water stain, the one like Texas plain as a map, telling Delia about geography and everything again. Telling how it was when her Old Mister was alive and her Little Mister played out on the mosses like Delia and Luther did now. How it was when Old Miz was a little girl living right down the road her whole life till she married Dom Matrill and they moved in here and planted that oak yonder it would take five grown men to reach around now, wouldn't it? Say yes! Then the boarders came after Old Dom died and they broke the fine white wedding plates and knocked the handles off the tea set and lost her mama's sugar spoon down between the cracks in the floor . . . Old Miz cried at this point every time, her tri-whiskered chin trembling.

Delia listened. There was the part coming up about the snake and the one-leggedy chicken. It was coming up soon now so Delia sat ready, listening.

Earlier, when Ruth — Old Miz Matrill's daughter-in-law — was pulling on her rubber support socks and tying her shoes twice and walking away in her green hat, she had told Delia, "Lissen now. You set right there and lissen till I get back. Just going to run up to town, get me some Camel's tomater soup. Bring you'n Luther some Chiclets. You be a good girl, won't taken me long."

So Delia had sat there and listened, but just when she got to the part about the chicken and the snake, Old Miz Matrill fell asleep, yawned right into sleep in the middle of her telling, and lay wide-mouthed under the Texas stain, snoring like a dog. Delia listened.

Delia watched Luther dragging his lawn chair across the yard to set up his position on the sidewalk. He had his railroad engineer hat on his head and his bandanna on his neck and his radio on his shoulder. Big fine radio running on batteries, the radio Old Miz Matrill didn't like. He listened to music. He didn't have to listen to Old Miz, even though she was his granny. He was older than Delia but no smarter. He couldn't read. He couldn't write. He was almost a man but he didn't know it. And he'd never be a man, but he didn't know that either, and they said hush she'll hear you when Delia heard them tell that, but Old Miz had said it anyway, "What he never had, he'll never miss." But his mama had been against doing it to him, whatever it was, and still cried against the doctors and Old Miz, saying it was their fault, from the beginning, for he'd have been as good as anybody else's son if they'd birthed him right, but it went on too long before Old Miz got Ruth to the hospital and then he was born and born blue, she told Delia that all the time, and said, "That's not passed along in the blood, that's accident," but Old Miz had had her way about it, and Ruth still cried about it, and lay on

224

her sofa and sniffed and told Delia that the old woman had wanted to see her son's line end there, so there'd be no more claim on her from Ruth's side. That's what Ruth thought. That's what she told Delia all along. Told and told. How the old woman hated her from the first.

When Ruth took Luther and Delia to pick poke sallet down across the field toward the dead end, they gathered a sackful in no time. Ruth scolded, "Delia, don't you tear those leaves, you worsen Luther. Watch me how. I'm a good hand . . . My mama taken me to the mill and me only eight years old, taken me and left me and said, 'Keep a sharp eye out and don't run your fingers in the machines and don't sass back to the boss,' and I were a good hand for them, and a good child to my mama, putting my pay in her pocket every time till I marry with young Dom. Made him a good wife too. Hard worker, ask anyone." She'd look off toward the woods, red-faced, mouth working, out of breath from running through her grievances and virtues. Old Miz had hated her from the beginning. Had wanted "better," and didn't mind who knew. Ruth had told Delia all about that. "Because of my bad eye was why," Ruth said. "Because of that, and me seeing sharper with one than her with two. It weren't borned in me bad, it went bad later. Coal oil poultice my mama laid on it to draw out the sty was what put it out. Burned it white. That was all it were, nothing wrong in my blood, an accident." The same thing she said about Luther. Who had such a quiet way to him, and nothing in his looks to give a clue, so it might have been any young man setting up his chair on the sidewalk to watch for trains and truckers. They leaned on their air horns and whistled and waved, and Luther waved back. Delia listened.

Old Miz was still snoring. Ruth had said, "Set right there," but after a while, when all there was to hear was the snoring, Delia eased off her chair and went over to the window, squinting through the cracked pane toward uptown. She couldn't see Ruth anywhere, couldn't tell if Ruth had already gone into the P.O. with Old Miz's key on its dingy string to get the letters and send off the money orders. Delia lined up so she could stare right through the shade's pull ring, like a monocle. She swung around and peered through it at Old Miz. The dust from the shade made her sneeze.

The old woman never stirred, but maybe there was a flicker to the eyelids. Delia crept over and reached out a finger and tapped on the old woman's forehead, one little tap just to see if she were playing possum. "Hello," Delia said, but Old Miz was asleep.

Delia sighed and sat down again. The pendulum of the shade pull slowly stopped. "Lissen good," Ruth had said, but all Delia could hear was the traffic. The faraway coming-on train — more of a feel in the house's dry timbers than a sound — and the light siffling of the old woman's breath, the characterless hum of the electric clock, the slow seethe of the water heater in the corner of the kitchen where the balding broom stood.

Delia thought about how nice it would be on the sidewalk listening to Luther's radio and watching for trucks. But Luther wouldn't want her. Had said so, from the first morning Delia had come to stay in that house while her mama and daddy were working. Luther didn't like Delia. He had said that too. He had said keep away from his crayons and the little wooden man on his dresser. He had said keep away from his cigarettes, but when he wanted another one, he had asked Delia to get it from Ruth's purse. "Just to borry one is all," Luther told her. Under his mama's bed. And it was Delia who got caught, not Luther.

Luther made sure it happened, right when Delia had the pocketbook in her hands, like she was after money. It was all Delia's to explain and bear. Luther didn't say a word. He let her be the one. He was smart enough for that, to play hard with her like that.

Delia didn't tell. That was one thing she knew already — not to let them know you care how they treat you. Their triumph in her tears never came. She already sensed it was stronger not to break if breaking was what they wanted of her, and Ruth said now, "Girl, you flying high but you'll land in the cow pasture," and Delia thought of how Ruth cracked the eggs on the rim of the iron skillet and tossed the shells away. "I'm not yours!" Delia said, her only defense. "Talk to my daddy." And even if she had told them how Luther had set up a trap like that, Ruth wouldn't have believed her, not even if Luther had testified for Delia's sake. That's how she was, as if all the mean things Old Miz did to her had taught her how to be meaner, instead of reminding her how it could hurt. Ruth had snatched her pocketbook from Delia, getting as red in the face as Old Miz.

She said she'd tell Delia's daddy. She called Delia a snitch and wicked and wild like her mama, everybody knew it, she said, it was in her blood, and coming out every day bad and worse. On and on like that till Delia finally bit her on that righteous arm that kept shaking, shaking her. She ran out the front door and jumped off the porch, dumping the geraniums from the box on the edge, not on purpose but Ruth would believe what she wanted about that and everything. Delia kept on running and it was hours before they found her out in the brush pile with the stray dog and her puppies. Ruth had an earful for Delia's daddy that night when he came to pick her up.

She pushed up her sleeve to show the bite mark. And

227

she didn't fail to mention the cigarettes. James listened. He told her, "All right, ma'am," and took Delia by the hand to go, and added, "If you'd rather not keep her after this, just say it now," but Old Miz heard that, and called from her chair, "No refunds," which was how Ruth saw it, too, and since James had paid a full week in advance and since there wasn't really anywhere else for her — James's mama and daddy worked in the mill, too; all of them did — Delia went on staying at the Matrills' till her mama, Toni, came home. Never mind what some said, that this time she was gone for good; James paid only one week at a time, like an act of faith that Toni would be back soon.

Delia promised him she wouldn't bite anyone else. James talked that out with her. He didn't believe in whipping. Explaining was his choice. "I don't want to hear any news like that ever again," he said, kneeling to converse eye to eye.

She stood with her hands at her sides, looking down. She nodded.

"Delia?"

She nodded again but wouldn't look up.

"Delia, what is this?" He held out his arm.

She laid her hand midway of its iron length. "Strong," she said.

He almost laughed, but the pleasure didn't keep him from making himself clear.

"It's not fried chicken," he said. "You understand me? It's not corn on the cob. You don't bite people!"

"I feel so mean," she said. "Bad mean."

He thought it over. "Tell you what, next time, *yell*. But don't bite. Only an animal bites. You're not an animal."

"Am I like my mama?" she wondered. And now it was his turn to look away.

"I love your mama," he said.

They sat for a long time in the dark, listening to music on the radio, not talking. Then he pushed up out of his chair and clicked on the porch light. It stayed on all night. Whenever Delia woke, she could see the light leaking through her pinpricked window shade in little stars, and framed that artificial sky all around its frayed edges, reminding her to listen for Toni's homecoming, reminding her to hope, that there was still hope.

The next day, when her daddy took Delia back to the Matrills to stay, she parted from him quietly. "In only eight hours from now," James promised, the way he always did, and Delia didn't make a scene till he had backed his truck out and driven away. Then as Old Miz and Ruth exchanged looks, saying to Delia with a false sympathy, "Maybe your mother will come home today," and took her into their grim custody, Delia began to scream. She screamed and screamed, exhausting her rage and despair in shrieks. The women were afraid, and shut her in the front room till she had yelled it out. That screaming went on daily for a week, leaving her empty. The Matrills thought she was meeker afterwards, so they let her rage. She didn't break things. She didn't cost them any extra money. In fact, they made a little, on board, since Delia had lost her appetite. Once when Luther's cruel teasing got too much for her, she ran away to the brush pile where the stray dog had had her puppies — gone now, hauled away by the man from the pound — and she yelled again, like James had told her to do. Afterward, she was quieter. Paler. Thinner.

That spring the days were very fine. Delia took long runs in the field through the stubble from last year's corn, her palms stiff, fingers outspread, arms flapping, running till she was out of breath, laughing all by herself, or she'd whirl on the greening lawn, making herself dizzy-drunk till she fell and lay on her back looking up at the lurching sky. Ruth watched this new wildness with her good eye and always drew the same conclusion — "Like her mama." On the day Ruth took her and Luther to pick the poke sallet, Delia brought a handful and asked what it was for. Were they going to feed the rabbits in their weathered hutch under the oak tree?

Ruth wrung the tender leaves from the purple stalk and shoved them in the bag. "These for us. Pareboil 'em and eat and purify our blood." She gave a righteous, witchy nod, and Delia felt revulsion rise up in her.

"No," she cried. Suddenly she couldn't bear the bright leaves, and tossed her handful away. Their stems were purple-red.

"My blood's all right," she said. "No, I won't eat it and I won't pick it either."

Luther crowed, seeing her afraid. "Blood blood blood blood blood blood." He fixed on that and sang, "Bad blood." He'd heard it before. He shouted it, rocked in the sunshine and closed his eyes, happy.

"I won't eat it I don't have to —" Delia started to say again.

"You just better would, Missy," Ruth said, looking hard at her. Pointing that crooked finger. "You pale as loaf bread, look like a ghost, what you do." Luther was still crooning, "Blood," holding his hands up to the sun now, studying the red in the webs between his fingers.

Ruth hadn't been teaching Delia long, but she had already taught her fear, peril, superstition, and death. Ruth said if Delia got cut between her thumb and her pointing finger, she could die. And if she planted a cedar tree, when it was taller than Delia, she'd die if the tree didn't. And if she went out a different door from the one she came in at, she could die. And if a bird flew in a window and landed on her bed, she'd die for sure before New Year's. If she heard an owl, she had to throw a nail or a horseshoe in the fire and turn all her pockets inside out. And if she was laughing and a thousand-legger ran by, her teeth would loosen and fall out. And if an ambulance or a hearse went by, she had to touch green wood, or they'd come for her — or someone she loved — next. Ruth told her, "You can't be sure when you'll need one, you ought to carry a little green stick all the time, not oak or dogwood." She told Delia that every time she heard a siren. Ruth kept *her* green stick in her apron pocket, and one in her pocketbook for when she went to town. Luther wore his on a string around his neck. Delia slept with hers under her pillow, and every morning she put a little green twig in her daddy's lunchbox.

The old woman didn't believe in it, but when Old Miz fell and had her setback, Delia made her a green twig stick too. The old woman woke and found Delia in her room, just as Delia was reaching out to put the stick on the bedside table. Old Miz rared up quarreling and fretting. The lens had fallen out of her left eyeglass and she couldn't quite see. "Who's that messing in my things? Delia? Delia! You messing my things?" Delia left the stick on the table and ran out. Ruth came and took her into the kitchen and told her, "Don't mess with her. She don't believe. I done something even better anyhow. I slip a piece of Reverend Ike's prayer cloth up between her featherbed."

All this time Old Miz was cawing, "Stay outen my things, all of you, you hear?" Hammering on the night table with her dry fist to drive the point home. "Delia? You hear?"

But if the door fell open on its own, that's not messing. If the wooden latch on the wardrobe swung loose on its nail and hung itself at six o'clock straight up and down, so the door swung slowly open, that wasn't messing either. The weight of the wash dresses hanging on their nail was what made it swing. Delia never planned that, never took unfair advantage. Never touched. Just stood and looked in, breathing what she tried to hold her breath against, the moth-cake and mouse scent and the sweet dead fur of the red fox collar with its dull chipped glass eyes. The old hats in their dusty boxes gave of old straw. And there was Old Dom's hat right on the top. Old Miz kept it for wearing to the garden to pick lettuce and onions. She kept a pair of his dry hard-nosed oxfords too, to wear in the garden's mud.

Delia sat under the table playing with her little boats and Indian figures. If Old Miz thought Delia was watching her take out her change purse from her satchel, on the floor of the closet, she'd warn, "Curiosity killed the cat, Missy. Now you just run along and help Ruth," and Delia would go.

Sometimes they did laundry and Delia would hand the pins. Sometimes they worked in the garden, early, before the sun got high, gathering salad and peas. Delia liked that. She liked to pull onions. Liked the way they came out of the ground all at once, ready, as though the earth helped push, eager to be rid of them. Delia liked helping in the garden. She liked shaking the dirt off and piling things in the flat basket.

Luther helped too. When he held up the onion that had a twin bulb, he said, "Look what." He held it to his crotch and said, "Look what" again. Flapped it, pointing it at Delia, pointing it all around, whistling softly, like he was making water.

Ruth jumped at him when she saw. Tore it from his hands, wrung off its green top and flung the white bulb over the fence, like it was trouble itself she was ridding them of. She was fierce. "Lissen," she said. Ruth sounded scared. "Nobody saw it. Nobody." She kept slapping Luther's hands. "Lissen, boy, you play like that and they'll cut the rest of it off and send you away from me for now on." Luther started to cry in that way he had, rasping like a saw through dry wood, almost a laugh, but slack-faced. Slobbering.

So then Ruth reached her arms around him and held him till he stopped, but all the time she was beating on his back, hard, angry at the doctors . . .

"Chiclets," Luther said, when Ruth was trying to think of what to give him, because she was sorry. So then Ruth led them back to the house and pulled on her rubber stockings for the trip to town and told Delia, "Set right there and lissen," and Old Miz fell to snoring when the snake story was getting to the good part.

She was still snoring.

Delia wished Old Miz would wake, but on she slept in her recliner chair. A robin was singing in the wisteria arbor. Delia drew the bird's picture on the folded grocery sack, using Old Miz's grocery listing pencil. She drew it as a baby bird, in its nest in the flowering bush. The leaves and flowers were so thick they looked like clouds to Delia. She added a few more clouds and darkened them. All of a sudden she made a storm all around the baby robin alone in the nest, with lightnings and thick rain. It kept on raining till Delia had shaded the whole scene and only the bird's little eye looked out. She dotted the raindrops onto the paper, so hard the pencil broke. Not at its dull point, but in two, right in the middle. Delia was afraid. She wanted the old woman to wake up now, so she could confess. She even said, "Guess what?" but not very loud, not loud enough. She carried the pieces around the room with her, thinking what to do. Finally she went to the little box she brought her toys in each day and took out her favorite Indian, the one with the war bonnet and bow legs for riding a horse, and traded it for the pencil. She laid it in the tureen, with the other odds and ends, where she had found the pencil. In a minute she went and got the horse from her toys and laid it beside the Indian, because the Indian loved the horse and needed it to get about, though now it wasn't an even trade any more. She stood looking at the Indian and horse, then turned her back. She wouldn't look again.

Old Miz snorted, like water going out of the bathtub, but she didn't hear herself and wake up. Delia got a drink of water in the glass Ruth told her to use every time. She stood at the window, watching.

Luther was still sitting on the sidewalk in his chair, counting the trucks one-two-three and waving. Way off in the distance Delia heard the sound of a siren, tiny but growing. As it got bigger, Delia touched the green stick in her pocket. She watched the ambulance go by, all red and white — the lights flashing on top and all around — and she ran outside, drawn by the clamor, to stare, standing under the tree with the wisteria in it, surrounded by giddy bees. The siren faded away toward Marietta.

Delia saw Ruth coming home. She pointed toward the woman bringing two sacks, striding along, coming fast, her face all squinched up and red under her green hat. Delia said, "Luther, your mama." They went to meet her. Luther took the sack with celery sticking out.

"You seen the am'lance?" Ruth asked, bright-eyed.

"Sireen," Luther said. "I seen it." He made a siren sound.

Ruth looked down at Delia carrying the gallon of milk

in both arms. "I heard all the glory details uptown," she said. She hastened on past them toward the house. To Luther, loping beside her, she said, low, "Somebody done been shot."

Luther set his sack on the top step and began plundering for his treat. Old Miz pushed open the screen door and listened and asked at the same time, "Where's my Co-Cola? Who got shot?"

Ruth said, impressively, with a signifying twitch of her brows, "Somebody's daddy."

"What?"

Ruth nodded.

"The Lloyd Jesus!" Old Miz sat down hard on the papers bundled up for the Boy Scouts' paper drive, shaking her head, no, no, no. "Not *dead*," she said. "Not dead?"

Ruth just looked at her, breathing hard through her nose.

Luther had the Chiclets now. He pulled the red cellophane string and opened them, tapping out two for him and one like a tooth onto Delia's palm.

"I heard it uptown . . . May be on the radio by now," Ruth said.

Delia bit her Chiclet and asked, "Who?"

"Oh I caint believe it, it isn't so!" Old Miz cried out in her genuine agitation. She smoothed, smoothed, smoothed both cold knees with her gnarled hands. "Who would do a thing like that?"

Right then Ruth said, "Luther, you and Delia go wash your hands for lunch," and when they went, Ruth shut the door to the kitchen, like keeping a secret, soft, firm. Delia listened. She could hear them talking. She could hear the radio. She listened and listened, but she couldn't hear who.

Forenoon

DELIA AND RAIN were turning the rope and Nita was jumping. Nita just went on and on, the best of them, and would never miss, even playing double rope, even playing hot pepper. She could jump on into the thousands, her thick dark ponytail lashing the dusty clouds she raised with her bare feet. Her cousins, Sully and Fury, the twins, stood on the perimeter, pestering. "Let us throw," they begged. But everyone knew what to count on if you gave in: they'd pull the rope tight, knee high, tripping you. Or they'd hold up their turning arms so high you had to jump as high as a table to keep going. And Nita didn't want to stop now, not for any trick or claim; she was trying for a record.

"Don't you do it," she warned Delia about the twins. And Rain agreed, "Not me either," and slapped his hand away as Sully tried to muscle in.

Delia warned, "Don't lose count," and somebody on the edge of the little crowd said, "one thousand twelve, thousand thirteen . . ."

236

Delia was tired. She switched hands on the rope, and after only a minute or two found the weight of the rope so heavy she began to use both hands to turn it, but she wouldn't give the job to anyone else, even as tired as she was.

It was her first day back at school. It was everyone's first day back after Easter, and they had all had a week of holidays, everyone but Delia, who had missed it all, including the egg hunt, by having a fever. They had tried to sweat it out of her with ginger tea. She had been so sensitive to light they had taped the shade around the edges. She couldn't bear the least noise. The sound the tonic water made as it fizzed in the glass by her bed seeped into her delirium and she dreamed she was frying. She had the most terrible thoughts and intuitions, which she lost on waking. Her daddy bought a pair of heavy sunglasses for her to wear in bed. He held up a mirror for her to see herself and called her "glamour puss" and draped his blue chambray shirt over the lamp to guard her tender eyes. Her mama came in and sang softly to her, and turned her damp pillow over to the cool side. Delia's skin was so sensitive she couldn't bear the weight of the slightest cover. And during the worst of it, for three days, she didn't eat at all.

The doctors didn't know what to think, but they didn't think it was entirely the work of a germ. "What is she afraid of?" they asked Delia's mama. But Toni couldn't imagine what.

Waking in the shrouded blue silence of the sickroom, Delia would hold her breath, listening, listening. She listened for her mother's scuffs with those clear plastic heels making a patter across the rooms, Toni's laugh sudden as a sneeze at something absurd she had heard on the TV. Delia listened. She thirsted to hear her father, his low voice telling Toni about the day, his work shoes heavy as he stepped slow and tired. In the night waking damp from her broken fever, Delia would go on listening. In the silence she would rise, to creep trembling through the dark, sleeping house, resting in doorways, her feet stupid and rounded-feeling from the weeks in bed, heavy as they bore her across the cool linoleum.

Sometimes she found her daddy asleep in the chair in the front room, still dressed from the day. Sometimes she found them both in bed and they'd wake to find her between them, her arms around both their necks, holding on for dear life even in sleep.

In her dreams she heard voices, Toni saying, shrilly, "She's not made of glass, she won't break . . ." or lower, "All *right!* Did you think I'd leave while she's sick? Give me a little credit . . ." and her daddy's voice, slow, deliberate, weary as his heavy steps, "Why do you think she's sick?"

She would wake, heart racing, to have other memories rush up at her — Luther, like a shadow, his stupid secret and dirty laugh as he peered into their front door at a man and woman silhouetted in the dark interior, "kissing," saying it in a sniggering ugly way so that Delia wondered what could be wrong with that, and looked and said, unsurprised, "It's okay; they're my mama and daddy, they're married." And Luther had said, "My mama say Toni Racing kisses with anybody." And Delia would shout, "Liar!" and wake herself, and then she'd know she had been dreaming again, that same old treadmill of nightmare built on truth and terror. If they came to her, asking what she was afraid of, how could she say?

They blamed her sleeping medicine. The Racings all were allergic to codeine, growing wilder rather than tame. So James drove Delia down to the emergency in the middle of the night and the doctor on duty gave her a shot and she sank, quiet at last, into a dull reverie. She resisted sleep as long as she could, then went under.

She dreamed of wandering the roads. Not lost, but never home. Landmarks loomed but came to nothing. The caked dust on the blackberries, fruit perfectly ripe, so plain and real in her sleep she reached for it. She could smell the rank musk of the passion vine with its bitter green may-pops hanging unripe, not ready for tasting. Sudden-looming fences, tilting trees, odd perspectives on familiar haunts . . .

In the long grass lay the green brainlike fruits of the mock orange, at the midpoint of the way between home and Miz Matrill's. All the houses looking the same, mill town, cookie cutter houses, but only one was home . . . Now the dream would take on its habitual form, a dream she experienced nightly through the fever's duration:

Her mind fixed its whole attention on the mock orange tree, and knowing what came next, she'd sob in her sleep but, perversely, not wake, as though this nightly suffering were her penance, which she accepted and endured. She was standing at Reverend Lomond's fence, where the painted-out realtor's sign announced in uneven letters, FReSH on one side and DReSSeD RAbbiTS on the other. The hutch stood in plain view under the oak. Delia watched the preacher as he took the rabbit from the hutch, holding him as though he were about to dress him — as she would her doll — and then she saw the knife, long but not sharp, so that it took time and effort to saw off the rabbit's head, which, severed, fell into the grass at her feet. Delia watched it, in the dream, open-eyed, staring down at the rabbit star-ing up, its blood emptying, spattering the fallen mock or-anges. Sometimes, in the dream, it wasn't the rabbit hang-ing there from the mock orange tree, it was someone, it was herself, and Toni would claim Delia's head and James, her daddy, would claim her body with its pounding heart, and sometimes it was the other way, he'd have her head and Toni would have her heart, and Delia would thrash in her sleep, squealing like a rabbit, until they came to her, woke her, and held her, amused by the way she demanded, frantic when she woke, "Love me together together," and would never say why.

By Good Friday, she was better. She could sit up. They carried her into the front room and set her in the rocker, sliding a broom handle under the rocker legs so it wouldn't tip back too far. She was still lightheaded. Sully and Fury came by after the egg hunt at school and told her what she had missed. They didn't come in. They stood on the front porch and talked through the window to her. They had a basket of hard-boiled eggs, decorated and colored. Most were broken already from throwing them at each other, but there was a blue one without a crack and Sully handed it through the raised window to her. It was just the color of the best kind of sky, a blue violet like twilight in summer, and there were little flaws in the dye, little bare white flecks, like the stars. She loved it; loved its heft on her palm, its temperature not cool, not hot, its shape, its dearness, its saying: You didn't entirely miss Easter.

"I'm going to be an astronomer," Delia confided. "Mars is red and Venus is blue."

"You ain't —" they began to say.

"I'll live on a mountaintop and have a telescope right through a hole in the roof." She held the egg to her cheek, then to her ear, as though listening.

"You going to live in a *broken* home, what I hear," Fury said, jealous that Sully had given her so much pleasure with the blue egg. He spat.

Sully elbowed him, sharp, to hush.

But everything was spoiled. Delia threw the egg. Weak as she was, it went all the way out and past the edge of the porch and cracked in the grass. "No!" Delia shouted.

Sully and Fury went.

When Toni came running to check on the noise, there was only the empty rocker. Delia had put herself back to bed, the covers drawn up over her, shivering. On her way back to bed she had seen her mama's suitcase airing in the back yard, broken-backed across two lawn chairs. She pretended to be asleep and Toni left her alone.

Later, when she heard Toni's car keys chatter two rooms away, Delia yelled, "Where are you going? Are you going?" Are you going are you going are you are you are you going echoed in her brain, tinying away to a hot pinpoint of fear.

"Another country heard from," Toni said, coming to the door. "What, baby?" She had on her pretty shoes. "Had enough company for one day? You just rest. Mama's running up to the store for a few things. Maybe find you an Easter dress now you're fit to wear it." She cinched the belt around her town dress.

Delia sat up, the covers flung away. "I'll go with you," she offered. "Are you going far? Just to town? Just there and back?"

Toni laid a fever-gauging hand on Delia's forehead — cool — and pushed back the girl's bangs.

"Well . . . I don't see why not." Delia sighed in relief. She pulled on her clothes. They were a size too large, because of the wasting fever. Her eyes were a size too large too. She ran back for her sunglasses and even so still squinted at the daylight, at the world rolling past the car windows.

Before they left, Toni brought in her suitcase. She stowed it deep in the closet where it had been since her last leaving. Delia had watched. "Will you be needing it?" was

241

how she asked. Everything went into that question. It felt as though the words had grown in her chest, had now to be torn from her, leaving a raw wound.

Toni took her time answering. She was head deep in the closet, battling the shoebag and garments in dry-cleaner's shrouds. Her voice, from the dark, sounded strange, breathless, strangled, false. "I was looking for quilt scraps and decided to sun the mildew off that old case is all . . ." She turned and studied Delia a long minute before she explained, like a challenge, "Spring cleaning. Okay, bird?" After that, unable to take her shallow, quick eyes off Delia's deep slow vision hidden behind the sunglasses, she added, "Why? What did you think?"

It was time for Delia to say what, but she didn't. She didn't say anything.

Toni said, "It was a bad dream, that's all."

She bought Delia a scratchy, tiered, ruffled white dress, like a costume, and turned her into a knobby-kneed wedding cake. Her Easter frills rustled and crinkled around her like paper. She wore it — though she hated it — to her Grandma Jo's where her daddy James and his brothers brought their families after church. Delia was stronger than she had been in several weeks, but the excitement and clamor of so much company left her pale and shaky. She stood on the periphery of the game, sheltered behind her sunglasses, weakly watching the twins and Rain and Nita run on past in their bright new clothes, trampling the grass as they hunted — one last time — for eggs, leaving Delia behind, dizzy.

"You look like a little old granny," James said, and hung her basket up in a tree safe above the noses of the dogs. He swung Delia up and settled her on his shoulders, piggyback, and went on with the conversation he was having with his father. "But I *have* tried until I don't know anything else *to* try . . . I told her I'd even leave the mill, leave here. We'd go if that's what she wanted . . ."

"What *does* she want?" James's father asked, yawning, the yawn breaking into the slow, worthless brown-lung cough that was killing him. It took all his concerted breath to get the cigarette lit. He let Delia blow out the match.

"Little pitchers," he warned, before James could say more than, "She wants —"

He began, then didn't finish. But it wasn't his father's warning that stopped him, it was Toni, running across the lawn. James's brothers were chasing her in a pack at first — Buck and Moore and John Knox — barking like hounds as Toni dodged the trees and clumps of children. The pack divided then, to conquer, running her to earth. When she toppled, she fell slow and pretty, her new striped silk dress swinging and billowing full, settling around her like a bright afterthought. The open toes of her shiny red shoes turned up to the sky. Buck was the one who kissed her. He was thorough. He was always willing to push his luck.

"That's all you get," Delia's mama cried, laughing, beating at him weakly with her open hands. Her nails were lacquered red, and matched her earrings. Her belt. Her shoes. Her toenails. Her lips.

Jo Alice came to collect Buck, hauling him by the belt, saying in that low, convincing drawl, "Damn right's that's all you'll get," making them laugh.

Delia rested her chin on the exact center of her daddy's head, listening. She could feel the heat, the vibrations of his words as he said, "What she wants she usually gets. And there ain't a whole lot she's missed."

Toni had to have heard it. She stood there looking at him across the grass, stone-eyed. James swung Delia off his shoulders and set her lightly down. He didn't even seem to realize it was she. He just disposed of the burden of her, like luggage, like a doll. She stood watching them, shaded by the pink dogwood. They headed for the house in that Sunday-shod ground-covering stride. "I left my cigarettes in my jacket," he said to his father as he went. The screen door slapped. Toni was right behind him. Their voices tangled as they argued their way through the house. Delia felt cold. She went in to get her sweater off the pile on Grandma Jo's bed. Toni and James were in the bathroom, the taps running to cover their voices, but it was an old house. And an old argument.

"Obey like a damn dog? I've got two legs, not four," Toni was saying. James came out of the bathroom then, and Toni followed. They forgot to turn off the taps and the water kept on wasting down the drain. Delia stood with her back to the wall, between the radio and the sewing machine. For a moment all three of their reflections haunted the mirror across the room, then Delia was alone again. They hadn't noticed her.

"Two good legs," James agreed. "And between them you'll make your fortune."

"If there's a fortune to be made, I'll be the one who has it to do, I see *that* clear enough," Toni said, pushing past him, running out the side door, down the path to where Buck had the hood up on his truck and Moore stood listening to the engine while John Knox gunned it, in neutral. The wives were in the kitchen, claiming their platters and Corning Ware, dividing leftovers.

Buck said, as Toni whisked past, "Y'all going?"

"When it's over, it's over," Toni said.

Delia was running right behind her, trying to catch up, but Toni was so fast. In her hurry, Delia went right under her Easter basket where James had hung it in the tree. She didn't remember or care. In the car, she pulled the blanket up over her, but she couldn't stop shivering. The keys were in the lock, but Toni couldn't drive. She turned the radio on, anyway, loud, singing along. Delia fell asleep listening, waiting on James to come drive them home. James had to carry her from the car to her bed.

When Toni woke Delia to get her ready for school James was already gone to the mill. Now, on the playground, before books, while the high schoolers were still gathered waiting on their bus to carry them to the Consolidated, Delia and the others were playing, counting Nita's jumps as she pounded in the arc of the rope, going at a record-breaking pace. They were nearing two thousand now, and they were counting aloud. Delia felt like the day was long already, that she had been throwing the rope over Nita's dust forever, not just an hour.

She kept her eyes on the pit full of soft dirt Nita's feet had turned to pumice. She jumped barefooted because her mother had warned her about ruining another pair of shoes. Her last sneakers had held out three weeks before giving way at the toe. Nita's new pair, with the socks neatly rolled inside, stood clean on the swing seat.

At one thousand ninety-three Luther came running on a diagonal across the school yard, right at them. They never could tell about Luther. He might do anything, say anything. Just the sight of him loping earnestly along made Fury laugh, mean.

"Watch him," Nita said, holding her hands to her aching ribs.

"He could — put a hand — in the rope — tangle it up — or talk and — make you lose — count."

He wasn't enrolled. He was way older, too old for any school; he came to school to have something to do, somewhere to go. Not to learn. During music, he sat out in the hall on the floor, blowing spit bubbles, listening. He lurked around the office, too, overhearing things. Sometimes he mistold what he heard. Sometimes he got to deliver real messages if there was no one else to do it. He wouldn't even knock, but with his sense of importance, he'd just walk into the classroom, disrupting, making everyone laugh, all for a moment's attention.

Now he loped across the playground ducking under the slide, calling something to the older kids waiting in line for their bus. He headed for the swings, gasping out, "Guess what! Ja' Racing blowed his brains out."

Webb had already broken from the crowd of older students, dropping his books, running after Luther calling, "Hey! Hey!" but Luther didn't stop. The high school bus came and filled and went, and Webb never looked back. When he finally caught Luther, he grabbed a handful of his shirt and swung him around. Luther was way older. Luther was grown, such as it was, man-sized, but Webb stood in. "You shut your filthy lying mouth!" he told Luther. "What's the matter with you?"

Luther laughed. "Don't matter what you do," he said, in such a sensible way that Webb was convinced against his instincts. Luther headed on toward the rope jumpers. Webb ran too, but got there too late. Luther had already spilled it.

Delia was still turning the rope and Nita was still jumping. He was always talking crazy. Nobody believed Luther Matrill. Like the rest of them, Webb watched Nita's grimy feet pounding the ground, losing themselves in the dirt, lifting from earth with a smoke of dust. Along with the others, he counted, counted, as Nita's rise and fall in the morning air charmed terror away. Luther said it again, and Delia's arm lost strength, but honored its duty with the rope.

Mrs. Savage was on her way out to them. When Delia noticed her, with those puffy feet stuffed into their tiny shoes, trampling like hooves toward the jump-rope pit, Delia got scared. Mrs. Savage advanced as far as the slides; she couldn't cross the gravel in those heels. She lifted her arm in its wide bracelet and pointed, beckoned. They could see her fingers snapping for their attention. She called, "Boys and gulls, chirren, please . . ." Like a woman in difficulties, stranded on a shore. They must row across and rescue. Still, nobody moved. Not even Luther.

Then Delia noticed the others — their severe principal, Miss Victor, and Aunt Eden and Uncle Moore and others — men and women somber and watchful, like grand jurors making annual inspection. "Delia Racing," Mrs. Savage called.

Nita stopped jumping then and the rope fell across her shoulder. Delia's arm was half raised. For a few precious moments more there was the silence of unbelief, as they stared, adults and children, across the rocky gulf between. This wasn't choosing sides in Red Rover. This wasn't a question of finding the weakest, the strongest for a game . . . Mrs. Savage snapped her fingers again and called out, "Delia? Come along."

But Delia couldn't. She had fallen in some kind of fit. It was Webb who gathered her up and carried her in, rigid, her head thrust back, her eyes roaming, her jaw clenched. The doctors in Chattanooga and the doctors in Atlanta blamed it on the recent fever. During their tests — both physical and psychological — they determined that her eyes were weak and her brain strong — IQ 168 — and offered the opinion that perhaps her life wasn't sufficiently challenging.

"You'll have to talk to us, Delia, if we're going to help you," Dr. Gore said. But Delia had nothing to say.

Noon

"DON'T TALK," Ma Jo said. "Don't wiggle. Don't fidget. Can't you just stand still for one minute?"

Her grandma was taking the hem in Delia's new dress, not a grown-up dress but not a little-girl dress, either. It would do for joining the church in now, at Easter, and later on, for graduating up to high school in. When Delia tried it on in Rich's store, Ma Jo said, "Well, look at you, Miss Priss," and when Delia curtsied, Ma Jo gave a derogatory tug at the shoulder seams and sniffed at the price tag — "You could buy a whole bolt of cloth for that much, up home, and lace and findings too . . ." — and gathered up a handful of growing room in front — "You'll need it if you bud out like your Mama . . ." — and behaved in general as though it were a terrible dress, Delia knew better, had known from the moment Ma Jo had called her Miss Priss it would be her dress, the one for Sunday, when she would stand in front of all the congregation and say her promises to the church.

248

Ma Jo wasn't one to wonder long which end of the needle to thread, so while she had that spare hour in their rooming place, she took the hem. She was pinning it when the phone rang, and she sputtered pins out from between her lips the same way she had spat out catfish bones the evening before at the S&W. "Now who but God knows we're here in Atlanter?" she grumbled and went over to the phone on the bedside table to answer it.

Delia was standing on a chair to have the hem taken. She stood right there and looked out the window, resting her arms on the cool top of the window unit air conditioner, looking down into the yard next door. She could see a brick wall and white stairs going down, and around the trees in their little necklaces of picketed curbstone, the tulips and pansies burned in the early light. The starlings looked like pine cones scattered in the tender grass. Behind Delia, into the phone, Ma Jo was saying *no* not in her own voice but in a terrible new voice, just taking in breath and pushing out *no* over and over like a dog being dry sick on an empty stomach. Delia jumped down and her new dress lifted, filled, and she parachuted to the floor. She hit the air out of it with her hands to see where to land, where to run, to help. The straight pins in the hem kitten-scratched her bare legs. Ma Jo wasn't even talking into the phone, she was thrashing on the floor, her face grinding into the dirty carpet she had been fierce not to let Delia's bare feet touch.

"What? Grandma? What's wrong?" Delia asked her again and again, but Ma Jo wouldn't say. She was bad off. Delia couldn't find the medicine. She jerked open the hollow drawers of the metal bureau. She ran searching to the bathroom. She tumbled through the suitcase, then she thought it might have fallen from Ma Jo's pocket. She knelt on the floor beside the old woman and found the bottle. She forced the little pill between Ma Jo's blue lips. All the time Ma Jo was announcing in that tremendous new voice, "He's dead. Oh he's dead, he's dead, my boy's dead." She drew herself up to her knees the way she did when she played "Poor Kitty" with the grandchildren. She took to beating her head and hands on the floor, making Delia go crazy too. Delia shook and jerked, and crumpled down to rest her face in the new cloth of her dress, all the time praying, "Not my daddy, not *my* daddy, not my *daddy*," hoping to die before she heard that, but having to know, having to ask, taking Ma Jo by the arm and screaming now, "Who? Who!" till the old woman finally noticed her, and wildly staring, sat up, her knotty hands over her mouth pressing back the truth. It seeped out and around her white knuckles in a whisper, all the time her eyes roving back and forth as though she were reading the narrow verses of the Bible, her head denying slowly no no no.

"James," she whispered.

Delia's ears heard it but her mind wouldn't listen, wouldn't acknowledge the kinship because of being so scared, then she felt it melt through the obstacles. It sliced clean, the way it must feel to the lady in the magic show when the cookie sheet slides in between her top and bottom halves and it looks bad but she knows the trick to surviving it. Delia didn't know the trick. She heard her own voice saying, "Not my daddy," speaking gently, rebuking such a lie. It was no joke to play on a spring morning. Delia saw herself, not kneeling there by Ma Jo, but still happy, still standing on the chair looking out the window at the flowers and the birds and city sky.

"My sweet James," Ma Jo grieved.

Delia sobbed then. They sobbed together. Delia had

wanted it to be Buck, Rain's daddy. She had wanted it to be Uncle Bill Williams or Uncle Free or Uncle Moore or Uncle John Knox, any of Ma Jo's boys dead but James alive. Why couldn't it have been so, even now? Delia buried her face in Ma Jo's lap and begged please please please and Ma Jo kept on denying no no no. None of the uncles stepped between Delia and the firing squad at the last moment to save her, so that even though she loved them and they gave up life for her and she'd be sorry, she'd be saved, and glad. Lightning flashed down her arms and legs, stabbing down into her heels and fingers quick as a flash bulb, then fizzled out, dark, then cold water poured into the hot places.

Delia vomited. She spoiled her new dress. She moved to take it off, washed, then went back, in her slip, to help her grandma. She lifted Ma Jo and eased her onto the bed and loosened the laces tied over her righteous old arches. Ma Jo lay there, her arm over her eyes till Delia turned off that bare overhead bulb. The old woman was quiet only a moment, then started in again, denying, no no no no no . . . Delia crouched on the chair, her face on her knees, her hands over her ears to shut it out. Impossible.

Ma Jo sat up, groaning. She began distractedly pacing. "I won't believe it, I don't believe, I don't have to believe it, what am I doing way off down here, Jesus, help me to stand it . . ." She folded herself up like a fresh-ironed shirt, arms folded across herself flat and funny, her deep groaning tapering off into humming. She quieted herself and sat smoothing her skirt, ironing every wrinkle out with the heat of her hands. After a while she said thickly, "We'll go by the noon bus."

Delia lifted her face then, and stared. If only Ma Jo would put her arms around her and say, "Child, child, poor child," but she didn't even notice her. Delia was just one more ticket to buy, one more hem to take up, one more suitcase to pack. Delia knew why. *Because I look like my Mama.*

"Right now, Missy," Ma Jo said, getting started, clawing up the phone and dialing for a taxi and putting everything back in the suitcases they'd unpacked the day before, not even a whole day ago. To have come all this way and then go back to sorrow! Delia rolled up the measuring tape and zipped the pins into the kit. When everything was packed, they put on their traveling clothes still stale from the bus trip the day before. They were paid off with the landlady and waiting on the curb when the taxi finally got there.

"Don't lean back," Ma Jo told Delia as they got in.

"Hey!" the driver protested, then laughed. "Ain't no bugs on me," he said.

Ma Jo ignored him. She just rode. All the way to the Trailways station she was trying to catch her breath. Traffic was bad.

"How far?" Ma Jo fretted. "How long?"

"Keep your shirt on," the driver said. "Just over the next hill. Two more blocks."

But they didn't move up at all. "What's the matter?" she asked him, when the light had changed twice again from green to red and no forward progress. She held her pocketbook in both hands, like a hymnal. She was leaning trying to see. "What's holding us up?"

"Tires," he told her. "What's holding us up? The air in the tires!" he said, telling himself the joke the second time and laughing. He saw Delia in the rearview mirror and advised, "No use crying over it. No use busting a fuse."

Ma Jo paid him and got out. She wanted to be moving, even if it was on foot. Each step was that much closer home. She paid him the exact fare on the meter, counting it out to him from her brown snap purse. No tip. Delia carried the larger suitcase.

"So who died?" he yelled after them, reaching across the seat to shut the door.

"My daddy," Delia told him. It didn't sound true. She said again, "My daddy."

"Well, hell, how could I know?" he said.

Delia and Ma Jo straggled up the hill, frail-legged, wind-blown, grievous. At the corner Delia had to rest. Her hand burned from carrying that suitcase. Her palm was red and tender, as if she had been hoeing. Ma Jo didn't stop. She kept on plugging.

Delia ran to catch her, the suitcase dragging her back like an anchor seeking rock bottom. Up the street a man with an airhammer was chopping up the pavement. A fire truck stood blocking all lanes of traffic; its hoses and pools and rivulets had to be gotten across somehow. They picked their way through. After that, it was downhill to the depot. A policeman came out as they went in. Delia walked under his arm, right past his gun.

After they straightened it out about their tickets, Ma Jo phoned the Emory eye clinic to cancel Delia's appointment. Then they found the LADIES. Ma Jo warned, giving Delia her handbag to hold, "The tickets are in there." Delia held tight. When it was Delia's turn, Ma Jo warned, "Don't sit down."

Out on the platform again, they watched for the bus. "Clinic's rescheduled you," Ma Jo said, "They'll send a letter saying when."

The driver for the return trip wouldn't be the same one who drove them down, the day before. Ma Jo studied his badge, deciding whether or not to risk her life with him at the wheel. She gave his sleeve a pinch. She tapped. She said, "Come over here, Delia," and then she told the driver, waiting by his bus, "This is my boy James's child — we're going home to Pinedale." She asked the driver who his people were, said he favored the Dougalls, every now and then they sported a red-haired throwback, had his hair been red when he was younger, she thought so . . .

The line for boarding grew behind them. The driver said, "Welcome aboard, ma'am," and stepped back. Ma Jo chose seats near the front. A woman across the aisle had a lapful of cake boxes. Ma Jo looked but didn't catch the woman's eye.

"Wedding," Ma Jo guessed, loud. She liked weddings. She was humming a little. She seemed to have forgotten about Delia, and about James. She sat by the window, humming low.

They dieseled out of the dark garage into the afternoon, nosing down the on-ramp, bullying into the expressway's flow. When Delia glanced out the window, she could see Ma Jo's face reflected in the glass. Wet with tears. Ma Jo wiped them, then caught up Delia's wrist in her wet fingers and consulted Delia's Christmas watch, not letting go. "Thirteen minutes late already," she said. "Eight hours," she reckoned, including the layover, counting up how long till they got home.

She cleared her throat in that way that sounded like Buck changing gears in the old Chevy, low to second to high, quick. She hummed again, looking out the window at the houses going past, inspecting the Monday wash hanging on the lines.

Delia felt funny. Scared. Wanting them to go faster, but wanting never to get there. She had ridden down to Atlanta the day before, afraid because they were going to look into her eyes and take pictures with a light brighter than

the sun. Delia hated it. Hated the way Ma Jo teased her
the first time, saying they could see into her soul, see every
flaw, every wrong, every lie. Delia had been scared, then,
that her eyes so like her mama's would betray some terrible
thing — not that she'd go blind, but that she'd go away,
like Toni, and go bad like Toni, who "hated when she
should've loved and danced when she should've prayed and
never said a fare-thee-well when she left." But after Delia
got used to the visits to the eye doctors, who were kind to
her, she wasn't afraid of them, though she still hated it and
was always afraid of herself, of being a coward. It was all
she could do to endure the light that struck into her till it
washed her other senses away and there was nothing but
that light, now green now red as her pulse fed the nerves
with the dyed blood that gave the light its target during
the treatments and left her jaundiced for a week afterward.
There was only the disk of light inside her brain, and the
disk grew until it was the whole world and there was just
the light, so that she became disoriented, staring at the sun
that stared at her, and she was kindled like a star, lost in
the eclipsed void, her body trivial, forgotten — all she was
was eye — until the nurse would press Delia's skull more
closely against the brace that held her still for that burning,
warning, "Don't move," calling Delia back into herself again,
only transformed now to eyes, all eyes, eyes the size of
melons, white-hot, and her neck a mere stem like a morning glory's vine, and her spine and long bones gone to ten-
drils, and all of her stupid, exposed, like some blind cave
creature, blasted and stunned by that persisting, invading
beam against which there was no blinking, no defense, and
if she resisted, shuddered, or cried out and rattled the doctor, the treatment and agony went on longer, so that she
learned soon to endure it without flinching. But when they

had finished with her, and she took custody of herself again, sitting with her eyelids pressed shut, excluding them all, swoony in the sudden inner dark, filling herself again where the light had emptied, her brain draining its light-gorged sensations into her other nerves so that she became aware of her feet — feet! — in their shoes — shoes! — and the tissue crumpled in her fist, mushy with tears, and the tear-drenched front of her blouse, and the strong hands of the nurse as she unstrapped Delia's skull from the brace, the tear-slick chin cup, and the doctor saying out in the hall, "We did well today," and Ma Jo saying, "We're obliged . . ."

"Eight hours," Ma Jo said again, looking out the bus window, sounding as though she couldn't stand it.

Delia said, "In only eight hours from now," that farewell James had used in the mornings when he left her at Miz Matrill's and headed for the mill. Delia always remembered that saying. She used it, from the beginning, to mean goodnight. She hated to say goodnight, hated for the good times to end, for sleep — so mere and stupid a thing as sleep — to interfere.

She'd be out playing until twilight and they'd holler the first warning for bedtime and then another and then the last warning. They'd have to send someone, always, to fetch Delia. Usually James came calling for her. Rain and Nita and the twins and the others would be home by then; they never held out long. But Delia's daddy let her get away with it, that nightly postponement; it was just one more game. They were always playing games. They'd come back down the root-heaved sidewalk, their shadows dancing from streetlight to streetlight, laughing, joking. At Rain's, as they passed, Delia would detour up to the porch and yell it, and at the twins', and across the street at Nita's, and even to Luther up in his attic, Christmas lights blinking night and day, summer and winter, and across the creek, toward Webb's: "In only eight hours from now!" — making an appointment with continued life. Saying good night and good morning both. Then she and James would pass on by, laughing, talking nonsense, making up for the rest of the year when they'd be separated. Toni got school-year custody — "Which just *shows* you," Ma Jo said. "Don't talk to *me* about justice . . ." — and James got Delia summers and every year or so, in other odd months, as now, when Toni was honeymooning with a new husband.

No matter where or how well Delia lived, with Toni it was not the same as Pinedale, with James. Home was never anywhere but there, and summer for the others never started till she arrived. Even though she was smart at books, she liked summer vacation best, those long formless mornings by the river, the drowsy noons in the porch swing, the lasting twilight, playing under the first shy stars. Even after it was too dark to see the birds, she could still hear the swifts and swallows way up in the sky and the whippoorwill cutting low over the church roof, the semi trucks groaning, leaning around the curves on the business route, gearing down over the tracks, heading for the mill. The bus leaned now, and Delia imagined she was on her way home for happiness, for summer, and that she and James were about to take up where they had left off, and him not dead at all, and it not over, forever.

Delia tried not to think of her daddy. Tried to forget. To make it smaller, a tiny and separate and meaningless thing, the morning's terrible news. She watched it recede, as the figures and letters in the eye test do with every click of the machine, clear but small and not worth straining for. Delia noticed that the whole day looked like that, everything diminishing in her mind's eye to miniature. The world outside the bus windows looked like the little town under a Christmas tree . . .

They were coming off the expressway now, heading for the station. She opened her eyes and blinked at Marietta, whose dainty streets were all in bloom, white and pink dogwoods, azaleas, tulips. The traffic sounds, the sparrows in the eaves of the station — they were lurching into the parking lot now — the PULL sign on the door . . . everything looked so tiny and tidy and distant and cold. Ma Jo said, feeling it too, "Let's get the blood going in our feet," so they stomped around in the sunshine, but Delia was still cold.

Ma Jo was cold too. Her ankles had swollen. She had Delia reach over and untie her laces. They had an hour before their connecting bus for home loaded and left. Ma Jo kept looking at Delia's watch, the numerals so tiny and meaningless.

"Ought to be *doing* something here and now," Ma Jo fretted. "I could be hemming that dress if you hadn't ruined it. Come here, girl."

Delia thought Ma Jo was going to open the suitcase and take out the sewing kit anyway, but all she wanted was to brush a flake of bark off the back of Delia's skirt where she had been sitting on the edge of the planter.

"Stand straight. Don't lean like that or sit like you was common. Act a lady," she told Delia. Ma Jo pinched a coin up out of her little purse and gave it to Delia. "Buy us a *Journal*," she said. "Make sure it's this evening's." Delia brought it to her and Ma Jo looked all through it, twice, then said, "It's not in here yet. Maybe in the morning." She folded the newspaper back like new.

"You mean about the accident."

Ma Jo hadn't told Delia anything, as though truth were

258

just one more coin she might spend on her or not, and so Delia had believed it was an accident, all this time believing it was an accident that killed James: that he was dead in a wreck or plane crash or roof collapse or jackknifed rig, those perils she had prayed him safe against all the years since the day he walked out of the mill and started working at a string of restless jobs before he learned how to build houses and began to make his fortune. He had flown all over the South with a heavy construction firm, first. Later he had done built-up roofing. He had slept in motels. Had been in a fire. Had ridden a Cessna into a Kentucky field and walked away from the crash. Had missed by three paces being in the load that an elevator took to hell when the cable snapped. He had driven over-the-road for someone else, making enough for child support and gifts. All along he'd send Delia something wonderful and crazy and apt, by freight or special delivery — a guitar, a globe, a telescope, an encyclopedia, two crates of it, and Toni uneasy, saying, "You clear that crap out of this living room before Newt gets home, y'hear me?" Then gentler, "He don't care to be reminded, y'know, of there being anyone else, no matter how long ago . . ."

Ma Jo watched another bus come and go and then she turned to Delia, with a funny, long look, a look that said, "You're going to suffer, but it's for your own good." She told Delia, "You won't never forget this day."

Another bus drove in, not theirs . . . emptied . . . filled . . . left. They moved to the far side of the platform out of the fumes, out of the way. The benches were all filled.

"Delia," Ma Jo said, in that faraway voice matching her look. She was staring through Delia, at the plain blank wall.

"Yes, ma'am?"

They both looked at the blank wall. The sun beat down on her back now as Delia touched her fingertip to the rough mortar, traced around the bricks, waiting to hear what she had to.

"He took his own life."

Delia blinked and swayed.

She didn't understand at first what those five syllables had to do with anything. Then, when she decoded, she rejected. "That's a lie!" And Ma Jo said, "No ma'am, I wish to God it was. It's true the whole nine yards of it." But Delia wouldn't listen. She pushed Ma Jo away from her and stamped her feet as though getting mud off and pressed her hands over her ears and shouted, "Don't you *dare* say that! Lies! Lies! Lies!" as loud as she could. Ma Jo slapped her till she hushed. Delia was glad to be slapped; it felt real, but it broke her heart. It almost convinced her, almost knocked sense into her. Her inner tide was going out, fast.

She wanted to sit, knew she must sit, but there was nowhere. She started to rest on the upended suitcase but it seemed she was rising instead of sitting. Everything all around her went silent and colorless and tiny. Her own voice withered to a grit as she wondered, "Grandma?"

The old woman grabbed at Delia's blouse but she couldn't stop her from falling. Delia heard her sleeve tear and the suitcase go over and her own head thump the cold cement of the bus station apron . . . Night . . .

She woke gradually, flickering on like the fluorescent light in the broken Greyhound sign, not quite on, not quite off. Ma Jo's voice was saying, "You're just all right. Hungry is all," telling the crowd, "She missed her lunch in all the excitement."

260

A stranger brought her a Coke and some crackers. Ma Jo insisted on paying for them, counting the coins, slowly, from her snap purse. One of the men had lifted Delia onto the now emptied bench. She wouldn't lie there; she sat up and tucked in her blouse, embarrassed. "Please," she said. "Please."

The crowd went away and left Delia alone with Ma Jo, but kept looking back at them, speculating, talking them over.

Their bus finally came.

"I never once thought of feeding your face," Ma Jo said, disgusted with herself, with Delia. Not grudging exactly, but as though she had so many crosses to bear and Delia was just one more. Delia said, "I'm sorry."

"You might have mentioned you was hungry," Ma Jo said. She gave Delia another cracker.

"I wasn't," Delia said. "I'm not."

"Eat," Ma Jo said.

Delia chewed but couldn't swallow. Ma Jo reached across and pinched Delia's cheek, pinched hard. *"Cry,"* Ma Jo ordered. "Get that lump out." She gave Delia the handkerchief with the sweet shrub bloom tied in the corner, and when the bus came, she gave Delia the window seat. Beyond the dirty glass, trees and houses swam past through her tears. It didn't look like anywhere they had ever been. They were going fast, getting nowhere, and Delia thought they might be on the wrong bus, on the wrong road, getting more and more lost.

"We're not halfway home," Ma Jo said, as though she felt the same.

Every time they got up speed, rolling through open country, another little town would pop up and they'd have to stop to take on or let off riders. At every halt Ma Jo would hum in that worrying way and when they got going again, she'd say "pretty horses" when they saw horses, and "pretty little cedars" where there were cedars, and all along when they rode by pastures she'd say, "The cattle on a thousand hills . . ." Ma Jo kept tapping her fingers on her pocketbook, as though counting up.

Afternoon

THE FIRST STARS were out now. The bus toiled on and on, up through the foothills, around the S-curves, climbing gently. Now the landscape beyond the window began to look like home, the bus's headlights striking the pale trunks of the cucumber trees, the concrete pillars of the tall poplars, the bent and graceful redbuds, willows, alders. Not so much pine now, and all along they went by lumber plots and sawmills, the burner for the sawdust glowing red like a cigarette end. The moon was five days past full. Delia shut her eyes against it, against all the stars.

Ma Jo gave her a poke, tapped the window with her crooked finger, pointing toward the west. They were on a ridge now and the horizon was far. "That a planet or a sun? I forget everwhich it is."

"Planet," Delia said, looking. "Jupiter."

"Well, you always did sound sure," Ma Jo grudged. "James wouldn't hold it against you if you turned out to be an astronaut . . . Hah . . . Whatever happened to that spyglass he bought you. Paid on it for months, the best he could find to owe for, and he was always so proud. It was ever bit as good as Rob Pursang's and that was how it had to be with James, nothing too good for his Delia . . ." Ma Jo sniffed. "You couldn't tell him anything . . . Maybe he was doing it to impress Toni . . . God knows . . ." She went on and on.

Delia shut her eyes again and tried not to remember, not to think at all. She pushed James and Toni out of her mind. To do that, she thought of Webb. How he had teased her, finding her in the dark the night they had all driven up the ridge, a friendly car full of them, going to see the comet Kohoutek.

When they came to the summit clearing, where there was the most sky, others were already parked there, a bivouac of strangers, but not for long. Soon everyone got acquainted, passing field glasses back and forth, sharing the telescope.

It had been so clear a night. Clear and cold. They had stood quietly in the cold dark, Delia, Rain, Ma Jo, and Carol. Webb — Carol's brother — and James teased Delia because she seemed afraid to put her eye to the scope. Her whole ambition toward astronomy had muted and altered since that night she had met the full moon through Rob Pursang's lens, falling to her knees because it was so much more of a moon than she had suspected, huge, luminous, cold and unexpectedly true, not some little coin of light to carry in a mental pocket and know odd facts about but a world to itself, unknowable, with a dark side. And James, not understanding what had happened, went out and bought Delia an identical telescope to Rob's, which arrived at Toni's by UPS and which Delia could hardly bear to touch. It might have been a cannon. That was how Delia felt about it — as though it were some instrument of war — something to defeat the magic and mystery of the universe, to betray the privacy of stars. She could not tell James that, could not disappoint his pride in such a gift. She wrote him that it had been rainy, but that when the weather turned, she would have the good of it. She did not say how it made her feel even more lost and lonely to have the machinery of cosmic trespass at her command, to know how much there was of the void. The stars were far, but she could know them. Better, perhaps, than she could know James, home in Pinedale. He wrote and said aim it his way, he'd leave the porch light on . . .

Delia looked down instead of up, that fall. She pored over her trigonometry book and steadied her mind on symbolic infinity rather than the universal sort. Webb called her moody and the others called her sulky at Christmas when she came home to Pinedale. That night on the ridge watching the stars, he found her in the dark, her arms stubbornly stuffed up her sweater sleeves in a mandarin pose, withdrawn past her chin into the buttoned-up wool, her eyes determinedly downcast.

"Now look, honey," Webb said, "you've come all this way, and so has the comet. Why don't you look up? You can see it without a telescope." He pointed. "No, more yonderways . . ." She turned so he was speaking to her back; she wouldn't look. "Like a waterfall, sort of. Way off. Or a bride veil. You see it like that, you'll want to see it better. *Look,*" he told her. He held out the binoculars; she wouldn't take them. "It's really something, won't be another one for years and years . . . Now's when."

They stood there on the edge of the world. All the valley lay below. Far, far off were the little lights of town. The wind had fallen to no more than a breath. She turned and looked up where Webb was showing her. Kohoutek was a smudge, just a smudge. It made her lightheaded to crane so hard. She swayed, then stepped back from the edge of the cliff.

"You won't fall," Webb promised. "I've got you."

She let him hold her as she raised the glasses to her eyes. He stood behind her, helping her focus. He stood warm at her back, his arms strong around her and suddenly he was a stranger, someone unknown to her, not the Webb she had grown up with, but rather a man, one of her daddy's workers, and the tobacco scent of his hands as he focused the binoculars for her warned her stomach — a quick minnow leap and flutter of pleasure or fear; she shivered, and then she was steady again, only chilled through, and burning. It was a revelation, like the moon through Rob Pursang's scope, of a world of unexpected peaks and pocks. She ducked out from under Webb's arms and walked back to the car.

"Sulking again," they said. Webb watched her go, but didn't follow. The others waited in meek file for their turn with the telescope. It was another hour before they left, then they headed for Chuck's Hut for BBQ. And that was the night James told them — sitting with Carol on one side of the booth — that he was going to marry her. Ma Jo stretched her old grasp out, clutching, not quite reaching them across the dinette table, saying, "Carol, Carol," and to the others, over her shoulder in the next booth, "He needs Carol," her bitterness and surprise not in the least neutralized by the smile she formed, her teeth just showing, the corners of her lips twitching with nerves.

"Right away," James was telling, answering *when?* And that meant that Webb would be family. He stood by James during the service; he was best man.

266

"A sweet little wedding," Ma Jo called it, with a proper homecoming afterward, all the Racings and their wives and children there. Delia stayed with Ma Jo that summer, giving James and Carol room. The mill had closed by then and the mill houses from Tater Hill to Silk Stocking Row were up for sale and James had plans for at least Tater Hill. He wanted to make it what it ought always to have been. He intended to try. Even though it meant he and Carol would have to live lean for a while; she was more than willing.

"James always hated mill town," Ma Jo wrote Toni that Christmas, always keeping her posted, on a Christmas card covered in her crabbed script. "Hated the lint that killed his daddy and all the same lives lived under same roofs." She told Toni how he had plans to renovate, had spent good money with an architect and when they finally agreed, the plans astonished everyone — modern shapes, odd angles, solar collectors, rough siding, custom colors and every house distinct. They were written up in the Sunday magazine, and it was called a renaissance. Ma Jo kept the Xerox of it in her Bible and sent the original, with color photos, to Delia and Toni in Maryland, with the sentence calling it a "million-dollar project" highlighted. She didn't tell her what James said, more than once, "It's all on paper and all of it hocked hilt-deep to the bankers."

"Well if she thinks I'm jealous, she's wasted her stamp," Toni said when she read it. They had quarreled like that, by mail, for years, reading between the lines, believing the worst.

Toni, in that war of nerves and long-distance mauling, got her revenge the next summer when Delia stepped off the plane and no one knew her. She was all jacked up and painted, in high heels and a cocktail dress — Toni's —

267

sunglasses dimming only a little her technicolor eyelids and false lashes. Delia's hair was covered under a frizzed wig puffed out full, bleached white as a shirt. She was smoking too, one of the complimentary cigarettes from the airline. Ma Jo took a long look and began to cry, said she knew they'd lose her and they'd lost her. Said, and not for the first time, "no more conscience than a cat," giving Toni full credit for "tarting Delia up, for sending her out cross-country smelling like a Decatur Street whore." James told Ma Jo to hush, that'd be enough, but it did no good. Finally he took Ma Jo's face between his hands and said, "Don't shame us, Ma," and she struggled free to gasp, "Me? Me!"

She had wet her handkerchief in the public fountain and was going to scrub some of Delia's paint off right then and there but James wouldn't let her. "You think she favors her?" James asked, smiling, as Delia tottered across the terminal with her suitcases.

"Halloween is in October," Ma Jo grumbled.

"I thought it was Toni," James marveled.

Ma Jo said, "You'd do well to keep your mind off old business. I'd say you've got your hands full as it is."

He drove fast.

Ma Jo warned him, "You caint outrun it. You have to outlive it," but he went even faster, like there was an emergency, like it was life or death to get Delia safely home. Delia felt it too, that need to have summer begin. She sat forward watching as they tore along, their wake leaving the roadside weeds flat. When they came to the town limits of Pinedale, Delia took off her shoes. She hardly waited for the car to stop in the drive, and ran in her stockings across the lawn and up the steps, calling to the world at large, "Oh look everything's the same not a thing's changed here I am!"

But that summer was different from day one. To be home wasn't enough. Delia didn't understand what had happened. Her face wore a searching look, a listening look. There was a new tracing of lines between her brows, but for any merriment she was merrier than them all and yet through it all she had that attunement to some distant footfall or news that never came.

Some said she was as wild as ever, but they didn't mean evil, they meant game, they meant that she had that willingness — like her daddy, like all the Racings — to gamble it all, high stakes or low, just to have a chance at laughter. The Racing side came out in her in a few days and the Yankee side, Toni's uptown ways, wore off and left her barefoot and busy with her cousins, running from daylight till dark and from one house to the next catching up on a year of missed news and gossip. Aunt Eden even found time to teach her to crochet, and Delia's purple potholder, her only finished article, got itself mailed back to Toni, whose response a month later was a postcard saying "Thanks what is it?" and Delia, who had learned to crochet to keep from biting her nails, invested in a nail-wrapping kit, when her own grew too slowly. But she didn't like long nails once she'd bought them — they interfered with her guitar playing, her doghouse building, her grip on the softball bat, and her typing for James two days a week, helping Carol with the company's books.

But still, they looked good for a couple of weeks — "grown-up nails," Delia called them — and they were the reason, as she got reacquainted with her family, that she held out her hand, to shake, rather than hugging as always in years past. She stinted no one as she made herself welcome back, serving herself up in those elegant handshakings, in blown kisses, in embracings. Something sweet for everyone, like refreshments at a party, until there was nothing left in herself but a hollow sourness that sent her, frowning, off to sit for hours on the riverbank, watching the water tongue its way around the sandbars. Sometimes she rode with James out to the building sites and gathered blocks and scrap to make into bird feeders or rabbit boxes. James showed her how.

One noon in July when the phone rang, James was home to answer it. He had driven back for some milk for his stomach — his ulcer had been bad lately — and a little sleep if he could manage it. But he couldn't rest, had to answer the phone, always eager to answer the phone. Like Delia, always listening for news, a habit formed years back, when Toni had left them hoping she'd come back, so that they had all that restless energy, and love to spare, and sad eyes.

James came back from the phone, frowning. "Ah . . ." he said. He rubbed his chin. He took up Carol's iced tea and sipped from it. "There's been a little incident out at the Crossing."

Ma Jo looked sharp. "Who's hurt?"

"Webb."

Carol stood up, quick. Delia wondered how she managed it, when she had suddenly lost all strength herself, and just sat, and managed only to say, "Tell me!"

Everyone looked at Delia, then at James.

"Concussion, not a bad one, and a broken arm. Overnight in the hospital, that's all."

"We'll go," Delia said, for all of them. But she couldn't move. She thought she might be ill. Then she realized, *I love him; that's what this is.*

It surprised her. It gave a sick joy, like a quick tooth. *Well I love him.* She laughed. Everyone had already left the house and she was still sitting there, her hands stupid and fluttery. She didn't remember how she got to the car, but as they rode along, she thought, *I love Webb Brannon.* That was that. It was so simple she laughed. It was so true she wanted to cry. Then a shadow came over her heart: *He's a man already and I'm still a kid. Why should he wait for me?*

Suddenly, she wanted to hurry, if running would do it, to get herself in proper order to please him, to claim him. What did she have to offer him? In despair she studied the flat profile of her chest in the hall-tree mirror. Always she had clung to childhood, and now it seemed her downfall, now when she was so eager and there was too much catching up to do, and she'd miss her chance with him. She began standing very tall, and always wore shoes now, shoes with a little heel, a terrible penance and trammeling for her, and overnight her nail-chewing ceased. She pestered James till he bought her contact lenses, too, and just when things were settling down in her spirit, and she was getting used to herself and had found things to say to Webb, it turned September and she had to fly back to Toni for the winter.

As Delia was halfway up the steps to the plane she whirled and headed back down past the other passengers, looking wild, like the child she had been. She ran back to them. Never in all those commuting years had she ever allowed herself a backward glance, would just turn and board, not even waving from the window, swerving from one camp to the other, a clean break, shuttling between the halves of her life. But this time she backtracked, kissed them all again, insisting, "You *be* here when I come home! All of you!" and Ma Jo weeping, held her close, predicting, "We're losing you," and Delia denied thrice, "Not true, not ever, not Delia." She broke from them and fled up the ramp to the plane, hiding her tears behind sunglasses, so no one could see how much she minded or accuse her of what she had spent her life denying: that she loved one parent better than the other. She fell asleep on the plane and woke when they landed in the north, where autumn had already come; it was like a dream, her summer, a dream between flights . . .

Ma Jo was shaking her now, on the bus, and saying, "Wake up and find your shoes, we're nearly there." Delia looked around. Up ahead was Bully's store, the lights on the KOOL sign blinking. The bus paused just long enough for them to step down, then it swayed on north toward Tennessee. Ma Jo found change for the phone and was already dialing.

It was Buck who came for them. They could hear his truck way off, backfiring. He loaded their suitcases in back. Ma Jo rode in the middle, between Buck and Delia. When Buck got his door shut — third try — they just sat there a minute. Dead silent. Because of what came next, what had to, what must, be done.

According to Ma Jo, what came next was Corton's.

"No," Buck protested. "He's not ready yet, they said maybe noon tomorrow."

"He's my boy," Ma Jo said. "I'm going to him . . . I'll walk if I have to. Open the door, Delia, let me out."

Delia didn't.

Buck argued some more but Ma Jo had her way, as ever. Buck cranked the truck and drove angry, finding most of the potholes, shaking everybody up on purpose, as if he was hitting them with his fists, and Delia's shoulder bruised itself against the door as they bounced. Buck squealed his tires, roared and ground the old truck across town to the undertaker's, slewing to a stop under the awning. "I'm telling you again, they're not open," Buck said. Ma Jo didn't listen and didn't care. She hammered the door and the window alongside the door till Corton himself came downstairs and opened up for her. He led them through all the dark rooms, clicking on dim lights. At last they came to the room where James lay.

Ma Jo didn't hesitate. "Walked right up like a dog to its dinner," as Corton told someone the next day. She crooned, leaning, patting, kissing, talking to James.

Delia held back. Buck told Corton, "I *told* her tomorrow." Corton sighed. He and James had been friends. "The poor bastard," he said. He put his arm around Buck's shoulders.

They had forgotten Delia. She went into the GUESTS and vomited. She took her time washing up, pressing cool damp toweling to the back of her neck, to her eyes, letting the water run on her wrists. When she came out, Ma Jo was calling for her in that do-your-duty voice. Delia could hear her asking Corton, "You'll be able to make him look like his sweet self?" Touching, lifting, looking at James as though she were shopping at Food Town for a Sunday roast. "And the hair . . . Delia's hair matches, maybe you could —"

Delia knocked into things as she ran. She got the side door open and kept on running. It didn't matter where, but she was heading home, where else? A mile in the dark, down through town, across the iron bridge, up school hill, cutting across the playground, running for her life yet all the time not a soul only the dogs after her, and they were her friends. She knew them all. She outran them all. She was always the fastest. Always in motion from first bird-song till the evening star. Any race they set for her she always won, running all summer long like she was making up for lost time, and the one time tearing down school hill on a dare and couldn't stop, all the other kids dropping out of the race but Delia going faster and faster, pressing her advantage and strength to the limit, as usual, till she fell headlong and never slowed, never screamed . . . Laughed. Laughed when she should have been afraid. Faster and faster till she rolled through the final bare red clay, raising a cloud of rosy dust, and fetched up hard against rocks and lay there, dead to the world.

All the Racings are fair, but Delia was white as bond with blue bruises beginning to show. So still and quiet she lay, the other kids thought she *was* dead. An ambulance came and carried her away. She lay on the hospital bed like something left behind after a party, something folks would claim later when they finally missed her. Not as though she were sleeping, for when Delia slept, she was always in motion too, as when awake, the covers coming loose from their tucks and winding up, tangled, on the floor and the pillow choked flat in her arms and Delia holding onto it, so it, so anything, couldn't get away.

She had a shock when she got to the house. It was all lit up like a celebration and a block away she could hear the talk and confusion and what sounded like rejoicings, all the mourners with their fine appetites and jokes. Delia stopped short of going in. She wished she had a stick and the strength to drive them out of her daddy's house, the way Jesus drove the dove sellers out of the temple.

The light was on in the playhouse, too, the little summer house James had built for her when she was seven. She heard the twins, shrill and hyper, way past their bedtime still playing, this one night of the day on which all the rules were broken. Rain was with them, her dreamy voice chanting, rhyming, quoting, singing the way she always did. She wanted to be an actress. She slept with her baton.

Rain was saying, "James!" then a scream, then, "No, let me try it again it was more like this: *James!* and then she knelt." They were rehearsing, replaying the events of the morning, as though it were something they had seen on TV, or a myth they acted out of a schoolbook. They had Carol's squeeze bottle of ketchup for blood. Rain squirted a little on the towel she was wearing for a long skirt.

Sully cried, "Gimme," and took the towel and flapped it, settling it over Fury's ketchup-smeared hair. "Jesus Christ cover the dumb sonofabitch," he quoted.

Then Fury sat up, and they recast themselves in other parts. Every part had its meat and moment. Who played Carol got to scream with bloody hands. Who played James got to die. And the sheriff's role had the cursing to recommend it. They chose their new roles and started it over again, arguing in asides from the improvised script. Delia, who had been resting, catching her breath in the shadows, had heard enough, all her questions — the ones Ma Jo and Buck wouldn't reply to — answered in full. She ran at them now, screaming *You stop that, you stop!* and dragging Sully up from under his shroud, and throwing the plastic pistol into the creek.

Someone came out onto the back porch calling "Delia?" calling "Chirren? Bedtime . . . Delia, is that you?"

But Delia wouldn't go in. She slipped around the playhouse to its blind side, out of the arc of the porch lights, and concealed herself there in the shadow, her back to the wall. She let herself feel; she let herself cry at last.

Evening

DELIA, AGE SIXTEEN

WEBB STEPPED SO SOFTLY she didn't hear him coming. He stood there in the dark a moment before he lit his cigarette. She saw herself — in the flare — in his eyes.

"I brought you something," he said. "Something for you. Mind if I sit?"

They propped against the same wall and for the length of a cigarette didn't speak. She was going away. She had finished high school early and was going to college, the first Racing to go on past high school, the only one ever to get a diploma by age sixteen. The college was way up north and she was going to be gone soon and wouldn't even be back for summer, the first time that she hadn't had that to live for.

"What did you bring me?"

Webb handed her a long slim box — jewelry? a locket! — and she tried to unwrap it slowly, not grab and tear into it. The box opened on a hinge of ribbon. They were in shadow for a moment as the moon went behind a cloud. He held up his cigarette lighter for her lamp, shading the little flame in his cupped hands because the wind had risen, was stirring the willows, rattling them like sleet.

"A fountain pen," Delia said, bravely. The sort of gift an uncle might give. She swallowed and said thank you. There was a little card enclosed. On it Webb had printed, "Maybe you'll write me." But he had changed his mind about it, had scratched "me" out and had written instead "a book."

"Tell me something," Delia said. "You've got to tell me the truth, I won't have a lie —" but she never finished the question, just jumped up and brushed off her jeans and said, on tiptoe, "Kiss me goodbye . . . I can stand it if you can . . . It'll have to last awhile . . . Make it good . . . I won't look back . . . 'Bye," and tore herself free and ran, a moment in the dim light, then into the shadows of the willows, and the river and life came between her and Webb.

The river and life and Tom Gray.

Night

IF SHE HAD HAD to say whom she loved, it would've been Webb. She'd known that ever since that day when she was fifteen, when he was hurt and it hurt her too. She'd known him as long as she could remember and it was so natural to love him, it was like something planted way back that had grown slow, rooted deep. It wasn't the sort of love that begins or ends, just is and will be, forever.

So what was it, then, about Tom Gray?

He was a lab assistant, a graduate student with his own researches and apparatus, and his advanced work and habits were silent, complicated, sure. For the most part all the lab assistants left the freshmen to make their own mistakes. They graded them rough and without sympathy, to weed out the weak and uncommitted. The assistants moved among the younger students lofty and unyielding, dogmatic in their instruction, terse in their praise, fierce in their critique. Delia's notes often received only a check mark, a simple indication that she had not made a major error. Her records were neat, coherent, honest. If she had trouble with apparatus or procedure, she'd run the test again, with a passion for certainty, for ironclad proof.

Still, she had problems. Being youngest in class, she somehow offended and drew the attention of her professor, who did not believe her advanced placement was earned. He set out to humble her, to push her to the limits and make her cry for quarter, or cry like a child, to eclipse her with his rude and determined brightness and crudity, as though there were some contest to the death between them. He had a reputation for unkindness. "It isn't just you," some of the other students consoled her; they were taking the course for a second or third time, and they knew.

"I don't mind," Delia said. She worked harder. She was one of three in the four sections who passed the first test. The professor called her to his office and asked, "So how did you do it? You must've cheated, but how? I'm interested, that's all; the others who passed it have all taken the course before. I kept records on it; maybe you saw a copy of the exam or something?" He reached across her in the little office to take a book off the shelf, allowing his arm to brush her breasts. She said, "If that's all, then, sir, I'll be on my way . . ." and left him standing in the door, watching after her.

Delia didn't like him, but she wasn't afraid of him. She *was* afraid of the acids, though. She feared them beyond reason. It wasn't healthy respect — it was terror, it was phobia. She had been like that since high school when her chemistry teacher, who was in the middle of being divorced, took off his wedding ring and dropped it in a bottle of aqua regia and watched it dissolve.

She acknowledged the power over flesh that all dangerous things wield, but more terrible to her than the actual dissolution was the symbolic, and she became clumsy with the bottles of reagents. It was a silly thing, like being afraid of the moon after seeing how vast and cold it was through Rob Pursang's telescope. It sometimes seemed to Delia she would always be battling her emotions about things. That was why she preferred science, the pure and absolute numbers and laws.

In high school, her lab partner poured acids for her. Now she worked on her own, and she had more than the experiments to master, she had to conquer that old and silly fear. All around her lesser students were managing well. She ruined so many experiments by clumsiness that she had to work extra on weekends. Gradually she controlled her irrational reaction to the acids, mastering hydrochloric first, her heart pounding but her hands steady. She could always control her behavior more easily than her feelings; she could appear to be calm even when she was not, to seem poised, happy to be arriving or leaving whatever occasion in her life, fearless, carefree, to walk lame in bloody shoes without limping. She approached the acid test as a problem in manners. She would *act* the way she ought, never mind how she felt . . .

One by one she learned to pour any acid, from the weakest to the strongest. The only thing she needed was time; she worked much slower in lab than the others, and this proved to be her downfall, for the lab tests were timed, and the experiments had to be timed as well.

She sat on her stool in front of her apparatus and considered changing her career and plans. The clock ran and ran. The assistant urged her to get a move on. She gave her notebook a little flip to shut it, the pages still empty where purpose, procedure, data, calculations, and results belonged. All the others worked on, serious, as she began to take down her experiment.

Tom Gray, who floorwalked the aisle opposite to her

work area, waited till the other assistant had passed then came around to Delia and took the acid to the fume hood and poured, steady, sure, without asking or commenting at all, the way a harried mother might hurriedly stoop, tie a toddler's loose shoe, then move on into the day's duties without loitering for thanks. How had he known? She didn't have time then to marvel, but she was grateful, and her gratitude took the form of sharper noticing. But she didn't have to search Tom Gray out, for after that incident on the exam, when she needed help he was there, without making a fuss or playing favorites. He seemed to be doing his own work, seemed to be borrowing something for his own research, and the others never realized what was happening.

When Delia missed a week of classes because of flu, she had to make up two skipped labs, and was working late one evening when she heard the sound of breaking glass in the adjoining workroom. Not an unusual sound nor was it followed by the urgent noises of emergency — cries or running feet. Delia finished titration and went to the store-room to replace a borrowed burette clamp and stepped in fresh blood on the floor. At first her mind, concerned with her own experiment, didn't comprehend; then she realized, Someone's hurt. How long ago had she heard that glass break? She stepped through the preparation room into the other lab and said, "Someone's hurt?" Tom Gray was holding his clenched fist under the running tap. "You," she said, watching the water dyed rich with his life gurgle down the drain of the sink. "Yeah, I am," he agreed.

There was no one else; it was up to Delia. And when it was up to Delia, she never asked permission or stopped to pray. Ma Jo had always called her a "self-starter." Now Delia grabbed up a handful of pulp towels and pressed them to the cut. She said as she jammed the rough paper on the wound, in which she had seen the white tendon exposed, "Direct pressure," as though reading it some-where. "Pressure to the point." She pressed. The papers soaked through in a few strong pulses.

She fought his blood like fire, hooked a stool over with her foot and sat him on it. "Are you weak?" she asked him. She spared a glance to his face to see if he were pale, clammy, going into shock.

He was smiling! He was amused! All this fuss over a cut!

When she saw that smile she let up for a moment, as though she had misjudged the seriousness. "Just how bad *is* it, you think?" She peeked under the bandage . . . *"Bad,"* she assessed as the blood surged again. "You'll need stitches."

He said, "I'm just going to pour some iodine on it and forget it, it'll stop bleeding soon."

"Soon as you're hollowed out," she said. But he had the iodine in the other hand and poured it! When he flinched and cursed, she blew and blew to cool the sting of it, blew till she was lightheaded.

"Take it easy," he told her. "It's not CPR."

She had him press towels till she could get some gauze, and then she wrapped it, bound it tight and fashioned a massive white mitten. "Keep it high," she told him, then stepped back to survey her ridiculous handiwork.

"Like a boxer," she said. "The winner."

"I'm both of those," he said, and then she knew that much more about him. He was looking at her with such quiet confidence. It disturbed her. She felt awkward. The way she had felt the summer she learned to swim and the hairy lifeguard held her in the water, crisp across his two arms, encouraging her, "Float, float, relax and float, sugar, trust me and let go and float," and she sank like a rock every time from the simple burden of his touch . . .

The bandage Delia had made was very white against Tom Gray's deep tan. She asked him, "Are you a lifeguard?"

"Hell, no," he said. "Can you drive?" He handed her the keys and she got him over to the clinic for stitches. Somehow their books got tumbled in the car, and she had custody of his German dictionary for the weekend. There was a fragment of *Faust* hastily translated. Delia thought Tom Gray had written it. When she told him, "That's very good," he said, "Thanks." Maybe he didn't know she thought he had made it up, or maybe he just didn't mind if she thought so. She looked at him through brighter eyes.

Once in lab he borrowed her watch to time an experiment while he used his own as a stopwatch. She unclasped it from her wrist and handed it across to him. He raised it to his lips and smiled. She couldn't look away.

It was only a matter of time before he asked her the question with the one word of her name — "Delia?" — gently asked, not to be unasked, the question between them because he was male and she female and every question has an answer and *no* was not the answer, *no* was a denial of the question not an answer, and after a time Delia realized with some wonder what the answer was and she spoke it, not halfheartedly, not reluctantly, not furtively, and she was not at all concerned about what had been or would be, only about what was happening — now! — in the moan-praised, eradicating moment.

It was like the strange green fruit of the passion vine, the maypop's rank peel and inner rind, the bitter astringent savor if you pick too soon, but if you time it perfectly, it falls golden, its full flavor of Eden like nothing foreseen, earthy as marl and rare as angels.

That was how it was about Tom Gray.

Midnight

Delia's black dress was wrinkled like a map of every mile of the way home. The crepe just hung on her, swung around her like a bell, one of her maternity outfits. Maybe that was all she had, Webb thought, the only thing black . . . He was glad James couldn't see her like this, bone-weary, used-up, and used to it. The black of the dress bleached her color till she was almost as pale as the time she tumbled down school hill and lay dead at the bottom, out cold . . .

She and Tom Gray had walked in around midnight. She went straight to a chair, looking left-over. She had seen the cars and lights as they drove up, had seen the FUNERAL sign posted and the wreath on the door. That's how she knew that James was dead. That was her welcome.

She asked for the telephone to be brought to her so she could phone while she rested. She called back up north about her baby. Tom Gray's mother was keeping him. "Is

Jamie sleeping?" she asked her mother-in-law. She listened, then reported at large, "Jamie's sleeping." As though that were very important to her, to them all. Did Mrs. Gray remember to fill the vaporizer? "She's got the steam on," Delia told Tom. He nodded, shrugged, dull-eyed. She satisfied herself on a few more points, then gave the phone back, and while Tom talked to his mother about the trip down, and the news about James, Delia said, softly, "All day I've been praying" — not crying, but with a tremor in her true clear voice — "and Daddy was already dead." She glanced around, as though accusing them of keeping it from her. Tom Gray, behind her chair, his back to the wall, looked nervous, as though he were still detouring too fast over dark and unknown roads. They had really honked it down the Interstate, he was telling someone, as far as Knoxville.

Webb decided that Tom Gray was not a bad man, but he'd never like him. He didn't like the beefy good looks of him, didn't like the way Tom Gray's strong hand lay on Delia's shoulder, though it lay there lightly enough. Webb was glad when Buck called Tom away to the kitchen for a drink, and he was more glad that Delia didn't seem to notice Tom had gone. She said she wasn't hungry but she sipped a little of the Coke Jo Alice brought her.

"People always bring all this food," Delia was noticing again, "just at the time when nobody's hungry."

Webb stepped out on the side porch in the cool. From there he couldn't see the cars all over the lawn and everybody running in and out, talking, making a night, a party of it. Ma Jo went out and stood awhile beside Webb and didn't say a word. Not one. She sighed, though, and in answer, so did he.

She had been busy all afternoon putting out her eyes

sewing black ribbon down every last bright stripe of her Easter dress, dousing the color like a fire, a pinch at a time, like she was curing something — shame or hate — the hard way. She wasn't talking to anyone, hadn't all day, even if spoken to directly. She had just hunched over the work in her lap, pick-picking with that needle, emptying a whole spool of black ribbon a neighbor had driven to Hammermill for on her exacting orders. She was still sewing when Delia and Tom Gray got there. She had taken a look at Delia, but hadn't got up, and didn't speak. When Delia had leaned and hugged her, she winced, as though in bodily pain.

Webb put his arms around Ma Jo now, but he couldn't comfort her, no one could. She clawed her way free and pecked back into the house. Webb stayed out there in the shadows, on the far end of the porch, settling in the swing. He was thinking how when Delia went away to college, there had been five years' difference in their ages, but now she had caught up, had passed him. The door opened and it was Delia, saying, "Are you there?"

She came over and sat beside him. "I was looking for you," she said. He didn't touch her, but she warned, anyway, "This is business," not in an insulting way, but desperately, like someone with no pencil and only one coin and repeating the life-or-death phone number over and over. "Business," she said again.

"What can I do for you?" Webb wondered.

Delia didn't say, just then. She waited — it was almost as though she were hiding — till some of the visitors left. They watched the taillights vanish beyond Tater Hill and then Delia said, "I want — tell me the truth — I won't have a lie — " and still she didn't ask him, only showed him, opening that little pocketbook to take out the .22, its nickel chrome flashing like a mirror. She had brought it all the way with her, going to fix who hurt her daddy. "Who?" she asked Webb. That was all she wanted to know. Then he knew she didn't know, no one had told her.

"Crissake, Delia," he said. "Oh, why didn't someone tell you!" Webb paced in his agitation. The porch wasn't big enough. He jumped to the ground and paced larger. She followed him, caught up, caught his arm.

"Who?" she insisted.

"Where'd you get this thing?"

Delia took it back from him, impatient. "Santa Claus," she said. "The Easter bunny. What does it matter where?" She put it in her pocketbook and zipped it out of sight.

That was Delia, Webb thought. Even as a kid she'd never looked twice at jawbreakers and doll shoes and autograph hounds. Fireworks and Buck knives and flytraps and creels and things with a how-to and why-for, peril, that was what Delia went for. But tenderhearted too. She had had a zoo for the orphaned animals a summer would bring her way. She even kept her dead kitten an extra day, holding out against hope, against all odds.

She used to lie on the bluff over the river and stare down into that dead sullen water for a glimpse of fish. The river always ran low and scummy in summer because the mill needed more water and gave it back hot. Delia would go fishing every morning, as if the lessons of all the days she'd had no luck on hadn't mattered at all. Hoping against hope, yet with that way she had too of expecting the worst all along, so when it came she wouldn't go to pieces. A temper like that earns a lot of teasing, a lot of practical jokes.

The summer she had turned sixteen, studying hard to be ready for that exam for advance placement, pretending she didn't care how it turned out but packing, just in case she got to go to college early, walking to meet the mail van every morning and when the letter with the good news finally came, she had set off running across the back lots, yelling and someone — who? maybe Webb himself, yes Webb — saying *Quick!* and Buck and Boyd and Billy and Red and James too had all lain down, and the roofers too, sprawling right there and then, and Delia not noticing anything just coming on running, whooping, calling till she got close enough to see them all lying around like they had been killed by gas or electrocution or some other terrible thing and before she could get too close they all sat up and laughed, and she was sore, oh God yes, she was sore, she threw a fit. Threw sand by the handful and chunks of cement and nails and a hammer through the storm door and then she threw up. She wouldn't let any of them near her, to help her, to apologize. She ran away and vanished for the rest of the day, missed supper and prayer meeting and the little family party after, to celebrate her good news.

Webb had finally found her, hadn't called, hadn't looked, just walked out in the dark and found her by the toolshed. He had a present for her, something he had bought the day she took the exam, that was how sure he had been she'd win the scholarship.

She didn't care about that. She was still mad. "Don't you *ever* do that to me again, you hear? Don't you ever let me hear I've survived you . . ." And she held him to her so fiercely he knew then he could have had her, she was his. He could have taken her then. She was offering. But when she kissed him, he let her go.

And Toni, who always did have a taste for surprise, wrote at Christmas, "Find a chair. Delia's got a husband. He'll do right nicely. They're living in a little place near school, cute as a button. Delia tickles me to death with her lists, getting her ducks in a row. She says she'll go on with classes as long as she can. She means to get her education. Has a job in the evenings to earn a little extra till the baby comes. I'd help more but I've been under the weather myself lately . . . Let's keep in touch . . ." Which is what she always signed off with and it might be a year before you heard another word from her.

It was true though that Toni was under the weather. Way under. She was bad off before her current husband, Walt, called Ma Jo in mid-January to say it was cancer. Toni didn't want him to call, but she couldn't stop him, she was that weak. He told them what the doctors had told him, "Six weeks." If she had let the surgeons cut when they first found it, it might have made a difference. Ma Jo said wasn't that just like Toni — "Rather lose her life than her looks" — and as it turned out, it didn't take even six weeks. "Toni was always fast," Ma Jo pointed out, but she sent flowers, from all of them. James wired roses and walked the floor. It was Delia who called and told them Toni had died. "There was nothing left, Daddy. You wouldn't know her," explaining why they chose cremation.

James kept a headache; he'd sit in the dark, just sitting and smoking. When Carol came in to coax him to bed he'd say he wasn't tired. "Old men don't need so much sleep," he'd tell her . . .

He got up early. Too early to be dressing for the day. Carol figured he'd come back to bed when he'd smoked a cigarette. She was getting used to his restlessness. She fell asleep again. When she woke the next time, and he still hadn't returned to bed beside her, she went looking. She didn't find him in the house, but she found him.

When Carol ran back and phoned Webb to come help,

Webb hadn't thought about how Delia would hear it. He didn't even know who had called her.

"Who?" he asked her.

"Jo Alice," Delia said. "Wasn't it?" She stopped, troubled, trying to get it right. She was very tired. It seemed like years ago, or never . . . . They had phoned her, they had told her James was shot, was bad hurt. "They didn't say *dead*," she told Webb. They had had to borrow Mrs. Gray's car, since it had better tires. They had left as soon as they had got the baby's things collected into the diaper bag. They had dropped the baby off with Tom's mother and filled the car with gas on Mrs. Gray's Gulf card and headed south. Every time after that when they stopped for gas Delia had called collect from wherever they were, asking, "How is he?" to anyone who'd answer the phone in James's house, sometimes a relative, sometimes a stranger, but every time they told her, "Unchanged, no change since morning."

The phone had rung, rung, rung, ladling Delia and Tom Gray up out of sleep, warm as soup, weak as broth, pouring them into the cold first light. It was too early for both of them. The sun was up, but it was too early when night was a continual drag awake, baby-interrupted, dream embers that never quite flame, a smoldering sleep-hunger that never went out, the baby's month-old mouth grieving for Delia, for Delia, always for Delia, so why should Tom Gray — he had pointed this out in a reasonable daylight discussion a week ago — with his own exhausting work schedule still ahead, nine to five, why should *he* rise? He couldn't nap during the day as Delia could. Why should Tom Gray get up and hush the baby's howl or the phone's intrusion, early or late? They had settled all this in Tom's favor — after all he was the one with the scholarship and grant — a week before, so when the phone rang Delia got up to answer it.

The news, five pulses away over the cold floor, wouldn't wait. She headed for it, unsuspecting. The robin in the hedge defrosted into its first arpeggios in Delia's right ear. Into her left ear like poison, the slow deadly seep of news over the wire woke her, woke her to grief.

She set the receiver back in its cradle gently then, and just stood there, her silhouette a wraith against the young day filtering through the broken blinds. Tom Gray roused, aroused, and said, "Look at me, lady, come here, forget the baby for an hour, I've got something for you," throwing back the covers for her to see, and when she failed to behold, failed to notice him at all, he exclaimed, "Ah, shit, what is it now?" and Delia couldn't say it yet, could only move to the closet and begin jerking things out, searching cold-handed in the dark and finding, from habit, her maternity clothes. She needed to shop, but there hadn't been time. She dressed in the dark, announcing, "I have to be there!" the way she had when Toni was dying, so that though he didn't yet know *what,* he knew right then that "another whole damn weekend's shot in the ass, I bet."

Delia said, again, "All the way down here I was praying for him." She took out the little gun and asked Webb, once more, "Who?"

Webb was too late to catch the door; it slammed between them, but he didn't miss anything. She was moving around the room from person to person, asking them *who.* She was smaller than Webb remembered her. Upstairs filled out some, but thin, too thin, the baby only rounding her off, but not fleshing her out.

She asked everyone, "Who did it?" That was what had kept her going, what still gave her the energy to keep on, and her no more than a husk. All those miles home, she had planned on revenge.

"That's all she wants," Tom Gray said, in the kitchen, when Webb went in to talk it over with Buck.

"Maybe James knows that, wherever he is," Buck said.

They had been hitting the Wild Turkey pretty hard. Webb stuck with gin. He had his own reasons. *It ain't courage but it's close, son* . . . When he drifted back to the living room Carol was saying to Delia, "I guess you'll have to hear it from me." Ma Jo wouldn't even look up. She sat rocking slow.

Carol and Delia went into the bedroom to be private. It was a few minutes before the door opened again. The house had cleared some, only kin remaining, closest kin. And Luther. He had on his Hawaiian shirt. He had lollipops in his hand like a bouquet. He was handing them out, one for everybody, his idea of a consolation, better than flowers. "You caint eat flowers," Luther was saying. They laughed. They were joking with him, nothing to do but joke him along. His whole life had been good stories and laughter. He showed up every time something happened. Not many cakes got sliced without Luther having a taste. He haunted the funerals too, coming into his gray hair gradually, like a good old dog going white at the muzzle. He still loved to cut the fool, as if he were a boy, laughing in that high whine like a jungle bird. Everybody hushed when Delia came out again. She stood there, halfway through the door, looking around. When she found Webb she steadied up, held fast. All the room between them and nothing between them and the last thing she ever told him — *I can stand it if you can* . . . *Kiss me* . . . *It'll have to last* — She wouldn't cry. Not Delia. Not then.

She flickered her eyes over all of them, the way she used to when they played school on the clay steps of the storm cellar and she was Teacher. She was always Teacher. No one knew so many answers as Delia. She rested in the doorway now, all black and white, like her own picture crooked in a frame.

Finally she spoke. She asked Webb first, she asked them all, anyone who might know. "So, who do I shoot?" Then she frowned, as though she were proofreading the whole story on a page. She cleared her throat and said, "I mean, whom?"

Funny thing was how they'd been waiting for Delia to get there so things could start, but now that she'd arrived, it was over. Somebody said, "Look at the time," and they began collecting the kids from the spare beds and hauling them home.

Delia was eighteen now. She stayed talking on and on. With the grown-ups. She always did hate to say goodnight.